Death Wish

LINDA HUBER

Death Wish

This book is dedicated to
Huntington's Disease families.

Also by Linda Huber

The Paradise Trees
The Cold Cold Sea
The Attic Room
Chosen Child
Ward Zero
Baby Dear
Stolen Sister
The Runaway

Prologue

He stood in the hallway, his stomach churning. The body was in the back of the van. In a metal box. And he was going to have to shift it all the way round to the back garden, then get it into the hole and buried, all without anyone seeing him. He wiped a hand across his mouth and down over his neck to his chest, feeling the slickness of sweat and his heart thundering beneath his ribs. It wasn't even dark. But he couldn't wait until nightfall; in this weather people slept with their windows wide open, and if anyone noticed him digging the garden at two a.m. – well, that would be it. How long did they give you for murder, nowadays? No, the afternoon was safer. The neighbours were out. Everyone was out. He shuddered, thinking about the woman in the metal box. The only way to be sure she would never be found was to keep her right here under his nose.

The sun hot on his shoulders, he went out to the van and opened the back. There it was, looking like an innocent large-sized metal box, but oh… Two tears trickled down his face; nothing in his life had prepared him for this. He grabbed the box and slid it towards him. Now for the wheelbarrow. He angled it by the van, pulled the crate out and – clunk! It was in the barrow. Trying to look as if he was transporting something perfectly innocuous, he manoeuvred the wheelbarrow up the garden path and round to the hole by the back green.

Now for the tricky bit, because of course, he couldn't bury her in the box. To decompose properly – and as quickly as possible – she'd need to be in the ground, where the bugs could get at her.

He took a deep breath, then snapped the lid open and oh *shit*, the smell. Retching, he closed his eyes and tipped the box. The body plopped to the bottom of the hole, six feet down, and he squinted through his eyelashes. This was the worst ever. Her hair… in a way it looked no different, but the skin was dark now, sliding off in places. The horribly stained clothes… He retched and spat bile, then grabbed a spade. Cover her, cover her, she was dead and oh, he hadn't wanted it to be like this. Some people deserved to die, of course. He glanced over his shoulder. Others were doomed to die. It wasn't fair.

Earth thudded on ghastliness, and she was gone. He shovelled until the hole was half-filled in, then jumped down and stamped until the earth was firm before heaving himself back out to continue. She had to be gone for good, because if she wasn't, he would lose everything. None of this was his fault, but he was the one who'd pay the price.

'Mummy! Come and help!'

He worked on frantically. Joya was back, which meant Martine was too. They mustn't see this, they mustn't notice. If they did, he'd be the one who was doomed.

PART ONE

BRAVE NEW LIFE

Chapter One

Several weeks beforehand, end May

Grandma Vee was sick.

Joya tiptoed across the landing and stood outside her parents' bedroom, twisting one of her plaits round her finger as she listened. They were arguing in whispers, and her mum was crying. Again.

'I don't know how I'm going to cope, Stu. In just a couple of weeks Mum'll be here for good and I'll have to watch her wasting away – she'll be in my face, 24/7. What if I go the same way? If I knew that would happen I'd shoot myself.'

The door was cracked open and Joya peeked through, holding on to the frame to keep her balance. She could see her mum reflected in the dressing table mirror, blonde hair mussed up worse than Joya's had ever been.

Her dad sounded like he didn't know what to do. 'For God's sake, Martine, having Vee here was your decision. And be careful what you say. Joya would be scared stiff if she heard you.'

'Joya's too young to understand.'

Her dad's voice came out higher than usual. 'And that won't last much longer. She's a clever kiddy for eight. So you'd better work out how you're going to tell her, and you know what you have to do first – get the bloody test done.

Odds-on it'll come back negative.'

'That is so not true – it's fifty-fifty and if it came back positive I'd shoot…'

Joya crept downstairs, the heavy feeling back in her tummy. It was the same old argument and she still didn't know what it was about. Grandma Vee wasn't like other people's grandmas. She couldn't walk without her zimmer for one thing, and she couldn't do up buttons any more, but apart from things like that she was the best grandma ever. She was great at reading Wanda the Witch and playing games. What did Dad think was scary? Maybe because Grandma Vee sometimes sounded funny when she was talking, only it wasn't really funny, because it made Grandma Vee sad.

Joya grabbed an apple from the bowl on the kitchen table and wandered into what used to be the dining room. It would be Grandma Vee's room soon, and it was all empty now, waiting for her dad to paint it. It was going to be brilliant having Grandma Vee here.

A crash from upstairs sent Joya scurrying out to her swing set in the garden. By the sound of things her mum had chucked something at her dad again. The fights were coming more and more often, and they were getting louder, too. Joya swung as hard as she could, her back to the argument.

The painters in the house next door were loading their ladders into their van, and Joya stood up on her swing to see better. They saw her, and waved before piling into the van and driving off. Joya waved back. The painters were funny. Her dad called them the bonnie boys because they both had Scotland t-shirts, and one had a St Andrew's flag tattooed on the back of his head. They'd been working next door all week and the house was nearly ready. Joya was looking forward to having new neighbours – they might have children. It would be lovely to have friends right next door.

Another crash from inside made her jump, but then her dad's laughter came through the open kitchen window, and Joya's middle lightened up. Was the fight over already? She jumped from the swing and ran back to the house.

Her parents were both in the kitchen, her dad picking up pieces of a plate from the floor and her mum leaning against the cutlery drawer and watching him with blotchy eyes.

Joya hesitated. If she went on asking, one day she might get a proper answer. 'When will Grandma Vee get better?'

Her mum came over and hugged her. 'Oh sweetie, Grandma Vee's... old. She won't get younger again, you know that's not how things work.'

Joya pouted. It was another answer that didn't mean anything, and it wasn't even true. 'Stevie's gran's old too and she can still ride her bike.'

Her dad joined in. 'Everyone's different, Joya. Your mum can swim fifty lengths of the pool without stopping. If I tried that it'd kill me. But I can dance – look!'

He grabbed her mum, and Joya watched as they twirled round the kitchen, swooping between the table and the cupboards. Her mum's head dropped onto her dad's shoulder, so it really was okay. Sometimes the Grandma Vee fights went on for days, with Mum crying in corners and Dad getting crosser and crosser, and neither of them answering Joya's questions. It was awful.

She knelt up on a chair and leaned towards them. 'You won't ever get divorced, will you? Stevie's mum and dad got divorced and that's why he stays with his gran so much.'

Her mum stopped dancing and rushed to squeeze Joya tight. 'Oh darling, please don't worry about that.'

Did that mean they wouldn't get divorced? Lovely

perfume filled Joya's nose, but her mum's arms felt trembly. Joya closed her eyes and squished into her mum's neck while her dad hovered beside them.

'Your mum's just... concerned about Grandma Vee, Joya, but we'll fix things, never fear. Let's have something to drink.' He opened the fridge and plonked a can of Coke on the table.

Joya grabbed the can. She wasn't usually allowed Coke in the middle of the afternoon. She opened it before anyone decided it wasn't good for her teeth and took it away again.

Her mum's mobile buzzed, and she fished it out of her handbag. 'It's Mum.' Her face looked as if she was going to cry again.

Joya felt like crying too. Grandma Vee was sick and it was getting worse.

Leo Mackie pulled up in front of the house and strode to the back of the van for his tools and the box of bathroom fittings. He stood for a moment, fingers itching to lift the packet of cigarettes lying beside his jacket. But he was trying to give up, because Ashley didn't smoke. He slammed the door shut and took a swig of whisky from his hip flask instead, staring up at the wide blue sky over Glasgow, shivering even as the heat soaked into his t-shirt. Nicotine withdrawal was hell, but he'd do anything to keep Ashley.

Leo balanced his tool kit on top of the box of bathroom bits and pieces, and went round to the back of the house. The painters had finished now, and he only had the finishing touches to add. Warm satisfaction pushed the craving for a smoke to the back of Leo's mind. He could be proud of this project, his most ambitious to date – a big detached house, built in the warm, red sandstone typical of the area, with lovely reception rooms downstairs and three good-sized double bedrooms upstairs. And the master had a fabulous en-suite. He was going to make a bomb with this one.

The painters had propped the back door open to let the air circulate, and Leo left his things on the breakfast bar and strolled appreciatively round the kitchen-diner. You didn't get more high-spec than this; it was like something in a lifestyle magazine. Knocking the kitchen and dining room together made a great family space, and there was a separate living room, not to mention the generous garden. The location was spot-on too; Langside was just minutes from Glasgow Central Station by train. Smiling broadly, Leo went through to the living room, another generous room with a lovely bay window.

This place would sell quickly, even nowadays. Plus, there was the additional bonus of an annexe flat built on the side of the house. It could be a granny-flat or a holiday let, or a practice of some kind – a nice little money-spinner for someone, anyway.

He was about to start on the downstairs loo towel rail when his phone rang. Leo frowned at the screen. Ashley's mother wasn't in the habit of calling him, and they'd seen her only yesterday. He tapped connect. 'Eleanor?'

She had one of those deep posh voices with a permanent twist of irony, which meant it was difficult to tell when she was being serious.

'Leo. I have a proposition for you.'

Leo sat down on the toilet seat. In the six months he and Ash had been seeing each other, he'd never got to the bottom of the mother-daughter relationship. 'She's an overbearing, mean cow,' was the reason Ashley gave for her dislike of

Eleanor, but while overbearing was possibly correct, Leo had seen no sign of meanness. Ash's dad had walked out last year, so Eleanor was probably lonely and trying her best to keep in with her daughter. And although Ashley never stopped complaining about her mother, who called her every day, Eleanor's dinner invitations – every second Friday without fail – were always accepted. Ash was a softie. Mind you, it wasn't easy to say no to Eleanor.

Now, he matched the irony in her tone. 'A proposition? Is this going to be an offer I can't refuse?'

'What would you say to a couple of hundred K for your business?'

Leo wiped the sudden sweat from his brow, glad she was on the phone and not sitting opposite him. 'A cash injection, huh? So what's the catch?'

'No catch.'

He didn't believe it for a second. 'So what's the no-catch?'

'I liked the sound of the property you were talking about last night, the one in Langside with the annexe. I popped by this morning while the painters were in and had a look round. Here's the deal, Leo – you help me sell my house, and we all move to Langside. You and Ashley take the house, I get the annexe, and I invest eight hundred thousand in your business. We split the profit the cash makes. What do you say?'

Leo had to stifle his gasp – eight hundred grand would make all the difference to his property business. But typical Eleanor, arranging her daughter's life. At the moment, he and Ash still had separate flats, but oh, how he'd love them to move in together. He swallowed, then cleared his throat.

'Have you discussed this with Ashley?' But Ash would have told him straightaway if she had.

'I'll leave it up to you to persuade her. You needn't say it's a permanent thing; it would be best if she thought I was only in the annexe until I found something else. Think what you could do with that cash, Leo.'

Visions of making a name for his business in the luxury flat sector were already swirling in front of Leo's eyes, and he struggled to keep his voice steady. 'Okay. I'll talk to Ashley, and get back to you.'

'Get back to me today, Leo.'

The connection broke, and Leo got up to splash water on his face. He stared at his reflection, a pleasant-looking, if he said it himself, guy of thirty. Not exactly Mr Universe, but nice thick dark hair and a good body. He was making a reasonable income buying and selling property and he had an amazing but relatively new relationship with Ash. He knew she was the only woman in the world for him – but did she feel the same? She liked him, the sex was amazing and they laughed about the same things, but she'd always shied away from any hints about a future together. And annexe or not, sharing a property with her mother was not going to be high on Ashley's must-do list. On the other hand, this place was Ash's dream home; she'd said as much last week.

Eight hundred thousand.

Eleanor was right. It was an offer he couldn't refuse.

'I want you to help me die, Martine.'

Shock jerked through Martine and she dropped onto the bed, searching for words. They were in Vee's flat, starting the packing and organising for the upcoming move to Langside. Vee was going downhill – Huntington's Disease did that to you – but there had never been any talk of suicide.

Until today. Martine gaped at her mother in the easy chair. Vee's mouth was working in the twitchy way it did now, and her hands were shaking even more than usual. Add to that the awful grey and brown straggling hair, and the baggy tracksuit… Her mother looked like what she was – someone who couldn't take care of her own appearance, and whose daughter wasn't doing enough. The guilt was there again.

'It isn't that bad yet, is it?'

Martine didn't miss the relief that flitted over Vee's face. Had she expected a downright refusal? Martine wiped damp palms on her jeans. It was so complicated – becoming her mother's carer while still in her thirties hadn't been in the life-plan. Martine still wasn't sure how they were going to make it work, and Vee's shock statement only reinforced her ambivalence.

'I don't mean this minute. I mean next year, the year after, whenever. I need to know I can go quickly when it does become unbearable.' Vee's articulation was slower than usual and more slurred. She was clearly in earnest.

Tears shot into Martine's eyes, and she turned her head away. It wasn't fair, springing this on her in the middle of boxing up the contents of Vee's cupboards. But then, nothing about Huntington's was fair. Little had she known four years ago, waiting for Dr West to give them the diagnosis, that her life as it was would end that day. He'd told them the basics, that Vee's funny twitches and mood swings were Huntington's Disease, which was hereditary. Vee's parents had died young in an accident, but one of them must have carried the gene. The doctor hadn't made it sound like a death sentence, but when Martine went home and googled, she saw it was exactly that, and dread had weighed heavy in her gut ever since. Her poor mother's situation now was about the worst thing that could happen to anyone's health, and oh…

You might have it too, you might have it too. The mean little whisper that snaked through Martine's head at odd moments when she was least expecting it. She'd managed to live with the fear while Vee was still in her own place, but soon now the horror was going to be under her nose, all day every day. Trying to ignore it was no longer an option.

Martine pressed cold hands to her cheeks. What else could she have done? With Dad remarried and out of the way in Australia, there was no one else to turn to, and Vee wasn't safe alone any more – the recent episode with a kettle of boiling water had proved that, even to Stu. And Vee wasn't kicking against the move, which spoke for itself.

Her mother was still waiting for an answer, her brow furrowed and her lips trembling. Emotion, or merely a symptom of the disease?

Martine swallowed. 'Give me time to digest it, and then we'll talk.'

Vee nodded, and went on cramming winter underwear into the bag on her lap. Martine's fingers itched to help, but that would put Vee into a bad mood for the rest of the afternoon. 'Use it or lose it – so for God's sake let me use it,' was one of her mother's most often-snapped sayings. It wasn't true – Vee could use what remained of her strength and mobility as much as she liked, but she would still lose it one day. One day soon, too. Death was on the horizon.

And now her mother wanted help to die. Dear God, how could she live with that?

Vee grunted as the bag of underwear slid to the floor. Martine swiped it up and pressed it into the corner of the removal carton, shrugging off Vee's impatience. It was mirroring her own feelings. And she was alone with the frustration, because Stu was ignoring the emotional stuff. His attitude was that everything would be fine if they faced up to it, and it made Martine want to scream.

But thank goodness, they were finished at last. Martine slid the zimmer towards Vee, who sniffed.

'I wish you'd leave it where I can get at it. I might have wanted to use it while you were in another room.'

Martine stared straight ahead. She would get comments like this every day soon.

Leaving Vee to trundle through on her own, Martine went to put the kettle on. Stu and Joya were outside in the communal garden, Stu pushing Joya on the swing, way higher than Martine liked to see. Shrieks of childlike laughter pierced Vee's double glazing. If only they were all in the garden, a normal family having fun together. Martine gazed hungrily at Joya as the little girl leapt from the swing and ran across the garden. Would Joya still be moving so effortlessly in a few decades' time? Stu was right, she – no, they – would have to tell their daughter about the family curse.

Martine blinked up at clouds scudding across the wide city sky. Summer was coming and no matter what happened, this would be a better summer for Vee than next year. They should do something worth remembering; she should be a good daughter to her mother, set an example, because heaven knows she might need Joya to be a good daughter someday too.

Her knuckles white, Martine poured the tea. 'Anything special you want to do this summer, Mum? We could borrow a wheelchair, get out of Glasgow for a day or two. Boat trip to Rothesay? Or we could take the train up to Mallaig.'

Vee lowered her backside onto a chair and manoeuvred

mere four weeks. He would have to work out a way to get Ash on his side, but the money would help with that. They'd be stupid to lose out on all that cash. Leo grimaced. All he could hope was that Eleanor would behave.

He spotted Ashley on her way down from platform ten, and jogged towards her.

'How's my girl?' He grabbed her for a kiss, his head swimming as her body moulded to his.

'Mm, all the better for seeing you. Why the mega-hug?'

Leo took her hand and pulled her towards the Gordon Street exit. 'I'm glad we're okay again about the house.'

She raised her eyebrows. 'Call it okay-ish.'

'It'll be more than -ish when you hear my news. But let's get a nice glass of fizz in front of us first.'

They found a table at Esta Noche, the new tapas restaurant, and ordered drinks and a selection of veggie tapas.

Leo grabbed Ashley's hands across the table. 'Good news. There's a flat in Clarkston that would be perfect for Eleanor and I'm almost sure I could get it.' It was one hundred per cent the truth. No need to say he wasn't going to try for the flat.

Ashley's face went rigid and she pulled her hands back. 'That's way too close. What's wrong with a flat in Bearsden, or Paisley? Or Edinburgh, for that matter.'

'Come on. You'll be saying London next.' Leo gave her his irresistible grin, relieved when a reluctant smile quivered over her mouth. 'Sweetheart, that's the entire plan. It's not far away, so she'd have no reason to refuse it. It's part of a complex for the recently retired, and there's a thriving Women's Guild attached to the church across the road – I checked – and plenty of charity shops around for her to volunteer in. It's perfect. I'm sorry I didn't consult you before accepting her offer about the house – that won't happen again. No more secrets, huh?'

Ashley sipped her wine. 'Promise me that. No more secrets.'

'Promise.' He sat back as the waiter approached with their order. 'More' didn't include the enormous secret he – and Eleanor – already had.

'And no lies, ever. I'll promise too.'

Leo raised her hand to his lips and kissed it, saying nothing. No lies... That was another story altogether.

Martine tossed her magazine onto the table and leaned back in her chair. She and Vee had been sitting on the patio for over two hours, but they'd long given up discussing Switzerland and suicide plans. After that, it was hard to go back to talking about the weather or the new cinema complex in town, and anyway, Vee had fallen asleep. Martine stared at the rise and fall of her mother's thin chest. Oh, Vee could be a pain, but they did love each other, they did. And one day she would watch as Huntington's killed Vee. Cold fear banished the affection in Martine's gut. Maybe one day Joya would watch the disease kill her too. And after that... The thought of her child developing Huntington's was unbearable. The test, the awful, terrible test – she would have to take it.

But if she had the gene... Martine pushed the thought away.

'Hi, Martine!'

The voice came from the right, and Vee jerked awake. Martine turned, not sorry for the interruption.

Leo was leaning on the fence separating the two properties, grinning widely while Ashley beside him simply

Chapter Four

Friday, 20th – Saturday, 21st June

'That's the books done.' Leo flattened the last two removal boxes and took them to the pile in the hallway.

Ashley was organising kitchen cupboards, and he went to give her a hand. 'You'll love the bookshelves. I did his 'n' hers, so your Jane Austens don't have to mingle with my Dan Browns.'

Ashley giggled, but followed it up with a sigh. 'Oh, Leo. I can't bear the thought that Mum'll be here soon, trying to boss us around. Have you heard any more about her flat?'

Leo knew it was time for another distraction. They'd had two days alone here, but reality was about to hit big-time; Eleanor was arriving tomorrow. He had to make this work from the very beginning – and he had a good idea about that. More than good, actually – it was a real flash of inspiration.

He put his arms around Ashley, and she tucked her head against his neck. 'I'll get news next week. And you should boss her right back.' Leo shuffled them over to the fridge and extracted a well-chilled bottle. 'It'll be fine, you'll see. She'll be quite separate, and her friends can visit her in the annexe. Come on – wine time. There's something I want to run by you.'

He poured Chablis for them both, and they clinked. Leo shook nuts into a bowl and led the way outside to the swing seat.

Ashley sank down on flowery chintz and sipped her wine. 'Leo, I don't mean to moan all the time. It's just – I love this house, but here I am, thirty-two and about to be living with my mum again. It feels like a huge step back.'

Leo flopped beside her, inhaling the intoxicating smell of her perfume. Two days had been enough for him to know that this was how he wanted to live the rest of his life. Here, with Ashley. In spite of the no-fags and all the removal work, he'd never been happier.

And now for the great idea.

'Don't worry, my love,' he said in a mock-serious voice, popping a cashew nut into her mouth. 'I'll keep her out of your hair. This house is a great opportunity – we can start a family. A baby, Ash. We both love kids, and you'd be a fantastic mum. How about it?'

For a second she was motionless, then to his dismay her face crumpled and she shook her head. 'Let's have the summer before we think about that, huh? It would need to be you and me alone here, anyway. You don't know what she's capable of, Leo – no way am I letting my mother near my…'

She choked, and Leo couldn't tell if she was angry or upset.

'…my baby. So there's no point even thinking about it until you get my mother into a flat of her own.'

'You're the boss,' said Leo easily, but his heart was thumping. Heck. What was going on there? She wasn't meeting his eyes. But – Ash loved kids. Earlier this year she'd temped for six weeks on reception at the new Children's Hospital, and she'd been full of the funny things the kids said and did. Leo pushed one hand through his hair. Should he have proposed first, suggested a wedding and then a baby? But she wasn't a traditionalist – neither of them was. He put an arm round her and started the seat swinging, relieved when she relaxed against him.

Leo was alone in bed when he awoke at seven the following morning. He could hear Ashley downstairs, and the smell of coffee was wafting through the house – and oh, Lord, it was happening. Eleanor would soon be here. Ashley's cousin was helping with the removal at Eleanor's end, after which Eleanor was driving her car across the city to Langside. They were expecting her and the van at eleven. And somehow, over the next few weeks, he was going to have to bring about the biggest mother-daughter reconciliation ever. Leo curled into a ball and pulled the duvet over his head, shutting the world out as the desire to light up burned through him. But he'd hadn't touched the fags for – seven weeks, two days, and counting. Onwards, Leo.

Ashley was hunched over the breakfast bar eating toast when he arrived downstairs, and he reached out and ruffled her hair. 'Hey, that's not a Saturday face.'

Ashley pushed her plate away and stared out of the window. 'You're right, it's not. Leave me alone, Leo. I need space.'

Leo made his breakfast cappuccino while Ashley sat leafing through a magazine, but it was clear she wasn't reading it. He swung onto the stool beside hers, his stage fright growing. 'It'll be all right, Ash.'

It didn't sound convincing even to him. Whatever happened, he mustn't let Eleanor get the upper hand today, but that was going to be easier said than done. Heck. Maybe this whole plan had been a mistake. But eight hundred grand – no one would refuse that. Ash would come around when she saw what they could do with all that money.

'It'll be hell,' she said, sliding down from her stool, her voice wobbling. 'So it's your job to make sure it's the quickest hell ever, okay?'

She lifted her mug and swept off up the hallway, and Leo glanced at the clock on the microwave. In three hours' time, Eleanor would be living in the annexe. He rummaged in the sideboard for the key to lock the connecting door, then followed Ashley upstairs. She was in the bedroom, slumped on the edge of the bed cradling a shoe box, tears shining on her cheeks.

Shocked, Leo sank down beside her. 'I'm sorry, Ash. I didn't realise what a big deal Eleanor coming here would be for you. I'll fix it, I promise.' But how could he?

Ashley clasped the box to her chest, her head bent. 'It's not just Mum moving in. There's something I haven't told you.' She opened the box and began to sift through the contents, all papers of various kinds.

Leo's throat closed as apprehension rose. What was coming now?

Ashley's cheeks were flushed, and a little pulse on the side of her head was throbbing. 'I'll never forgive her, Leo, never. And this is the worst possible day for her to be moving in here.'

He put his arm around her, feeling the tension in her shoulders. 'Ash? Tell me what's wrong?'

Ashley went on with her search, and Leo watched as she leafed through old concert tickets, menus, train tickets – the kind of mementoes people gathered, to remind them of happy times and holidays.

Her hands were shaking. 'Poisonous old cow she is. She ruined my life and she won't even remember what day it is.'

Leo gave her shoulders a little squeeze. 'What day is it, sweetheart?'

Ashley pounced on an envelope, then opened it and produced a grainy black and white photo. She stroked it with one finger. 'Know what this is?'

Leo began to feel sick. The little head, the indistinct face, tiny arms and stick legs. 'It's an ultrasound picture. Ash? Whose baby is that?'

She turned bleary eyes to look at him. 'I was bloody fourteen. A stupid girl who got pregnant. That's what *she* said. A bit of fun – that's what *he* said – in the cupboard at the youth club. He was in my French class at school and I'd fancied him for ages, but it all went wrong. He wasn't a bit like I'd imagined.'

'And Eleanor made you have an abortion?'

Ashley dropped the photo on her knee and bent low, her head in her hands, her entire body shaking. Leo rubbed her back, and she leaned against him, then straightened up and pressed the photo to her chest.

'Oh no. By the time she noticed it was too late for that. Thank God. I was stupid and clueless and the best thing that ever happened to me was my baby. I called him Harry and I wanted to keep him, Leo. He was so beautiful.' Her voice broke, but Leo couldn't tell if it was down to grief or rage. 'And she made me give him up. They took him away and he was adopted and I never saw him again, and I could kill her for it, Leo.'

Leo pulled her close and rocked her. Dear God, what had he done? 'And is today…?'

She nodded against his chest. 'Today is his eighteenth birthday.'

Joya lifted Snowball back into his run and closed the lid. The run was made of chicken wire so he still had lots of sunshine, and in there he was safe from foxes. Some big red foxes lived in the scrubland by the railway line, and it would be dreadful if any of them captured Snowball. She spread the sack on the roof to give him some shade, then ran back towards the house. Leo was at his kitchen window. Joya waved, and he waved back, but he didn't look happy.

Inside, Grandma Vee was watching a programme about old furniture, and Joya joined her on the sofa. Two men were talking about a wooden chair, and Joya leaned back, chewing one plait. This was boring, and she had a new Wanda the Witch DVD from the library – why didn't grown-ups like cartoons? A bang from the street had her running to the window. Two men were lifting a table from the back of a big blue furniture van. This must be Ashley's mum's stuff arriving. Joya skipped outside.

'Be careful!' The voice was sharp, and Joya pulled up short and skidded back round the corner of the house before anyone saw her. She peeked out at the scene on the pavement. A strange woman with the blackest hair Joya had ever seen was waving her arms at two men who were trying to get a table through the garden gate next door. They inched it in and vanished round the side of the house Ashley called the annexe. Joya's dad called it a granny flat, but the woman with black hair didn't look like a granny. She was more like a witch without a broomstick. But how could lovely Ashley have a witch as her mum? No one was looking, so Joya ran to the front garden wall and dropped out of sight behind a bush as the woman came back to the van.

'Leo! Take these pictures in, please. I don't want them damaged. Oh, for pity's sake. All this stress is very bad for my blood pressure.'

Joya peered through the bush. Leo and Ashley were there now too, but neither of them looked happy. Joya frowned. Wasn't Ashley pleased her mum was coming to live here? Leo was stomping back to the house with a big picture, and Ashley had both hands in the pockets of her jeans.

Ashley's mum sounded as if she was cross with Ashley. 'It's heartbreaking not to have Granny's dresser here. I wish I'd thought to have it in the living room, instead of the sideboard.' She pulled out a tissue and wiped her eyes.

'I thought Kevin took it? It's still in the family.' Ashley kicked at something on the pavement.

The witch woman sniffed. 'I suppose so. Have you met the neighbours yet?'

Ashley didn't answer, but Leo was back again. Joya inched closer to hear better.

'Yes. Martine and Stu Proctor. They have a little girl, and Martine's mother lives with them too. She has some neurological thing. You'll have to meet them.'

'I hope it's a quiet little girl. They must be glad to have the grandmother around. Family's so important, isn't it?'

Ashley put her head down and ran back inside.

'What's rattled her cage?' Ashley's mum was staring at the granny flat window. 'It isn't as if she's the one who's had to put half her stuff into storage. You can help me with the curtains now, Leo.'

Joya waited till they'd gone, then scurried back to the house.

'Ashley's mum has black hair just like Wanda the Witch,' she announced, running into the kitchen.

Her dad was opening a packet of spaghetti. 'Does she have a black cat?'

Joya giggled – it was a joke, wasn't it? 'I didn't see one.'

Actually, it was a pity Ashley's mum wasn't Wanda the Witch. Wanda was a friendly witch; she could have magicked Grandma Vee better, and made everyone happy again.

Joya's mum came in from the garden and threw a lettuce and some radishes into the sink and started to scrub them. 'Stu, could you take Joya to the park this afternoon? I've been trying all week to talk to Mum about going to Switzerland, but she keeps wriggling out of it. It's doing my head in.'

'Are we all going to Switzerland?' Joya wasn't sure she wanted to go. It was nicer to go to the beach in the summer, and Switzerland was snowy.

'No, just your grandma and me. There's a clinic, you see. You and Daddy can do something else here.'

Joya went to see the lettuce being twirled in the salad spinner. 'Will they make Grandma Vee better at the clinic?'

'I don't know, Joya. That's what we want to find out.'

Joya looked up. Her mum's voice had gone a bit funny, and her chin was wobbling.

'Ladies, would you like bolognese sauce, or pesto from a jar?' Joya's dad was hovering between the freezer and the cupboard, and his voice sounded funny too.

Joya blinked the tears away. It was horrible when you didn't know what was going on.

'Ashley, for heaven's sake, I need my pans on the higher shelf. Obviously, I use them every day, and with my back I can't be stooping all the time.'

They were in Eleanor's small kitchen in the annexe, and Leo could see Ashley bite back a retort as she began to rearrange the shelves. Leo stopped on his way to fetch more screws, and went to help shift the pans. Eleanor's mouth was tight as she watched them, and Leo began to feel like a schoolboy hauled up in front of the headmistress. He squeezed Ashley's hand when they finished, shocked when she pulled it away again. This was dire – if he'd had any idea of the true relationship between mother and daughter, he'd never have agreed to Eleanor's proposition; money or no money. Anger welled up inside him. Eleanor must be laughing her head off at them – silly little Ashley who hadn't told her boyfriend about the shameful adoption, and gormless, greedy Leo who put eight hundred grand before his partner's happiness. Or was he over-thinking this? Eleanor was probably convinced she'd done the right thing for her daughter, and the baby. And Eleanor was alone now, she'd be bossing them around as a substitute for Ashley's dad, that was all. Well, Leo wasn't going to stand for that.

'I'm looking forward to seeing Jim and Carol tonight, aren't you, Ash?'

Ashley had organised that evening's outing to the West End. At the time Leo thought it wasn't the most tactful thing to do on Eleanor's first evening, but now he was glad. They might as well set the bar early on. Eleanor was not going to live in their pockets. And as soon as he possibly could, he *would* find her a flat – one that was so bloody perfect she'd be happy to move out of the annexe, which was small with a very basic kitchen and bathroom. It wouldn't be hard to find her somewhere better. He would use all his powers of persuasion to get her out of this house ASAP.

But oh God – suppose she refused to go? Or withdrew her money?

The doorbell rang, and Eleanor tutted. 'Who on earth is that? And while I remember, Ashley, we must exchange front door keys.'

We definitely must not, thought Leo. He had one to the annexe, of course. That was enough. He trotted off to open Eleanor's front door, and found Martine on the doorstep, Joya beside her carrying a bundle wrapped in a tea towel.

'Joya and I spent the afternoon baking,' said Martine, indicating the bundle. 'We thought you might like a tea loaf.'

'Hello, come in.' Eleanor marched up. 'How very kind.'

Leo made the introductions, grinning at the way Joya was staring around. 'How do you like our annexe now that it's furnished, Joya?'

'It looks smaller.'

Leo choked back a laugh as Eleanor pursed her lips.

Ashley stepped forwards, her eyes glinting. 'Come on, I'll give you a guided tour. Don't worry, it'll take about a minute and a half. The place is titchy.' She led the way into the living room, barely large enough for a two-seater sofa and Eleanor's reclining chair.

Leo leaned on the doorway as Eleanor interrogated Martine about their home and about Vee. A little muscle in the corner of Martine's eye began to jump, and Leo almost smiled. Poor thing, she must be regretting her generosity already.

'Maybe Vee would like to come for coffee with Eleanor sometime soon?' he suggested, the idea popping into his head with a positive fanfare. If the two older women made friends, it would keep Eleanor out of Ashley's hair some of the time at least.

Martine's face brightened at the suggestion. 'I'm sure she'd love to. It's a lovely room, Eleanor.' She was looking around as she spoke, her gaze stopping at the DVD collection beside the TV. 'I see you like old films. Mum loves them, too.'

Leo caught Ashley's eye. 'Eleanor's a big Hollywood fan. I can see lots of film evenings coming up.' And what a brilliant idea that was. If only Vee was obliging enough to get on with Eleanor, and actually, she might. Eleanor could be amusing company when it suited her.

Martine moved to leave, and Eleanor took the tea loaf into the kitchen. Leo stood at the front door with Ashley, reflecting that the past ten minutes couldn't have gone better.

Joya trailed down the path after Martine, then ran back and pulled at Ashley's arm, whispering urgently.

'Your mum isn't a witch, is she? Because she looks like Wanda the Witch on TV.'

Ashley hugged Joya. 'No, sweetie. But she behaves like she should be, doesn't she? Don't worry, I'll protect you.'

Leo turned back inside as Joya ran back to Martine. Definitely, a good ten minutes.

Chapter Five

Monday, 30th June

It was the summer holidays. No school today or tomorrow or the next day.

Joya tipped a handful of rabbit pellets into Snowball's bowl and added a carrot and half an apple. She would eat the other half in a minute. Snowball was waiting in his corner of the garden, and Joya opened the hutch door for him to scamper into the run. She stroked the soft fur, but all he was interested in was his food – he always started with the fruit.

It was such a shame Frosty'd died. Joya pouted. One Saturday she'd taken out the breakfast bowl and Frosty was all floppy and funny, and she'd yelled for her mum, and they took Frosty to the vet's. The vet gave him an injection and he went to sleep. Not proper sleep, though, because he was dead. Joya rubbed her eyes. It wasn't nice when anyone died, though her mum said Frosty had gone to a better place. They'd buried him at the side of the garden, under the bush that had huge pink flowers every spring. It *was* a lovely place. Joya glanced over. The flowers were gone; they never did last long.

Back in the kitchen, she was eating her half apple when Grandma Vee tapped in with her zimmer. Joya beamed at her grandmother. It was going to be fun today, just her and

Grandma Vee. What a good thing she'd come to live with them.

'Joya, love, I must have left my reading glasses at Eleanor's yesterday. Could you pop over and get them?'

'Okay.' Joya finished her apple and wiped her sticky fingers on the tea towel, but her mum was at work so there was no one to give her a row for not washing them first. Grandma Vee and Eleanor were friends now. Joya's dad said they were the gruesome twosome because they were the same age and they both had wrinkly hands and necks, but Joya thought they were completely different. Not a twosome at all.

She trotted down the garden path, her footsteps slowing as she approached the gate. Eleanor was scary. She had a loud voice and even if she wasn't a witch Joya was never sure if she was joking or not, so it was hard to know what to say to her. Joya trailed along the pavement, then stopped. Oh, good, Ashley's red Smart car was in its parking space in front of the house. She could tell Ashley about Grandma Vee's specs, and they could go to Eleanor's together. Happier, Joya skipped up to Ashley's front door and rang the bell.

The door opened almost immediately. 'Oh – Joya. Come in.'

Ashley closed the door again almost before she was inside, and Joya stared. Ashley's face was red and blotchy, as if she'd been crying. Something was wrong.

'Grandma Vee left her reading glasses somewhere yesterday.' Joya wound one foot round her other leg.

'They'll be at my mum's. Come and have some juice before you go for them. I could do with the company.'

Joya followed on through to the kitchen. It was so nice having a neighbour like Ashley. Leo was fun, but he joked a lot too, though in a different way to Eleanor, because he joked to make people like him. But Ashley was more like a friend than a grown-up.

Joya hoisted herself onto a high stool, and leaned over to see her reflection in the shiny black surface of the breakfast bar. This was such a posh house. Leo and Ashley must be very rich.

'Don't you have to go to work and make money today?'

A smile flickered over Ashley's face and was gone before Joya had time to smile back.

'We've both taken the week off work. We're going to attack the garden, but of course Leo can't keep away from his office. I hope he'll be back soon.' She poured orange juice into two tall glasses.

'I can help you. I'm on holiday now too.'

But Ashley wasn't listening. She was staring at the pile of post at the end of the breakfast bar, and her mouth had turned downwards again.

'Did you get a nasty letter?'

Ashley sighed. 'No. That's the problem. I keep thinking I might get a nice one, but then it doesn't come.'

'Who from?'

'Someone I – knew – a long time ago. I thought he might get in touch this summer, but he hasn't yet. There's still time, I suppose.'

Joya squinted at the microwave and worked out it was nearly ten o'clock. Grandma Vee was waiting for her specs. She drained her glass and set it on the bar.

'Can you come with me to get Grandma Vee's specs? Please?'

Ashley stretched out a hand and Joya grabbed it.

'She's scary, my mum, isn't she? Come on, then.'

They walked round the side of the house to Eleanor's front door, which was funny because they went right past the inside door into the annexe in Ashley's hallway. Maybe it was stuck.

Joya rang the bell and they waited until Eleanor opened the door.

'An emergency, Mum. Vee's specs are here.' Ashley strode through to Eleanor's living room, not letting go of Joya's hand.

'They're on the coffee table. I was going to—'

'No problem. I'll see you later when Leo gets back.'

In half a minute they were back in front of Ashley's door and Joya hadn't had to open her mouth. Ashley didn't seem to like her mother much either. Was that why Eleanor was living in the annexe and not in the house like Grandma Vee?

Joya took the glasses. 'Thank you.'

Ashley smiled, and it was a proper smile this time. 'Any time, Joya. Are you doing anything nice in your holidays?'

'Me and my dad are going to Edinburgh while Grandma Vee and Mum go to Switzerland, but I don't know when, exactly.'

'Switzerland! Goodness.'

Joya blinked. There it was again, just like Stevie's mum and his gran, and Miss Harper at school. People looked funny, and then they went quiet when she told them about her mum and Grandma Vee going to Switzerland. There was something about Switzerland that nobody wanted to talk about, so why did her mum and Grandma Vee want to go there?

'Me and my dad are going to see the penguins at Edinburgh Zoo,' she said.

Their own front door banged open and Grandma Vee's

voice shook out. 'Joya!'

'Off you go.' Ashley gave Joya a quick hug, and Joya hugged back. Poor Ashley, waiting for a nice letter that never came.

Martine tipped her bucket of weeds onto the compost heap at the bottom of the garden, and wandered back along the side fence towards the house, inspecting the flower border with determined satisfaction. At least the garden was going well. This was their fifth summer here, and her hard work was showing results. Plants and shrubs bloomed alternately all summer. The rhododendrons were finished now, but the peony roses were still hanging in there, and the phlox was going to be spectacular this year, mildew permitting. And yet – the garden had changed; everything had changed. This was no longer the sanctuary she had created. Martine stood still, tears burning behind screwed up lids. No, that was wrong. The garden was the same; it was her life that had changed.

She glanced next door, where Ashley was raking unenthusiastically at the old vegetable garden she and Leo had spent the afternoon digging up. The other woman's t-shirt was damp with sweat, and Martine winced sympathetically. 'Did you have a big garden at your last place?'

Ashley dropped the rake and came over to the fence. 'I had a balcony, and it was enough, to be honest. Mum had a garden, though.'

'Is she settling in okay? I'm guessing she has less space here.'

'She does, and she keeps trying to invade ours, but I'm determined to stay separate. I'm so glad she's chummed up with Vee.'

Martine was glad too. Vee and Eleanor had spent a couple of evenings last week watching DVDs in Eleanor's flat, drooling over Cary Grant and laughing at Doris Day. Vee's lack of friends in Langside was a problem – she wasn't fit enough to get out on her own, and the park and the library were up a killer hill anyway. Apart from the twice weekly outing to occupational therapy, her mother was at home 24/7, except when they took her places in the car.

She pulled a face at Ashley. 'Not so easy, is it?'

Ashley shrugged, staring back at the house, and Martine waited. On the surface, she and Ashley were in a similar situation with their mothers, but the other woman didn't seem to want to confide in Martine.

After a moment's silence Ashley changed the subject. 'Joya said this morning you and Vee are off to Switzerland for a few days. That won't be an easy trip.'

Martine clutched the weed bucket to her middle, the sick, heavy feeling churning round in her gut. There was no escape. *Take the test, help me die…* What on earth had Joya said? Had the child understood the ramifications of 'going to Switzerland'? No, that wasn't possible – but she may have picked up on the fact that this wasn't going to be your usual tourist trip. And of course, Ashley was a medical secretary; she'd know about things like this.

'Mum's considering assisted suicide,' she said bluntly. 'It's something for way down the line, but we want to look at our options.'

Ashley picked at an uneven bit on the fence. 'I wondered. A friend of a friend has MS and he's thought about it too.'

Martine opened her mouth, then closed it again. Their friendship was still too new for her to start the 'actually it's Huntington's Disease so Joya and I might have it too' explanation with Ashley.

'She's stable at the moment. We're hoping things'll stay like this for a while.' But they wouldn't, would they? It was already more like Joya looking after Vee than Vee in charge of Joya while Martine was at work. Martine's stomach churned anew. She'd been so happy to go back to her job when Joya started school, but now the prospect of becoming a full-time carer was looming. A door banged next door, and Martine looked past Ashley to see Eleanor walking towards them, an empty washing basket under her arm.

'Hello, Martine. That veggie patch is a mess, Ashley. I can't think why you don't just get someone in to lay it to grass. You know your fingers are as green as the average beetroot.'

'Laying grass isn't rocket science, Mum. And I'm not finished yet.' Ashley's mouth was a red slash.

Eleanor snorted. 'You never will be at this rate. I'll get the washing in, then make supper for the three of us while you continue here, shall I?' She winked at Martine and strode off towards the dryer that was twirling gently in the breeze.

Ashley's shoulders sagged. 'She's a – pain in the bloody neck,' she said in a low voice. 'Oh, well. Better go.' She trudged back to the middle of the garden.

Martine tidied her tools into the shed and went back inside. Why on earth did Ashley have her mother in the annexe? They all seemed well-off; surely separate homes would be preferable to bickering all the time?

Vee was in the living room watching EastEnders, and a rush of painful affection swamped Martine as she saw her mother's little smile. Half a second later Vee cackled aloud, her voice breaking, and Martine flinched. If only it was MS. Would she be more cooperative about helping Vee die here at home, if it was? Martine stood still, her mind racing. She might be. Oh, this was complicated.

'Joya's in the bath,' said Stu, coming downstairs with an armful of muddy pink clothes.

Martine jerked out of the misery and joined him in the kitchen. 'I'll go up in a minute. She told Ashley about Switzerland. I've no idea what she's picked up about the Huntington's.'

Stu pushed the kitchen door shut with one foot, and Martine could see both anger and resentment on his face.

'Joya's way too young to be burdened with this. It's enough that Vee's not well and isn't getting better. I can't understand why you don't take the test, Maxine. If it's negative, your life'll be a hundred per cent better and you know it – and you'd be able to tell Joya the Huntington's stops with Vee.'

She knew it. 'It might not be negative.'

'I don't see why knowing you'll get it is worse than not knowing, and dreading it. It's not as if you're living for every moment and having a great time, is it?'

She knew that too. But terrible hope was better than no hope at all, wasn't it? Martine slammed her hand down on the table top.

'I wish you would try to understand what this is like for me. I want to get Mum sorted first, Stu. We'll listen to what they say in Switzerland, and take it from there.'

'Then for God's sake get booked and go. This is no way to live. Not for any of us.'

He was the voice of reason all round tonight. But why couldn't he be more supportive about what it meant for her? Martine was aching for a hug and a few remarks about loving and standing by her through whatever was coming.

Stu probably thought he was doing a good job here, but he was ignoring her fear. Not to mention ignoring the fact that her mother wanted her to do something illegal. Loneliness chilled through Martine, and she shivered.

Her mum was coming upstairs; Joya could tell by the tiny, fast footsteps. She began to scrub her legs with the flannel. It was more fun when her dad bathed her. Her mum would say she had too much bubble bath in the water, and it always felt like her head was going to come off when Mum was washing her hair. Her dad just gave it a quick skoosh with some shampoo and that was it.

'Let's get you washed and into your jim-jams. Were you good for Grandma Vee today?'

Her mum's face didn't match the cheerful way she was talking, and Joya nodded energetically. 'Uh-huh. I got her specs back from Eleanor's. Ashley helped me. I think she's scared of Eleanor.'

Her mum laughed, but it wasn't a real laugh. 'I think we're all a bit scared of Eleanor.'

Joya thought about this. 'Grandma Vee isn't.'

'Grandma Vee's different.'

For some reason Joya felt like crying. 'I wish she wasn't.'

'So do I.'

Chapter Six

Tuesday, 1st July

It was four in the morning when Martine awoke, fighting to sit up, her body covered in sweat and her heart racing. Grey dawn was filtering through the curtains and casting dim shadows on the wall. She'd been dreaming – such an awful dream; headless children running around like chickens shouting, 'Heads or tails, heads or tails?'

And that was it exactly. Heads she had it, tails she didn't. Stu had hammered the nail on the head last night – there was no certainty she'd inherited the Huntington's gene, yet she still spent her life dreading it. There *was* terrible hope, but she wasn't hoping it, was she? So she might as well take the test and know the worst.

Martine lay back down, pulling the duvet under her chin and listening to Stu snoring beside her. It was time to be sensible. She would schedule a test and go, and she'd ask Vee to come with her. It was time to work on her relationship with her mother; she had no wish to end up like Ashley and Eleanor. And no one knew how long Vee's personality would remain her own.

If the test was positive, she would start to live the day with a vengeance. And if it was negative – she could do anything. Plan her retirement, learn to ski. Have another baby.

Martine lay still. The memory of Joya's first four years was both precious and painful; four years when they hadn't known about the Huntington's. She'd been so happy to be a mother, at the start of family life, planning another baby soon and oh, what wouldn't she give to regain that happiness. If the test was negative, she could. She and Joya didn't have nearly enough fun together any more. It was horrible, seeing the hurt on Joya's little face when Martine was too worried to be patient. Worse still, for the past few weeks Martine had been forced to stand by as her child built a relationship with the woman next door. Joya and Ashley giggled and whispered and had fun together – exactly what Martine was longing for. If only Joya beamed at her the way she did when Ashley called over the garden fence.

Tears trickled down the sides of Martine's head towards her ears. How very much she wanted to live.

At half past eleven, Martine put the vacuum cleaner away and sank down on a hard kitchen chair. Thank God she wasn't working today; she was dead on her feet after her broken night's sleep. But Joya was at Stevie's, Vee was at Eleanor's, Stu was at work – she had me-time now, hallelujah. She was about to put the kettle on when Ashley knocked on the open back door.

'Fancy a ploughman's? Just you and me – Leo's sneaked off to a building site.'

Martine didn't need to be asked twice. They wandered up to the Unicorn and took their cider and plates of cheese and pickle out to the garden. This was more like it.

Ashley fanned herself with a paper napkin. 'This is the hottest summer ever. We could be in Greece, not Glasgow.

Great for the kids, isn't it?'

Martine sipped her cider. 'Joya's in her element. Any family plans of your own yet?'

The split-second silence before Ashley spoke told Martine that this was another touchy subject. Hell, could she and Ashley only talk about kitchens and gardens? The other woman's smile was going nowhere near her eyes.

'Maybe someday. I – I had one as a teenager, and he was adopted.'

Martine reached out and squeezed Ashley's arm. 'That must have been hard.'

'It still is. He's old enough to find me this summer. I really hope he does.'

'Can't you search for him?'

Ashley stared. 'I've always assumed it was a one-way thing in the other direction.'

Martine shrugged. 'I don't know. Have a look online.'

Ashley nodded, then busied herself with a chunk of Brie. Martine cast around for something else to talk about before Ashley thought to ask why Joya was an only child.

'How are you finding Langside, now you've been here for a bit?' Sometimes, superficial was best.

'Let's go for sushi.' Ashley stopped in the middle of Buchanan Street pedestrian precinct.

Leo was already turning towards Central Station and the five o'clock train to Langside, but he changed direction immediately. After a hard hour or so's shopping, sushi was a good idea. 'Why not?'

Ashley tucked her free arm through his and he smiled down at her. They didn't often spend an afternoon in town

– for one thing, shopping was easier in one of the centres on the outskirts of Glasgow, and for another, Leo wasn't a fan of the whole shop-until-you-drop experience. But he'd needed shirts, and Ash wanted to go into town, so here they were.

Of course, going for sushi was nothing less than an excuse not to go home, where Eleanor would be waiting with some valid reason to come and see them, but still – Leo was as keen to stay away from her as Ash was. He shivered. What would Ash do if she found out that Eleanor was in the annexe for keeps? She might leave him. Hell, no – he had to find a way to make Eleanor *want* to leave. Easier said than done; the old bat was revelling in having her daughter around to boss.

It was early, and the sushi restaurant was less than half-full. They sat at the centre table, watching as the band of dishes revolved in front of them, and Leo ordered wine. Ashley picked out a few plates and they settled down to share, Leo searching for a topic that wouldn't lead him into dangerous Eleanor waters.

But Ashley started first. 'I want to find him,' she said, waving her chopsticks at him.

'Who?' As soon as the word was out Leo realised who.

'Harry. My baby. He's eighteen now. I've been wondering if he would get in touch, but… Anyway, I don't know if I *can* contact him or if it can only happen if he starts.'

Leo poured more wine. This was an excellent project to keep Ashley busy, every bit as good as having a baby.

He put on his most encouraging expression. 'Social services would be able to tell you. Did an adoption society take him?'

'I don't know. Mum made me say I wanted her to deal with everything, and she didn't tell me anything. And yet…'

She mimicked Eleanor. '*Family's so important, isn't it?* Hypocritical cow.'

'Do you know his name?'

Tears welled up in Ashley's eyes. 'He was Harry Frew last time I saw him.'

Leo laid his chopsticks down. 'I guess they'll have given him a different name. Call social services in the morning.'

'I was thinking more a private detective, now we have some money. Or one of those people-tracing services you see on TV when they're looking for people's heirs.'

Leo was silent. A private detective sounded expensive, and now that he was determined to get rid of Eleanor, her eight hundred grand wasn't as certain as it had been. Finding her a lovely flat she'd actually agree to would be tricky. The heat in the restaurant vanished as a chill swept through Leo. He couldn't risk losing Ashley.

'Great ideas, both of them. You could compare services and costs online.'

Ashley beamed. 'I'll do that. And I'm wondering what Mum knows. If she knows Harry's new name, or even who adopted him, I might find him myself on social media.'

'Wouldn't he have gone to a foster family before he was adopted?'

'I don't know. But I've been looking online, and it said in some circumstances, the birth family can get updates about the baby after adoption, from a social worker. And you know what a control freak my mother is. It's not impossible she had something like that in place at the beginning and didn't tell me.' Her eyes met his, then slid away.

Leo gave her a quizzical look. 'And you want me to find out?'

Ashley touched his cheek. 'Please, Leo. If I ask her, I'll

get upset, and then she'll be horrible to me for being so soft.'

Leo kissed her hand. 'Of course I'll talk to Eleanor.' Which would mean being very, very nice to the old witch. But if Ash found Harry herself, they wouldn't need to pay a PI.

Ashley took a plate of makizushi as it passed by on the band. 'I'll start looking tomorrow. Thanks, Leo. You're such a love.'

He aimed a kiss at her head. 'Eat your sushi, miss. I'll tackle Eleanor tonight.'

Huddled under a too-small umbrella, Leo rushed along the side of the house to Eleanor's front door. Heavy rain had started while he and Ashley were on their way home, and the garden path had turned into a small river. The communicating door inside remained unused, in spite of pressure from Eleanor. Leo had no wish to be wandering around in his boxer shorts and come across Ashley's mother in the kitchen; there was a lot to be said for locked doors. He'd been tempted tonight, though. Up until now they'd managed to avoid the key swap by telling Eleanor they'd had to order new ones to replace a couple that were faulty.

Leo pressed the bell and heard the bing-bong in Eleanor's hallway.

The surprise on her face turned to a coquettish smile when she saw him. 'Oh – I thought it was Vee and I couldn't understand her coming out in weather like this. And for heaven's sake, Leo, don't let that daughter of mine bully you into not using the internal door.'

Leo dropped his umbrella into the stand behind the door. 'I've come to finish your kitchen cupboards, if that's okay.

I've got the right screws now.'

She followed him through and put the kettle on. 'I'll make tea, shall I?'

Leo had anticipated this, and grinned in the dimness of the cupboard. So far, so good.

'We found a great present for Janine's baby in town,' he remarked, when they were sitting at the kitchen table with Lapsang Souchong in Eleanor's blue and white Royal Doulton in front of them. This was true. They had reached a stage in life when their friends were having babies all the time, and Leo was conscious of a feeling of – not jealousy, but… who was he kidding, of course it was jealousy. He swallowed.

Eleanor sipped her tea. 'What did you get?'

'There's a wood turner at the top end of Buchanan Street and he makes personalised stuff. We ordered a rattle and a little bowl with *Emily* engraved on them.' Leo took a deep breath. Now for it. 'Ash told me about her baby. Giving him up must have been so hard for you both.'

There was a pause for half a second, then Eleanor cast her eyes heavenwards. 'Did she say that? It would have been a lot harder if we'd kept him. A dreamy fourteen-year-old isn't cut out to be a mother, believe me.'

Leo bit back a retort. She would clam up if he antagonised her. 'Oh, I know. She was only a child herself. Have you any idea what happened to him?'

Eleanor stood abruptly and poured a glass of water. 'Pass me my pill box, would you? It's behind you on the worktop.'

Leo handed over the little enamel pill box where she kept her medication. Eleanor was a big natural remedies fan, taking countless pills and potions every day, for everything from her supposedly high blood pressure to her falling arches. Leo said nothing as she emptied three or four pills and capsules into her hand and tossed them back all together.

She sat down and fixed her eyes on his. 'I thought it best if there was no further contact. It's water under the bridge. T– ah, the baby will be a young man now, and I'm sure he had a better upbringing than he'd have had with Ashley. She's so immature – look at her, thirty-two and still working in a temp agency. All she's done with her life is travel around and enjoy herself.'

Leo was silenced. What the hell had he done? He'd gone into business with a poisonous old trout, that was what, and there was no way he could buy her out again any time soon. And that slip of the tongue there – *did* she know the baby's name?

'I believe you can get yearly reports about adopted children, nowadays,' he remarked, making sure he sounded casual.

Eleanor's expression couldn't have been more neutral. 'Possibly.'

Leo held her gaze for a second before her eyes swivelled away. She wasn't enjoying this, but he could tell by the set of her chin that the subject was closed.

He stood up. 'Thanks for the tea.'

Ashley was waiting with an open bottle of Chianti on the breakfast bar. As soon as he went in, she poured two glasses. 'Any joy?'

'Unfortunately not, though I think she might know the baby's name. She said "T–" and then broke off. But she's not for telling us. She really is something, your ma; I've a good mind to go and search her place when she's out. She might have something floating around in a box under the bed.' Leo took a large swig of wine, then another, and breathed out slowly. He'd needed that. All this stress and no fags was doing his head in.

Ashley sipped too, her face alive as he'd seldom seen it. 'T… It could be Timothy.'

'Or Thomas. Or Travis. Or Titus.' He raised his eyebrows at her.

Ashley giggled, then sighed. 'I hope not. It might be Tony. But without a surname I still can't search for him.'

'So why don't you bite the bullet and do something here with your mama tomorrow, while I rifle through her flat?'

Ashley put her hand in front of her mouth and giggled. 'Oh Leo, we can't do that – can we?'

All Leo felt now was anger. 'Ash – she made you give up your baby. She puts you down every time she opens her mouth. And she might be sitting on the very information you need. Invite her, Vee, and Martine for coffee tomorrow morning, and I'll do the needful. She'll never know.' He refilled his glass.

'Martine'll be at work. But Vee and Joya might come.'

They looked at each other, then Ashley lifted her phone.

Chapter Seven

Wednesday, 2nd July

Joya hugged her knees, leaning back against Grandma Vee's leg in Ashley's living room. The floor wasn't a good place to sit because she couldn't see Grandma Vee properly, but she didn't want to be beside Eleanor on the sofa, and Ashley's cardie was booking the other armchair even though Ashley was in the kitchen making coffee. Joya giggled inside – Grandma Vee's leg was making funny, trembly feelings against her back. It was a bit like the massage chair she'd tried once at Braehead shopping centre.

Grandma Vee gave her shoulder a little poke. 'On you go and help Ashley, Joya.'

Joya pushed herself to her feet. Grandma Vee was a great one for helping, but this time Joya wasn't so sure. 'I might break something.'

'You can take the cutlery and paper napkins,' called Ashley, and Joya skipped through to the kitchen, going the long way round the back of the sofa to avoid squeezing between Eleanor and the coffee table.

Ashley was unwrapping an apple cake. 'Do you want orange juice or cola, Joya?'

'Or milk!' Eleanor's voice came almost before Ashley had finished speaking, and Joya stifled another giggle when

Ashley scrunched her nose up and mouthed, 'Or milk' while shaking her head in the direction of the living room.

'Juice, please.' Joya lifted the flowery paper napkins and cake forks, and followed Ashley, who was carrying the coffee jug and cake. She'd rather have had cola, but Eleanor might have started talking about ruining her teeth and getting fat. Juice was safer. She flopped back down beside Grandma Vee's chair as Ashley poured the coffee.

'You've forgotten the—'

'I haven't forgotten anything, Mum. I've only got two hands.'

Eleanor started to cut the cake and Joya spread Grandma Vee's napkin on her knee for her. Paper napkins tore, so it was better if someone did that for Grandma Vee. Joya checked her grandmother's mug, but Ashley had remembered about filling it halfway. Ashley was kind like that. Joya slid over to the coffee table and forked up her cake.

Eleanor started talking about Switzerland, asking Grandma Vee what part she wanted to visit. Grandma Vee sounded a bit funny when she replied, and Joya sighed, chasing the last few crumbs round her plate with her fork. She couldn't lick her finger and gather the crumbs up because outside manners counted when Grandma Vee was here too. And she still didn't understand why people sounded so awkward about her mum and Grandma Vee going to Switzerland. Joya glanced at Ashley. She was picking at her cake, and her face was like what Grandma Vee would call a wet weekend. Didn't she like apple cake?

'More coffee for Vee, Ashley,' said Eleanor, making it sound as if Ashley had done something wrong.

Joya shivered, leaning to the side to give poor Ashley more space. How very lucky she was that her mum was nothing like Ashley's.

Eleanor was still talking about Switzerland when Leo came in. He went to kiss Ashley, then winked at Joya, but his eyes didn't crinkle properly when he smiled. He cut himself an enormous piece of cake and took it through to the kitchen, which made Eleanor tut.

Joya inched back from the coffee table. No one was offering her more cake and it was bad manners to ask, but that didn't mean she had to sit here all the time. 'Can I go out to the garden?'

'Sure,' said Ashley, while Grandma Vee's breath was still rustling before she spoke. 'Come on, I'll show you the strawberry plants.'

It was better outside. The strawberry plants were in the sunny spot near the kitchen window, and they had lots of pink berries already. Joya started to count them, but soon gave up and ran off down the garden to look at the redcurrant bushes while Ashley and Leo stood talking. A few minutes later they vanished into the kitchen, and Joya went back to the strawberries. Would it be rude to try one? She had a feeling it would, and they didn't look very ripe yet anyway. She was turning away when she heard Ashley hiss through the open kitchen window.

'Oh *God*, Leo. Why is nothing ever easy?'

Leo made a shushing noise, and Joya heard the kitchen door close before he spoke again. 'I suppose it was a long chalk.'

'It would be so much easier if I knew his name. He's my baby and it's like he's dead, Leo, and it's all Mum's doing.'

Joya froze. She could feel her eyes stretching wide open.

Had Eleanor killed Ashley's baby? That would be why Ashley sometimes looked so sad and worried, and why she didn't like Eleanor. But didn't people who killed other people have to go to prison?

She raced into the kitchen and grabbed Ashley's hand. 'Is your baby dead?' It came out in a funny squeaky whisper – it was such a horrible thing to have to ask.

'Joya darling, no – come outside and I'll tell you all about it.'

Ashley took her right up to the back of the garden and Joya sat on the wall while Ashley told her about the baby who'd gone to live with another mummy and daddy because Eleanor said Ashley was too young to look after him.

'But Joya, it's the biggest secret ever. Heaven knows what Mum would do if she knew I'd told you.'

Joya swallowed. Eleanor might send her to live with another mummy and daddy too. People mostly did what Eleanor wanted, she had noticed that. 'I promise I won't tell.' She reached out to Ashley and gave her a lovely, squishy hug.

It wasn't long before Grandma Vee called to say it was time to go home. Joya turned at the gate to wave to Ashley, and saw how Leo was staring at Eleanor's back as she went round to the annexe front door. His face was saying 'I hate you', and now Joya knew why. Poor Ashley and Leo, not being able to have fun with their baby and watch him grow.

Leo went back inside, Ashley following on, mopping her eyes. And no wonder. That must have been a real mad hatter's tea party, and Joya's question was enough to tip anyone over the edge. It was odds-on Harry was still alive

– but were birth parents informed, if a child they'd given up for adoption died in an accident or whatever? It didn't seem likely.

'Ash, baby.' He pulled her towards him and she sagged against his shoulder.

'Oh, Leo. On Monday, when Martine was talking about Vee going to Switzerland and not coming back, all I could think was, I wish it was my mother topping herself. This is a beautiful house, Leo, but... I can't go on like this.'

A band of tension started at the back of Leo's head and radiated round to his forehead. This was what he'd been dreading. But now at least he had an answer for poor Ash. 'We'll get that changed as soon as we can, love. I'm going to see a couple more flats next week – we'll insist she takes one.' He tried to sound strong and reassuring, and the search for a flat for Eleanor had even become true, but Ashley wasn't convinced.

'She'll do what she likes and you know it.'

'I'll make sure one at least is irresistible, don't worry.' Exactly how he was going to do that was anyone's guess. But Ashley needed distraction as well as support, and the best distraction under the circumstances was her son. Leo made a point of checking the clock. 'This might be a good time to call social services and start the procedure to find Harry?'

Ashley blew her nose. 'I found a people-tracing company online – I'm going to try them first. They're based in Glasgow. It'll be less official than social services.'

Leo's fingers tapped on the kitchen table. This sounded like another idea that might turn expensive. But what the hell – if it made Ash happy, it would be worth every penny.

He held Ashley's hand as she called and explained the

basics of her story. It seemed to be a fairly standard request – the person on the phone asked a few questions, then told Ashley someone would call back within a day or two to organise a meeting 'to discuss how they would proceed'.

Ashley ended the call, her eyes bright with hope. 'That went quite well, didn't it?'

Leo managed to grin – but it *was* good. Bugger the expense. 'See? You can do this. You're not a fourteen-year-old any longer. Now let's get those grass seeds into the ground. Come on, woman.'

She laughed, and the tense band round Leo's head relaxed. He was keeping her happy. He slid a bottle of white into the fridge and followed her outside.

But Ashley was right. It would be easier if it *was* Eleanor going to Switzerland to top herself.

Chapter Eight

Thursday, 3rd July

'Thanks for fitting us in.'

Martine put her phone down and rubbed her eyes. She'd been up half the night with Vee, who'd developed a hacking cough and a cold. Or rather, a steam inhalation and a dose of paracetamol had given Vee a reasonable night's sleep, but Martine had lain awake, alternately listening for a sound that might mean Vee needed her, worrying when she heard no sound at all, and creeping downstairs in the dark to see if her mother was still alive. And now she'd had to take the day off work. This was the first time she'd needed a whole day off to look after Vee, but it was unlikely to be the last time – how long would it be tolerated? Her boss had been understanding about Vee, giving Martine a job backstage at the bank instead of on the counter, which allowed her to organise her hours to suit her new home situation. Most of her colleagues knew about the Huntington's, and they must all be wondering if Vee had passed the disease to the next generation. To her. Martine pictured the sympathetic expressions and muffled whispers she'd encounter next time she walked into the bank, and she felt like howling.

Instead, she put her head round Vee's door. 'Doctor

Shepherd's coming at half ten. I think he might send you for a chest x-ray, so we could be looking at a visit to A&E.'

Vee shrugged, her face flushed and miserable, and Martine went to put the kettle on.

Joya was at the kitchen table, stringing glitter beads and frowning. 'Why is Grandma Vee going for a chest x-ray? Am I coming too?'

'The doctors can see what's wrong better when they look at an x-ray,' said Martine. 'Of course you're not coming. Your grandma's more than enough for me to cope with. I'll call Stevie's gran.'

'They're all away in Morocco. Stevie's going to ride a camel.' Joya looked wistful, and Martine swallowed. She shouldn't snap at the child – poor Joya, she wasn't having much of a summer.

'We'll go somewhere nice very soon, I promise,' she said, stroking fair wisps of hair back from Joya's forehead. 'Who would you like me to phone? Lorraine? Or Sasha?'

Joya stood up to see outside, and Martine followed her gaze to where Ashley and Leo were bent over something in their garden.

'Can I go to Ashley's?'

Sick at heart, Martine stared into the child's hopeful face. But no wonder Joya wanted to go next door. Ashley was much better at all the fun-mummy things than she was.

The hospital was only fifteen minutes away by car, but the doctor organised an ambulance. Vee was whisked straight through A&E, Martine following on, racked with yet more guilt because Dr Shepherd thought it might be pneumonia. Trembling, she thanked the ambulance crew, then stood to the side as the team of medical staff surrounded her mother. Pneumonia wasn't a big deal nowadays, was it? But then, you couldn't compare Vee to a normal sixty-six-year-old. Martine stood listening to the jargon about IVs and U+Es. Vee was propped half-upright, an oxygen mask clamped over her face and a very young doctor attaching a drip to her arm.

An older woman in scrubs came over to Martine. 'We're taking her to x-ray in a moment. Why don't you grab a coffee while she's gone?'

Martine watched as Vee was wheeled out, looking much frailer than she had done at home. 'Will she be okay?'

The woman patted her shoulder. 'Once we get the right medication started, she'll feel more comfortable.'

Martine trudged through to the snack bar and bought a latte and a cheese and pickle sandwich, then sat in the corridor outside Vee's empty treatment room. How she hated hospitals. But then who didn't, when they were a patient? Or a patient's daughter who might become a patient too in a few years. Some Huntington's sufferers developed symptoms in their thirties – so any day, the first tingling, the first jerk could herald the start of her death. Tears welled in Martine's eyes. She would have to take the test; the uncertainty was heavier now than a positive result would be. She chewed her way through half the sandwich, then flung the rest into the bin and sipped her coffee. *What would she do if it was…?* No, no, she couldn't possibly take the test. God, this was the pits.

It was another twenty minutes before a doctor came to sit beside her. 'It *is* pneumonia, but it isn't very advanced. They're taking her up to a ward. The antibiotics will kick in soon and she'll feel a lot better.'

'Is it a medical ward?'

'Yes – 14B. Don't beat yourself up – pneumonia can develop like lightning, especially when people have other issues like Huntington's. I see Verena lives with you – are you coping?'

'More or less. But–' Martine cleared her throat. She should phrase this without mentioning Switzerland. 'We were wondering – if Mum was going somewhere, um, abroad, to see another doctor, would she be allowed to take her medical records with her?'

The doctor shifted in his seat. 'She can request a copy of her notes, and what she does with them is up to her.'

Martine stood up. 'Thanks. I'll go and see her.'

He gave her a brief smile and strode off. Martine sat with Vee for half an hour, then left her to sleep, promising to return in the evening. She treated herself to a taxi home, and stared out as Glasgow south side passed by. Wall-to-wall sunshine as far as the eye could see, and she had never felt this hopeless. Vee was going to need even more care when she got back home – how would they cope?

The first thing Martine heard when she opened the front door was Joya, chatting to presumably Ashley in the kitchen, and she fought back resentment. She could have done with quarter of an hour's peace and quiet before dealing with her daughter, and she wasn't going to get it.

'Where's Grandma Vee?' Joya's eyes were huge, and Martine forced herself to sound upbeat. Hospital stays might turn into regular occurrences.

'They're keeping her in for a day or two until the medicine works. Don't worry, she'll be home soon. Have you been good?'

'She's been an angel,' said Ashley, and Joya beamed at

her before turning to frown at Martine.

'We forgot Snowball's breakfast.' She lifted the rabbit's food.

The kitchen door banged behind the little girl, and Martine opened the fridge and poured two glasses of juice. She and Ashley sat down at the table, and Martine grasped her courage firmly. With Joya safely outside, this was a good time to 'fess up about Vee's condition. She told Ashley about the Huntington's, leaving out her own fears.

Ashley gave her arm a quick squeeze, sympathy all over her face. 'Oh, Martine, it must be so difficult for you. I temped in neurology a year or two ago, and I remember one family with Huntington's. They were so brave.'

Martine looked away. Not like her, then. 'There's a test, but I haven't had it yet.'

Ashley nodded. 'If you ever need help with anything, give me a shout. I can look after Joya tomorrow. And I understand completely about going to Switzerland. Does Vee know what they'd – do, to end her life?'

Martine sat tapping her glass. Of all the crappy conversations she'd ever had, this must be the crappiest. 'It seems to be a combination of strong drugs, either pills or in a drip, and apparently it only takes a minute or two before you lose consciousness. But… she wants to die here.'

'Oh. Would she be able to – do something here?'

'It would have to be pills, and swallowing's getting more difficult. And she'd need to take a massive overdose, and then she might be sick, or…' Martine's voice tailed off.

'God, it's so unfair. And there's no other way, is there?' Ashley pulled a face.

'Short of buying her a gun, or doing something complicated with the car exhaust, no. And that would be murder.'

'I've often wondered why they don't allow assisted suicide here.'

'I don't know. But even in Switzerland, she has to start the drip herself. And – I can understand what she's doing and I'll support her fully, but I'm so scared I might have it too. I could be talking about ending my own life some day.'

It had burst out of her. The big fear, the one that was driving her crazy. Imagine lying there in a foreign country, a stranger inserting an IV into her arm. Then reaching out and starting the flow of drugs, watching as poison dripped into her bloodstream and– no, no, no.

Before Ashley could speak there was a crash behind the back door and Joya's footsteps thudded down the garden path. Appalled, Martine leapt to her feet and yanked the door open. It hadn't been shut properly. Snowball's bowl lay in shards on the step, and Joya was swinging away, her back to the house.

Dear God in heaven. How much had the child overheard?

Chapter Nine

Friday, 4th July

Leo stared across the patio, which was looking a lot better now the decking was down. Taking a week off to get things sorted here had been well worthwhile.

Ashley came over to join him. 'Joya'll be here soon. She might want to talk about Vee and her illness, Leo – what on earth would we say? I don't know how much Joya knows about it.'

Leo put his arm round her. 'If she wants to talk, you can either answer, or tell her she should be having the conversation with her parents. It won't be a problem, trust me. When's she coming?'

'Half an hour. Martine's going to the hospital at ten, and she'll either bring Vee home, or sit with her for a while.'

Ashley's phone buzzed, and Leo went to make more coffee. He would have another look for a prospective flat for Eleanor this afternoon. She had given him a couple of cold, significant stares yesterday – did she suspect he'd been rifling through her drawers? Maybe she'd demand her money back, and as most of it had been used to buy three old houses his team was due to start renovating next week, it would be months before he was in a position to repay her.

'Hi! I'm so glad you've called so soon!'

Leo turned. Ashley was clutching her phone to her ear and there was an illuminated quality about her face that made Leo think of Harry. He dropped back into his chair and listened to Ashley's side of the conversation.

'Saturday morning – tomorrow? ... That would be perfect ... Um, I'd really prefer to meet somewhere more, neutral ... Lovely. Thank you so much.'

She ended the call and waved the phone at Leo, her eyes bright. 'We can meet the people-tracing woman in town tomorrow morning, and she'll explain about finding Harry. We've to think of all the questions we want to ask and all the details we know about him. Oh, Leo –once they start searching, they could find him any time! Then all we'd need to do is get Mum out of here, and we can start to live again.'

She danced across the room and kissed him.

Leo felt sick. Finding Harry might end up being easier and quicker than removing Eleanor.

'Sounds promising. But don't forget, we can use the opportunity while your mother's still here to find out what she knows about Harry. We won't kick her out this afternoon.' If only.

'She's hardly likely to tell us now. I saw the way she looked at you yesterday.'

'She might tell someone else, though. We're doing Martine a favour, looking after Joya – get her to talk to Eleanor.'

'Oh, that won't work. Mum'll chew Martine up and spit her out the same way she does with me. Anyway, poor Martine – she has enough to cope with.'

'For Pete's sake, Ash, what happened to positive thinking?' Leo tipped a slosh of whisky into his coffee and took it outside, irritation making it impossible to sit still. He wasn't usually a morning drinker, but all this with Eleanor and now Harry and no fags... It was too much.

The sight of Ashley's mother pulling rhubarb did nothing to soften his mood. 'Making crumble, Eleanor?'

She raised her eyebrows. 'Jam, though it's none of your business. It's the Woman's Guild Fayre this weekend. And Leo – you won't have the opportunity to look through my property again because I'm having my locks changed.'

She swept inside, and Leo stared. *Her* locks changed? What a bloody cheek the woman had. Or... could Eleanor argue that the annexe actually belonged to her, given that she had put forward her eight hundred grand and he had used some of it to buy this place? Hell. What kind of person came to live in a place where she knew she wasn't welcome, then set about being as unpleasant as possible? He flung himself into a garden chair, slopping coffee over the new decking. Frustration was still uppermost when Joya and Ashley joined him.

'Ooh – your strawberries are much redder now!' Joya dropped to her knees at the edge of the strawberry bed.

Ashley pulled a berry and handed it to Joya. 'You can try one, but they're not quite ripe yet so don't pinch any more while no one's looking. Want one, Leo?'

It was a peace offering, and he accepted. 'Mmm. Another few days'll do the trick if we get some sunshine.'

Joya went to sit at Ashley's feet, nibbling her berry. 'It's not sweet.' Her little voice was plaintive, and Leo and Ashley exchanged glances. Poor kiddy, she had a lot to deal with.

Ashley bent forward and took the remainder of Joya's berry. 'Tell you what, darling. You stay here and help Leo pick some mint, and I'll whizz up the hill and buy us some ripe strawbs. We'll make strawberries and ice cream, and peppermint iced tea. How's that?'

Joya's face shone, and a lump rose in Leo's throat. She was kind, was Ashley, even if she was weak with her mother. He would have to get Eleanor out. Soberly, he showed Joya the mint at the back of the garden, and she picked a handful of leaves.

'Grandma Vee likes peppermints. Can I take some for her too?'

'Sure. Why don't we pot up a few sprigs for you, then she can have some any time she wants?'

Digging up some mint and potting it kept Joya busy for several minutes, and Leo's thoughts returned to Eleanor, making jam in her kitchen, knowing more about Harry than she was letting on… and funding two-thirds of his business. And for the life of him he didn't know what to do about it.

Joya broke into his thoughts. 'I'm going to be very very nice to Grandma Vee because she's very sick and she won't get better, my mum says, so we want to make her happy while she's not old and dead.' She patted the earth down in her little pot of mint.

Leo wiped his brow. 'Sounds like a plan.'

'My mum says Grandma Vee might die before I'm grown up – but that's a long time, isn't it?'

Mentally, Leo applauded Martine. 'Years and years. What are you going to do for Grandma Vee?'

'We're going to Rothesay because she used to love going there, and we're having all her favourite meals, too.' Joya blinked into the pot of mint, her lips trembling. 'I don't want anyone to be dead. Are you sure Ashley's baby isn't dead?'

Leo took a deep breath. He should have gone for the strawberries; Ash would be better at this. 'Sure as sure. Ashley's baby went to live in another family, that's all.'

She was staring at him, her eyes huge. 'Was it Eleanor's

fault?'

Leo wiped sweat from his neck. 'Sort of. I don't know everything about it.'

Joya sniffed. An idea flashed into Leo's head and he looked at her speculatively. 'Um, Joya – could you–'

He stopped. Could she what? Ask Eleanor where the baby went? He must be mad, considering for even half a second that an eight-year-old would be savvy enough to put a delicate question to a poisonous old bat like Eleanor in such a way as to get the info he needed. Eleanor would see through that in two seconds flat.

'Huh?'

He could see the non-comprehension on her face. 'Nothing. Listen, there's the car. You can show Ash your mint.'

Joya sped across the garden, the pot of mint for Grandma Vee clutched to her chest.

'These are the new meds. Your GP will look in tomorrow, that's already organised. And here's your appointment for a repeat X-ray in ten days. Any questions?'

Martine accepted the pills and appointment card while Vee shook her head. The nurse pushed the wheelchair through the ward doors and out to the lifts, Martine following on. They would have to get their own wheelchair; the odd outing would improve Vee's quality of life no end. And after last night's chat to Joya about doing fun things to make Vee happy, they'd have to follow up on some of the ideas the child had produced. Martine tried to smile as the nurse helped Vee into the car, which Stu had waiting by the entrance. They'd been lucky this time, but her mother was frail. She'd obviously been doing some thinking in hospital, too – the first thing Vee had said when Martine walked into the ward that morning was 'I want to book for Switzerland, Martine. Whether I do it here or there, I need to get things sorted and getting more information's the first step.' Martine felt hopeless just thinking about the trip now. How on earth were the two of them to manage alone in Switzerland?

Home again, she settled Vee on the sofa and switched on the television. Fortunately, there was a gymnastics tournament on, and Vee was happy to sit watching girls who didn't look much older than Joya tumble about the arena. Martine went through to the kitchen. A quiet cuppa with Vee first, then she'd get Joya home again. Kettle on, she sank onto a hard kitchen chair and propped her head on her hands. Stu had rushed back to work after doing his chauffeur duty, so it was up to her to stay off work to look after her mother. Again.

The kettle boiled, and Martine rose to her feet, stumbling against the table – her leg! Oh God oh God, she had pins and needles all the way down the back of her leg to her knee and she couldn't walk properly, it felt so odd. Was this it? The start of the end of her life? No no no... Sweat broke out all over Martine's body, and her heart began to race. Panting, she limped round the kitchen, feeling the prickling sensation decrease gradually, then vanish. Was it–? It couldn't be. But of course it could. And she didn't know, because she hadn't had the bloody test. Panting, she stamped on the floor. Her leg felt normal again, but that didn't mean it *was* normal. Forcing the panic down, Martine dropped a teabag into Vee's mug and half-filled it with water. The mug was shaking more in her hands than it would in Vee's.

'Here you are, Mum. I'll just pop up to the loo, then go

for Joya. Be back in ten minutes, okay?'

Martine fled up to the sanctuary of the bathroom, buried her face in her towel, and burst into tears.

She couldn't stand this; she literally couldn't stand it.

'That was yummy.' Joya scraped her bowl clean and beamed across the breakfast bar. Ashley'd bought the nice ice cream from the Italian shop near the new Victoria hospital. They had it at home sometimes too, for special times like birthdays, but her mum said it was too expensive to eat every day in summer.

Ashley was nearly finished too, but Leo was only halfway through his. He didn't seem to be enjoying it much.

Joya was astonished. 'Don't you like it?'

Leo spooned two half-strawberries and a plop of ice cream from his bowl to hers. 'You can help me. Ice cream before lunch is more for youngsters like you and Ash.'

Joya giggled. Leo was nice, but sometimes he was difficult to understand. Back there in the garden... what had he nearly said? But it was safe now with Ashley here too, and Leo was being funny again. Joya looked outside. Eleanor was hanging washing on the whirligig at the side of the garden. It wasn't fair, Eleanor had lots of things Grandma Vee didn't have, and she could do things like hang up washing. And she had taken Ashley's baby away.

Ashley and Leo were holding hands across the shiny breakfast bar, looking at each other and smiling like Mum and Dad did after a fight. Would Ashley have another baby someday? But Eleanor might take that one away too – had they thought of that?

The washing was flapping in the wind and Eleanor was

gone. Joya licked her spoon one last time. 'Can I try your swing seat?'

Ashley gathered the bowls together. 'Little baby mini-swings, okay? I've seen the way you go into orbit on your own swing.'

Joya sped outside and lay back on the swing seat. Ashley was so nice, she deserved another baby. Joya hugged herself at the thought of helping with baby baths, then pushed the ground away with one foot, blinking as the sky swayed above her. Swinging like this was like being on the rowing boat last summer when they'd all gone to Largs, and her dad had taken her rowing, and then they went for knickerbocker glories and Grandma Vee finished hers first. Some of the sunshine went out of the day, and Joya stopped swinging.

'Hello, Joya. How's your grandma today?'

Joya shot to her feet. Eleanor had sneaked up while she was watching the sky. She looked round frantically for Ashley or Leo, but they were inside, and Eleanor was waiting for an answer.

'My mum's at the hospital and she'll bring Grandma Vee home today if the medicine's worked. I think.' Joya licked her lips. It wasn't easy to be sure, her mum had been so strange and sad yesterday, and this morning too.

'That's good news. Vee'll be glad to be back in her own home, where she belongs.'

Why did Grandma Vee belong at home and not Ashley's baby? And it wasn't Grandma Vee's very own home – she'd had to leave that because she was sick.

Joya squinted at Eleanor. 'Grandmas often live alone.'

'It's nicer for everyone when they have family nearby.'

'Even babies?' It was out before Joya had time to think. She shivered. Eleanor was going to be cross now, and sure enough, her mouth had gone all stiff.

'Babies need a good home too.'

Eleanor tapped back along the path in her high heels and Joya stared after her. Grown-ups were always saying one thing and doing another. She wandered round the strawberry bed, trying to forget the fright Eleanor had given her. What a lot of berries there were. Maybe next time Ashley could make ice cream and strawbs from her own garden.

Inside, Ashley was wiping the breakfast bar. 'Holidays at home are no good, Joya. You end up working harder than you have to at work.'

Joya perched on one of the high stools, nodding. Her dad was on holiday soon but they had nothing planned, and with Grandma Vee sick and Mum all cross and peculiar it was going to be no fun at all.

The doorbell bing-bonged, and Joya slid to the floor. 'Is that my mum?'

'Let's go and see.'

Joya followed Ashley to the front door. Sure enough, her mum was there, and her face was dull and flat as well as cross.

'I'm home again, Joya, and Grandma Vee's back too. Ashley, thanks so much for having her.'

'Martine? Is everything – is there anything I can do?'

Joya swung round to see Ashley better. She sounded the same as she had the day Grandma Vee lost her specs and the nice letter hadn't arrived, almost like she was crying. Her mum's hands were gripping Joya's shoulders so hard it hurt, and she shrugged away. What was happening?

'We're okay, thanks. Mum has antibiotics and the doctor'll check her tomorrow. It was just a scare, that's all. Joya, what do you say to…?' Her voice faded away.

Joya went to Ashley for a hug. 'Thank you for having me and for – everything.'

'Come back soon, Joya. Don't forget your plant for Grandma Vee.'

Joya ran to get the pot of mint, and when she came back, Ashley was frowning and her mum was halfway down the garden path. Joya trailed after her. It might be better not to mention the ice cream before lunch.

By late afternoon Leo had done everything he'd set out to do in the garden that week. The grass was cut, and new grass sown where the veggie plot had been. He'd repaired the broken sections of fence at the side, too. And if it hadn't been for Eleanor and her accusing eyes boring into him every time she went past, he'd have been happy. Thank God she'd gone out this afternoon.

No sooner had the thought crossed his mind than he heard Eleanor's Golf pull up in front of the house. The annexe stood where other properties in the area had a double garage, so the front garden was paved to make room for three cars to park. It didn't look bad – Ashley had planted ornamental grasses in tubs on either side of the front door, and she had window boxes with red and pink begonias, too. Leo swallowed. Ash was trying so hard to make this place a home for them, but Eleanor was ruining everything. Leo turned into the kitchen, pausing in the doorway when he heard Eleanor's strident tones in the front hall.

'–and tell that boyfriend of yours that getting children to make loaded remarks is despicable. I won't have it, and I won't have either of you snooping round my things. I'm having the annexe locks changed. It's my home and I can do as I like in it.'

The front door slammed. Ashley hadn't said a word.

Leo sidled into the hallway, trepidation making him stumble over his own feet. 'Ash? What was all that about?'

Her chin was wobbling. 'You tell me, Leo. But I've come to the end of my tether. I've tried to ignore my mother's attempts to make my life a misery, but it's not going to work. And that didn't sound as if she was talking about living here for a few weeks like you said. So, you can undo whatever arrangement you've made with her and get her out of here, because either she goes or I do.' She ran upstairs and this time it was the bedroom door that slammed.

Leo went back to the kitchen and poured a large whisky. His mind was clear, like ice. Eleanor had to go. How soon could he repay her? He jotted on a flyer for a Chinese takeaway. Eleanor had loaned him 800K. Most of it was now tied up in three properties, each of which should bring in a nice profit – but not for another couple of months, even if he got everyone working overtime. Could he borrow money somewhere else to pay Eleanor off? But hell, even if he repaid her, she'd still be here in the annexe. What would persuade her to move?

The whisky was working; he felt more in control. The problem was, Eleanor wanted to be here. Maybe she just liked being near her family? But that didn't ring true, somehow.

Horrible certainty swamped into Leo's mind and he began to feel sick. Eleanor wasn't here because she liked having family nearby to boss around, was she? No, she was here because she got some kind of sadistic pleasure out of tormenting her daughter. So anything he said or did in an attempt to get her out would be like feeding the trolls on some dodgy internet platform. Eleanor must be enjoying their discomfort; she'd be revelling in it.

And if he didn't get Ashley back on side, he would lose her and be left alone in a house he couldn't afford with Eleanor clamped to the annexe. That was *not* going to happen.

Leo yelled up the stairs. 'Ash! Emergency meeting. Now! Bring your iPad.'

The relief when she appeared, the iPad in one hand and a questioning expression on her face, was immense. He couldn't lose her – they had to work on this together.

Ashley was silent as he confessed. Her eyes were red. Leo poured another whisky, and a glass of wine for her, and for a moment they sat in silence.

Then Ashley spoke. 'What the hell, what the *bloody* hell did you think you were doing?'

Sweat broke out all over Leo. 'I, uh, it seemed like an offer I shouldn't refuse. All that money. But–' He reached across the table and grabbed her hand. 'I was wrong, and I'm sorry. I'll fix it, I promise.'

Her hand lay passive in his. 'You should have told me. I want this to work, Leo – but without my mother. Long term, that's non-negotiable.'

'I know. I didn't realise what she's really like. Does she get her kicks out of stuff like this?'

Ashley sighed, then sipped her wine. 'She's always been very controlling. What can we do?'

'I'll have the money back by autumn, but that won't shift her from the annexe. Can you think of anything that might?'

A tired grin flashed over Ashley's face and was gone. 'A plague of spiders. She hates them.'

Relief swamped Leo again. It was going to be all right. She was joking with him.

'Let's make that Plan B. What else might persuade her to

go?'

Ashley drummed her fingers on the table, her brow creased. Then she nodded. 'We should do what the advice columns say and get out of the victim role – we have to up our game, and I know a very good way to do that.' She sipped her wine, her eyes thoughtful. 'All we have to do is ignore her completely. And if that doesn't work, we'll make sure bad things happen to her. Just little, tiny, bad things. Lots of them.'

Chapter Ten

Saturday, 5th July

Martine glared at the alarm clock – twenty past five. She wouldn't get back to sleep now, not with Stu snoring for Scotland beside her. She eased out from under the duvet and grabbed her bathrobe. This was worse than the sleepless nights when Joya was a baby.

She made coffee and took it to the living room, settling into the corner of the sofa, feet tucked under her. Those pins and needles... It was time to organise the test, but that would take a while. You had to see a counsellor or psychologist first, and talk through the implications of knowing the result. She would start the process next week, and soon the uncertainty would be over.

And today she would make a list of the things she wanted to do if she did have it, and make sure she did them. Like going up in a hot air balloon. And visiting New York, and swimming in the Pacific...

Martine shook her head, her throat closing as tears threatened. Who was she kidding? She wouldn't do these things. She wouldn't have the heart. The depression would scoop her up and claim her; she knew it would.

But... there was always Switzerland. Martine swirled the last of her coffee in the mug. That trip to Switzerland was actually a very good idea. She'd be finding out for herself, too, so if the test came back positive, she'd have the details at her fingertips. She didn't need to face up to the disease; if the result was positive, she could go on her own trip to Switzerland well before she reached the stage Vee was at. It wouldn't be for years, of course, but how comforting to know exactly what she could do if...

Martine stared at the photo on the bookcase, her, Stu, and Joya at Disneyland in Paris last year. Huge and happy smiles. It was before the start of Vee's big decline, and they'd been clueless about what Huntington's would mean for them. No – she hadn't been clueless. She'd been burying her head in the sand. She was good at that. Martine trudged back to the kitchen.

Stu had put the kettle on. He was a tea person first thing. 'You're up early. Did Vee sleep all right?'

Martine closed her eyes in despair. She hadn't even checked on her mother; what kind of a daughter was she? She hurried out to the hallway and stuck her head in Vee's door. Steady breathing was all there was to hear, and Martine returned to the kitchen.

'Stu, I was thinking about Switzerland–'

'So was I. Let's damn the expense and go all together, the four of us, when we're both on holiday this month. It could be a fun time as a family even though it would have – undertones – for Vee. Why don't you go online today and see what's available?'

Martine nodded. If he was coming too, the journey would be a lot more manageable. She dredged up a smile. 'Good idea. And I'm going to get the test scheduled this summer too.'

His relief was unmistakable. 'Well done. Things'll be

fine, you'll see.'

A moment beforehand she'd felt comforted that at last he was helping, but misery and solitude loomed again as soon as he said that last sentence. There were no guarantees things would be fine. Martine turned her head to hide the tears, but he'd already seen them.

'Oh, Martine, love, please get a grip. You can't go on like this. I don't know what more I can do.'

Something snapped inside her and the words spat from her lips. 'More? You're not doing anything. You're leaving me alone to face how to kill my mother, not to mention possibly having a deadly disease. And one of these days I won't be here any longer and then you'll be sorry.'

His eyes widened. '*Martine–*'

He reached for her, and Martine allowed him to hold her. He thought he was saying the right things. If only she could take comfort from empty words.

'I'm okay,' she said into his t-shirt. 'I'm sorry. Don't worry.'

Saturday morning in Glasgow city centre wouldn't have been Leo's chosen time, or place, for a meeting with someone who was going to find your long-lost relative, but Ashley was delighted to be, at last, on the journey towards finding her son. Leo couldn't spoil her joy, especially after yesterday. They arrived at a very genteel tea room near the cathedral, and settled down at a window table to wait. Anna Wilson, the thirty-something woman from Track Back Adoptions, arrived ten minutes late and ordered coffee and home-made crumpets, so Ashley ordered the same for the two of them as well. Leo sighed inwardly. Social services would be better at this, and they wouldn't make him eat crumpets, too.

Conversation was general while they slapped butter on the crumpets, but Leo couldn't help feeling that Anna was weighing them up. And in spite of her thirty-two years, Ash did sometimes come over as naïve. Leo had no intention of being taken for a ride, but on the other hand he had no idea what searching for Harry would cost them. Which made him naïve, too, of course. It wasn't a good feeling.

'Okay,' said Anna, leaning forward. 'At TBA we can help with your search on different levels. One is through social services, like you'd thought, to check adoption records and so on. We'd find his current name there. Another way is social media. That's the kind of thing your son might be more likely to try first, if he wanted to find you, it's the easiest way to start. There are forums for finding your relatives, and I can go on different platforms for you and see if anyone who might be Harry has posted anything, and also leave a query on your behalf. If that brings no results, we can go the more official route. If we find him, it's up to him if he wants to meet you.'

'And if he doesn't?' Ashley glanced at Leo and he gripped her hand.

'In that case I'd be able to give you whatever information he agrees to – which might be none at all. We're very particular about confidentiality, but we'd make sure he knew how to contact us if he changed his mind.'

'How long will it be before we hear anything?' asked Leo, beginning to warm to Anna and her service. At least she wasn't promising them the earth.

'Hard to say. It's summer – an eighteen-year-old may well be picking grapes in France, or setting off on a gap year somewhere. But we'll get back to you, rest assured.'

The next fifteen minutes were spent going over all the details Ashley knew, then Anna left, having accepted Leo's offer to pay for the coffee.

Ashley pulled a face. 'Sounds like we might be in for a wait.'

Leo signalled for the waitress. 'You've waited eighteen years, babes. Another few weeks won't make much difference.'

'I so want to meet him, Leo. I hope he agrees quickly.'

'She has to find him first. But I wouldn't worry – you hear all the time about people getting in touch with their birth parents.'

They drove to the West End, where an exhibition of orchids was on in the Botanic Gardens. It was part of the plan to ignore Eleanor, who usually arrived uninvited on Saturday, wanting lunch after her stint at the charity shop. Leo wasn't particularly interested in orchids, but it was something different and it gave him time to think. This breaking free of Eleanor was going to take more than a few outings, and the one thing they mustn't do was antagonise her. Eleanor digging her heels in was exactly what they didn't need.

Martine stood staring out of the living room window. The feeling of being strong enough to schedule the test was gone. And now that they were all going to Switzerland, this wasn't the best time to start the process anyway. *Excuses, excuses*, said the voice in her head, and Martine shrugged. Excuses was dead right, but the trip was enough to cope with at any one time. Decision made, she heaved a sigh of relief.

'What's making you look so happy?' Vee was standing in the doorway with her zimmer.

Martine crossed her arms. 'I've, um, decided to postpone starting the test procedure until we're home from Switzerland. Time enough in a couple of weeks.'

Vee turned and clicked her way back to her room. 'You're a spineless coward, Martine.'

Martine pressed her lips together and turned back to the window. Her mother was right, but Martine didn't care. At least she didn't have to face the demons yet.

Chapter Eleven

Sunday, 6th July

Grandma Vee's voice from her bedroom was louder than usual, and crosser, too. 'Oh, for pity's sake! Martine!'

Joya switched off her Wanda the Witch DVD and crept out to the hallway. Something was wrong with Grandma Vee today. She'd snapped at everyone at lunchtime, and she hadn't wanted to go outside to see the new flower tubs on the patio.

Joya sidled into the bedroom. Her mum was in the garden so she probably hadn't heard Grandma Vee's shout. 'Mummy's outside. Shall I get her?'

Grandma Vee was sitting on the bed with her feet on the floor and her trainers on. 'Bring me the zimmer, please, Joya. Martine put it where I can't get at it again. She has a memory like a sieve, your mother.'

Something was definitely wrong. Joya's heart began to thump. She took the zimmer to the bedside and watched as Grandma Vee struggled to her feet. Her dad said they should get a proper hospital bed that went up and down, but Grandma Vee didn't want that. Joya held the bedroom door open while Grandma Vee lurched out and turned towards the kitchen.

'Come and help me with my pills, Joya.'

Joya wasn't supposed to touch the pills. But it was all right when Grandma Vee was there too, wasn't it? She stood on a chair to open the cupboard above the dishwasher where the pills were, then Grandma Vee showed her the right one and Joya pushed it out of its plastic bubble and left it on the table beside Grandma Vee while she half-filled a beaker at the tap. Grandma Vee tried to pick up the pill, but it kept rolling away from her fingers, and she banged on the table.

'Damn thing! Put it in my hand, Joya.'

Grandma Vee never swore. Joya's middle twisted so hard that it hurt. She put the pill into a trembling hand, and Grandma Vee crammed it into her mouth and grabbed the beaker, slopping water all the way down her front. A big loud swallow that sounded sore, and the pill was gone.

Joya didn't know what to do, then she saw the colander beside the sink with some vegetable scraps for Snowball. Grandma Vee's eyes were closed, so Joya said, 'I'm taking Snowball his lunch,' and ran outside.

Her mum and dad were sitting with the laptop at the little round table under the apple tree.

'Grandma Vee wanted me to help with her pill, so I did.' Joya dropped to the grass at her mum's feet, still clutching the colander.

Her mum stared. 'Oh no – I forgot to give Mum her pill after lunch.' She looked as if she was going to start crying, and Joya ducked her head. It was horrible when grown-ups cried because it meant everything was terribly wrong.

'No matter, she's had it now.' Her dad was still tapping away at the laptop, and Joya picked at the grass. He hadn't noticed how sad her mum was.

'I'm supposed to be taking care of her and I can't even

remember–'

'Martine, your mother had her lunchtime pill at two-thirty instead of one o'clock. It's hardly the end of the world.'

Joya peeked up again, and her mum gave her one of those smiles that wasn't really a smile at all before rushing inside.

Joya's dad stretched his arms above his head and grinned at her over the laptop. 'Another time, give your mum or me a shout, huh? The wrong pills can make people very sick, you know, especially strong pills like Grandma Vee has.'

'Grandma Vee showed me which one.'

'That's okay, this time. Your mum's tired, Joya – she needs a holiday, so we've booked one. Come and see where we're going!'

'The seaside?' Joya crawled round his chair to see the laptop. A picture of a mountain and a plate of cheese were on the screen, and she could read the word at the top. They were going to–

'Switzerland?'

'That's right. Grandma Vee can talk to the doctors there, and we're staying in a lovely hotel beside a lake. We can go swimming.'

Joya didn't know what to say. Every single person she'd told about her mum and Grandma Vee going to Switzerland had looked scared. 'Isn't it scary there?'

'Scary? Not at all. We're going a week on Monday. You'll love it.' He closed the laptop. 'I'd better make sure Vee hasn't roasted your mum alive about the pill. Why don't you go and ask Ashley if she'll take care of Snowball while you're away?'

He marched across the garden and Joya blinked after him. The Grandma Vee fights were different now – it was more often her mum and Grandma Vee fighting. Joya trooped across to the side fence. Ashley was painting the old bench near the back of their garden, but she came over when she saw Joya waiting.

'How's things? You're still on holiday, lucky thing. I go back to work tomorrow, but I have more time off in a couple of weeks. That's the advantage of temping, you have different jobs all the time.'

Joya relaxed. Ashley was never cross or having funny secrets, and she didn't talk down like other grown-ups either.

'We're going on holiday a week on Monday. Can you look after Snowball, please?'

'Ooh, I'd love to. You can show me what to do. How exciting – where are you going?'

Joya fixed her gaze on Ashley's face. 'Switzerland.'

'Oh! Is your grandma – um, is she…'

'She's going to talk to the doctors. And there's a lake we can swim in.'

'Lovely. Leo, we're rabbit-sitting while Joya's on holiday.'

Leo was coming up the side path. 'Great stuff. We can set him on your mother. Sorry, Joya – we'll be very careful with him. He's not dangerous enough, anyway. Maybe we should splash out on a nice Rottweiler.'

Joya gaped. Was he joking? It hadn't sounded very funny.

Ashley gave Leo a little push. 'We'll need a much better way to bump off my mother than that. And a Rottweiler isn't part of my family planning, thank you very much.'

Joya pricked her ears up. Bump off? Didn't that mean kill? Surely they weren't… And – family planning was what it said on the notice at the baby clinic at the doctor's. Was Ashley going to have another baby?

She grabbed Ashley's hand. 'I don't think you should have a baby until Eleanor's gone.'

Ashley bent over the fence and hugged her. 'Don't worry, I won't. And I'll miss you lots while you're in Switzerland but I'm sure you'll have a lovely time.'

Joya hugged back. Ashley did good hugs, the kind Joya liked and her mum didn't do any more. How she wished Ashley could come with them to Switzerland.

Inside, Grandma Vee was watching gymnastics again, and Joya settled down beside her on the sofa. Sunday was a boring day when they didn't go anywhere. She peeped up at Grandma Vee. Her face was more lined today, and she didn't put make-up on any more. Stevie's gran always wore make-up, and so did Eleanor. But then – look at the way the TV magazine was trembling on Grandma Vee's lap. She wouldn't be able to put on make-up any more. It was like she was much, much older than she really was, so she might die before Joya was grown up after all. Or…

'Will the doctor in Switzerland have pills to make you better?'

Grandma Vee jerked, and the magazine she was holding tore. 'Yes. Maybe not this time, but I can go back. Switzerland's a better place for – pills.'

Joya watched a girl do somersaults all the way across the TV. A better place. Her mum said that was where Frosty had gone. He'd been all funny and trembly too.

Joya cuddled up to Grandma Vee. She smelled of shower gel and old lady.

'I'll always help you with your pills, Grandma Vee. You can ask me every day.'

PART TWO

THE PLAN

Chapter Twelve

Monday, 14th July

Leo closed the lid of the run while Snowball got stuck into his bowl of dried pellets and cucumber. The rabbit didn't appear to notice he was in a different garden with someone else providing breakfast, and Leo wrinkled his nose. He was a poor thing, all alone in there. But a second rabbit was hardly going to be top of Martine's priority list this summer.

Leo glanced at the deserted house next door. The family's flight was an early one – they'd be in the air right now. And he should be in his car, going to work.

The morning passed with the usual Monday round of building sites, and at twelve o'clock Leo was back in the car. He didn't often go home at lunchtime, but this afternoon he was meeting a prospective buyer in Pollokshaws, not far from the house, and he needed a shower.

To his surprise, Ashley's Smart car was parked in front of the door. Leo pulled up beside it.

'Anyone home?'

She was in the kitchen, stirring soup on the hob with her mouth turned down. 'Oh! Leo. I thought I'd come home for lunch to check on Snowball and… the post.'

She didn't meet his eyes, and Leo winced. They'd had no

word from Anna yet, and the wait was driving Ashley nuts.

He dropped a kiss on her head. 'Ash, Anna would phone or email, if she found Harry.

'I know. But it's hard, Leo. I'll have no peace until I see him. Have some soup, there's plenty.' She ladled minestrone into a bowl for him, and Leo perched beside her at the breakfast bar.

Ashley lifted her spoon, her lips trembling. 'I keep seeing us in the hospital when he was born. He was so sweet, and I loved him, Leo. I should have kicked and screamed and yelled that I wanted to keep him. Why did no one see that Mum was overpowering me?' She blinked back tears.

Leo spooned up minestrone, hearing Eleanor's Golf pull up outside. Would the old bat come to the door when she saw the cars? She'd been unusually quiet this last week; their tactic of coolness and unavailability was beginning to pay off.

It was a relief when Eleanor went straight to her own quarters. Leo stood up to go for his shower, and at that moment Ashley's phone rang. She grabbed it.

'Anna!' Ashley pulled Leo to her side, and put the phone on speaker.

Leo hugged her. Hopefully he'd be celebrating with Ash tonight, not drying her tears.

'No real news yet, but I thought I'd call you with what we've got.'

It didn't sound like the most positive development. Ashley was hyperventilating beside him, and Leo rubbed her back.

'We've located Harry – that's not his name now. He's been asking questions in Facebook groups about finding birth parents, but it all looks pretty tentative. We confirmed it was him using the National Records of Scotland and his date of birth. We haven't been able to make contact yet, and according to his posts, he's travelling in Europe at the moment. He was supposed to be coming home last week, but he's extended the holiday. Kids, eh?'

'Where does he live? What more did you find out? Is he–'

'I can't talk about him, Ashley. I'll be in touch when I can tell you more. Sorry you're having to be so patient.'

Ashley ended the call and leaned against Leo, tears escaping closed eyelids and trickling down her cheeks.

Leo stood cuddling her, then moved across the kitchen to pull a bottle of bubbly from the cupboard. 'Dry those tears, baby. Because you know what this means, don't you?' He put the bottle into the fridge.

Ashley shook her head.

'We can celebrate tonight. Harry's alive and well and having a good summer. And he's been thinking about looking for you.'

Ashley nodded, taking deep breaths. 'Leo, I swear when I find him, I will never lose him again. I could kill my mother for splitting us up like that.'

Leo went back for another hug. 'So could I, baby. So could I.'

Martine pushed the new wheelchair through the arrivals building while Vee sat clutching her handbag on her lap. Zürich Airport was like the set of a sci-fi film – the floor reflected the people hurrying along it, and there wasn't a dirty mark or scrap of litter anywhere. If the rest of Switzerland was like this, Vee's death could be the most luxurious part of her life. If she opted to die here. One day.

Joya was trotting beside the wheelchair, pulling her

small pink suitcase and craning her neck in all directions. 'Everything looks new. Is the hotel all shiny too?'

'Let's hope so,' said Stu. 'Swanky, huh?'

Two minutes later they were negotiating a building site on the way to reclaim their baggage, and Martine laughed at Joya's expression.

'Be nice when it's finished, huh?' And maybe the next time she and Vee came it would be. The fact that they were here at last was making her almost lightheaded, like being tipsy, and it felt good. She was coping, facing up to the implications of the family curse. Okay, her mother had been furious that Martine hadn't made the appointment with the psychologist yet, but then the one thing Vee had never been through was the horror of being handed a death sentence before her symptoms started. Martine tightened her grip on the wheelchair as the feeling of well-being melted away. All this talk about coping was nothing more than whistling in the dark; she was in the biggest funk ever, but she had to hide it from Joya.

'All right, Joya love?' Vee's voice came out much too loud and slurred, like a drunk woman, and Martine saw her flinch.

She pulled a tissue from her pocket and handed it to Vee, whose cheeks were pink with embarrassment. Two teenage girls were staring at them, but they dropped their eyes and hurried on when Martine stared back.

She wasn't coping at all, was she? This was the worst time she'd ever lived through. Ever.

They had two rooms at the hotel, and if you went into her mum and dad's room and then into the bathroom, you could

108

go through another door there and you were in Joya and Grandma Vee's room. It was so funny. Her dad said it was called a Jack and Jill bathroom, but Joya couldn't think why.

Grandma Vee was lying on her bed with her eyes shut, and Joya stood at the window looking out over a lovely blue lake. If she peeked to one side, she could see mountains, but they were quite far away. There was no snow anywhere, in fact it was a whole lot hotter than Glasgow, and there was nothing scary anywhere either. What a pity she couldn't tell Ashley not to worry about her. Joya skipped across to her own bed.

'Joya, for heaven's sake stop running around. Grandma Vee's tired.'

Joya plumped down and looked on as her mum unpacked the cases. It sounded like she was tired too; her voice was dull.

Grandma Vee sat up, but it was a struggle. 'I'm fine, Martine. Tell me what's out the window, Joya.'

'There's a huge big lake but you can see the other side, and there's trees and a sort of park and people sitting on the grass and going swimming, and lots of little boats and a big one. Can we go rowing, Daddy?'

Her dad had come through the bathroom. 'I'm sure we'll manage that. Vee, I'm going to steal Martine and take her for a drink before dinner. I'll come and collect you two in a bit – and look, Joya.'

He pulled a bottle from behind his back. 'Non-alcoholic champagne for you ladies. And peanuts. You can have your own aperitif right here.' He popped the cork off and poured pink fizz into Grandma Vee's sippy cup and a glass.

Joya clapped her hands, and her dad laughed. 'Joya, you're in charge of refills for you both.' He took her mum's arm and they went out through the bathroom again.

Joya sat beside Grandma Vee on the bed and they sipped cold bubbles.

'Non-alcoholic champagne, huh?' Grandma Vee didn't sound too impressed. 'Joya, next time we come, we'll have a bottle of the very best real champagne, and you can have a sip too.'

'Ooh! When are we coming back?' Joya took another handful of peanuts.

'Oh, that's in the stars.' Grandma Vee made a funny face and waved her arm in the air, and Joya giggled. They were going to have fun here, she could tell. Switzerland was the best place ever.

'I made scones this afternoon – I thought you and Leo might like some.'

Eleanor was standing at the kitchen door, a tea towel covering the plate in her hands, the usual cynical smile on her face.

Leo joined Ash at the door as she accepted the plate from her mother. What was all this about? The only thing worse than Eleanor's sarcasm was Eleanor being nice for no apparent reason. There would be a reason, of course, and they were probably about to hear it, because without being downright rude there was no way not to invite her in.

Ashley was tongue-tied, so Leo stepped in. 'Thanks. Are you coming in for coffee?' He opened the door wider, but Eleanor was shaking her head.

'No, thank you – there's a film I want to see on BBC 2 in five minutes.' She tapped off back to the annexe.

Ashley closed the door, and Leo lifted the tea towel. Two

fruit and two cheese scones.

'Yum,' he said. 'No reason to waste them, is there?'

The scones were great, and Leo found a moment to regret the fact that Eleanor was such a class one cow. Imagine if she'd been a lovely old dear, baking for them all the time.

Ashley ate two mouthfuls of her scone and pushed the rest away. 'I hope this isn't a new trend. It'll only make it harder to eject her from the annexe.'

'If she was always like this we wouldn't have any reason to eject her,' said Leo.

'She gave away my baby!' Ashley spluttered crumbs over the breakfast bar, and Leo realised what he'd said. Hell. Talk about tactless.

He reached out to her, but she banged her mug into the dishwasher and stomped towards the door. Leo called after her. 'Ash, love, I didn't mean it like that. She'll be trying to get us to relax, so we'll accept her in the annexe.'

She turned, her expression both infuriated and suspicious. 'I don't like the sound of that either. Why are you so calm about her all of a sudden? Is there something I don't know?'

Ironically, there wasn't, now, but he could tell she didn't believe him. Leo bit his lip. Plan A hadn't worked. How the heck could they freeze Eleanor out of the annexe, when she refused to be frozen?

They would have to up their game. It was time to start the bad things.

Chapter Thirteen

Tuesday, 15th July

Joya ran back up the hotel garden to where her mum and dad were still having breakfast with Grandma Vee. It was brilliant here. She'd had muesli and orange juice and a croissant with jam for breakfast, sitting outside on the terrace, then she'd gone to explore the garden while the grown-ups had more coffee. They were all cross this morning, and Grandma Vee was crossest, but then she was the one going to the doctor. Joya slowed to a walk. Her mum had gone all huffy and quiet, like she did when there was too much work to do and no-one was helping. Her dad had started out cheerful, but he was scowling into a newspaper now. He must be looking at the pictures because it was all in German.

He folded the paper away when Joya arrived back at the table, and she smiled carefully.

'Can we go out in a boat today?'

Her dad put on a happy face. 'We'll do that after lunch, when Grandma Vee's resting. You and I can walk along by the lake this morning while Mum and Grandma Vee are seeing the doctor. There's a lovely swing park near the harbour, and we can look at–'

'For pity's *sake* would you please be quiet – or better still the two of you get off, and leave us in peace.'

Joya jumped in dismay. Her mum sounded as if she was going to cry, and people were staring. She moved closer to her dad. When he stood up he looked the same as the day Joya dropped a bottle of maple syrup on the garage floor and it broke.

'Call me when you're finished, then. Good luck, Vee. Come on, Joya.

Joya ran in front to press the button for the lift. It came straightaway and she stepped in, her dad following.

'Why is Mum so cross?'

'She's worried about the doctor's appointment, that's all.'

Joya thought about this. 'I thought the doctor here was going to help Grandma Vee.'

'He is. But it's still a complicated illness. We'll know more later. Let's take the towels – you might want to go paddling.'

'Yay!' Joya put the worry-thoughts away for the moment.

The clinic was half a mile up the lake from the hotel. Martine ordered a taxi; she didn't want to arrive for the appointment all hot and sweating after pushing Vee through the heat – the temperature was in the high twenties already. She sat in the back with the wheelchair after helping the driver fit Vee into the front, and watched blue water pass by on her right as they drove. This morning would either reassure her, or terrify the life out of her, and Martine wasn't in a fit state to be terrified.

The clinic wasn't a clinic at all; from the outside, it looked like an ordinary block of flats, four floors high. Judging by the nameplates beside the doorbells, there was a mixture of homes and businesses inside.

Vee was tight-lipped as they waited for the lift. 'This is a mistake. I want to die in my own bed at home,' she said, as soon as the doors closed behind them.

Martine could feel her heart thumping. She counted to ten. 'I know that. We're here for information only.'

Vee snorted.

Once on the third floor, they were shown straight into a consulting room where a doctor joined them a few minutes later. His English was perfect, and Martine strained to stay calm and remember as much as she could, aware that the man was speaking primarily to Vee, who was staring past him with an expression that would have silenced anyone who wasn't a doctor at an assisted death facility.

He explained the service offered, and the legal implications. Basically, there was nothing to stop Vee choosing her time of death. She would have to be examined by two doctors before the prescription for the drug was issued, but if she was in favour, her physical state made the doctors' agreement a formality. The only condition was that she had to administer the drugs without help, by opening the drip they'd put in her arm. She'd be unconscious in literally a minute. Martine found herself nodding – it was good to know, if she was ever in Vee's situation, that this place would help her die painlessly and with dignity. She wouldn't have to waste away and drown in her own secretions, seeing the horror and helplessness – and God forbid the fear – in Stu or Joya's eyes as she did so.

The doctor paused, looking expectantly at Vee, who inclined her head politely but said nothing.

'And if I develop it I'd be eligible too?' Martine flinched. She hadn't meant to squeak like that.

Vee banged her fist on the armrest. 'Don't be so

spineless, Martine. You're thinking yourself into the role of a Huntington's victim before you know you are one.'

The doctor's face was encouraging. 'Your mother's right. You can't plan until you know what's going to happen, and even if you do have the gene, you'll still have years of normal life.'

Platitudes again. Martine sank back in her chair, and Vee sat stony-faced

Ten minutes later they were outside again, armed with the necessary forms and information leaflets.

'We'll walk back. I don't care if it's hot.' Martine pushed Vee towards the lake path without waiting for an answer.

It was a perfect day, sunlight dappling through tall trees on their right. Insects were humming, and in spite of everything, the peace and the warmth of the day touched Martine's soul. Her steps slowed, and she lifted her face to the sun before staring out over the water. This would be a beautiful place to die – look at those hills and mountains beyond the blueness of the lake. She knew what she would do if her test came back positive.

The path was bumpy, and Martine's wrists were aching by the time they arrived at Vee's hotel room.

'I'll have a lie down,' said Vee, staggering from the wheelchair. 'I wish I hadn't come here after all. That clinic appointment was for you, not me. You're a selfish – oh, leave me in peace.'

Martine's bubble of reassurance burst, and she left the room without speaking. Vee was right, but she was sounding more and more like a stranger these days.

The motor boat was smaller than the one they'd had in Largs.

Joya sat down in the middle, opposite her mum and dad at the steering end. They chugged away from the harbour and down the lake. Joya turned her head. She was facing the wrong way…

'Sit down, Joya!'

Her dad spoke sharply, and Joya held on tight as she turned in her seat. 'I want to see the mountains.' She stared across the water. Everything on land looked tiny from here, like a train set. Just houses and trees… and she could see the outdoor swimming pool because it had a huge water slide and it would be so great – but oh, so scary – to swoosh down there, with all the twists and turns and tunnels. Maybe she could go with her mum. Still staring, Joya jerked to the left and her dad did a funny breath.

Joya pointed. 'Look – there's the hotel. And the place we saw this morning where the swans have a nest in the reeds.'

'We see them, but sit still. You don't want to fall in, do you?'

Joya inched along the seat in slow motion, then decided against dangling her fingers in the water. Her mum was still cross, and her dad didn't really like being in a boat. Joya loved it. This was almost as good as the seaside, even though there were no proper waves on the lake.

She hesitated. Was this a good time to ask about the pool? She decided to risk it. 'Mummy, can we go to the pool tomorrow?'

But her mum was staring towards land and didn't hear. Joya looked to see what was so interesting, but it was only the different places along the shore. As well as the pool, you could go swimming from the stony beach, and the park, and in front of the hotel too. Switzerland was a lovely place for swimmers. Her mum should be happy here.

116

'Mummy? Can we go to the pool tomorrow?'

Her mum turned her face back into the boat, and Joya's heart gave a great leap. Something had happened; her mum was sort of lit up inside, like when you could see the flame shining through the middle of a hollow candle. But – why?

'We certainly can. We'll make the most of our time here, don't worry.'

Her mum's voice was soft and happy again, and Joya heaved a sigh. It would be magic if this holiday made her mum like she'd been before, happy and friendly and fun, and it sounded like that was happening already.

Her dad cleared his throat. 'Let's go back and have an ice cream, huh?' He steered the boat in a big circle, and for the second time, Joya was facing the wrong way.

She would just sit quietly, though. While things were good again.

Joya tiptoed into their room, but Grandma Vee was lying on the bed with her eyes open.

'Hello, lovey. Did you have a nice time? What did you do?'

Joya plumped down on her own bed and bounced. First her mum, and now Grandma Vee was sounding so much better. What a good thing they'd come to see the doctors here.

'First we went out in a boat and then we went for ice cream instead of lunch and now Mummy's gone for a swim and Dad and me are going to get chips to keep us going till dinner time. Do you want some too? And did the doctor make you better?'

Grandma Vee pulled herself up. 'So much better I'll never

have to go back to him again. So I can start enjoying my holiday. Chips, huh?'

Joya helped Grandma Vee into her wheelchair. She didn't look much better, but maybe it had started on the inside and would soon work its way to Grandma Vee's arms and legs. It was fun, going down in the lift, just the two of them. Taking care not to bang into anything, Joya helped Grandma Vee steer the wheelchair outside to her dad at their table on the terrace, then stood on a chair to see if she could spot her mum in the lake. But so many dark blobs were bobbing around in the water it was impossible to tell which were men and which were women, never mind her mum. Joya sat down again and picked up the snacks menu. German was a funny language.

Her dad pointed on the menu. '*Pommes frites*, look, that's what we want.'

Joya listened proudly as he ordered, and Grandma Vee laughed.

'Joya, you're an advertisement for a happy child. It's lovely to see your smile.'

Joya beamed back. Why on earth had everyone at home had been so peculiar about Switzerland? They couldn't know how good the doctors here were. 'Did the doctor give you some new medicine?'

Joya's dad cleared his throat. 'Let's forget about doctors…' He stopped talking as the waiter arrived.

The chips came with ketchup and mayo and Joya tucked in. They were skinny little chips compared to the ones at home, but they were good. When they'd finished, her dad got out his phone to check the time.

'Martine should be back now. I wonder if she went straight upstairs.' He called her number, but no one answered, and he and Grandma Vee gave each other a funny look.

Joya's heart sank. Things weren't properly back to normal. Tears stung in her eyes. 'Is Mummy all right?'

Her dad had his ho ho ho voice on, like Santa. 'Course she is.'

Joya remembered how her mum had looked like a lit-up candle in the boat. At home she was always so sad and worried, then for a little while here she'd been happy, but now... Joya sat very still on her chair. Her dad and Grandma Vee were worried. With all her heart Joya wished that Ashley was here to make her feel better.

'Why don't you take Grandma Vee round to see the roses at the side of the hotel, Joya? I'll go and...' Her dad pushed his chair back and jogged down towards the lake.

Joya turned to Grandma Vee. Her face was frozen, and Joya swallowed hard. Being in Switzerland only made people happy for a very short time. Maybe people at home were right to be scared.

Martine sat panting on her rock, the sun hot on her back. She would burn; she hadn't put on sun cream. But what did that matter? Compared to the black uncertainty of her very existence, sunburn was nothing.

Clear water was lapping against the rocks; fresh water, not salt. The motion was mesmerising. Strands of green sea grass were waving up through the lake; they had tickled against her front and legs as she approached the bank, making her heart leap. She scratched a red spot on her leg – something had bitten her, too. She'd swum across the hotel bay to the stone beach, and nobody knew where she was. If she got to her feet now and jumped on a train, she could disappear and put all the bad stuff behind her. Or at least… Martine twisted to stare towards the road. No one was paying any attention. She could walk away unnoticed, in full sight of the other stone beach users. But as soon as she hit the village in her cossie, people would stare.

Painful longing rose in Martine's chest. How wonderful it would be, to escape the fears and pressures of her life right now. It was what she'd thought in the boat that morning and it had seemed like a revelation, a vision. She could just say 'no' to the bad stuff. She wouldn't have to watch Vee die; she wouldn't have to take the test. How peaceful that would be. And how impossible.

Martine stood up and waded back into the lake.

The path snaked through the rose garden. It was quite narrow, and Joya struggled to keep the wheelchair straight. She was panting by the time they reached the front entrance, and Grandma Vee's face was like what Joya's dad called 'cat's bum', but it wasn't funny today. Joya was surprised when Grandma Vee spoke nicely to her.

'That ramp's too steep for you, Joya lovey. Go in and ask the lady at reception to help us.'

Joya ran inside, and the big tall porter came out and pushed Grandma Vee all the way back to their table on the terrace. Joya stood on her chair to see the lake again, but there was no sign of her mum or her dad. She jumped back down and sat beside Grandma Vee.

'Do you think Mummy's back yet?'

'Let's give them five minutes and then go upstairs and see.'

Grandma Vee still looked worried and scared, and Joya

sat quietly until the five minutes were up. This was awful. She didn't know where her mum was.

As soon as Joya pushed the wheelchair out of the lift, she could hear her dad. He was in his bedroom and he was shouting, so he must be really cross. He never shouted like that when outside manners counted. Joya stood still. Her mum was back, but everything else had just got a whole lot worse.

Grandma Vee twisted in the chair to nod at her. 'Take our key from my bag, Joya, then push me in there and go and wait in our room. I'll help Mum and Dad sort things out.'

Joya did as she was told, banging her bedroom door behind her. She tiptoed into the bathroom, which was steamy and smelled of her mum's lemon shower gel. Joya stood at the other door, the one into her mum and dad's room. It was open a crack so she could hear everything.

Grandma Vee was talking. Her voice had gone all thick, like it did when it was watering too much and she had to wipe her mouth with a tissue.

'You'll have people in here complaining, Stu. And you're frightening Joya. What's going on, Martine?'

Joya could see her mum now. She was rubbing her hair with a towel.

'Nothing. I needed some alone time. I'm sorry you were worried, but you must see this isn't easy for anyone.'

'We came here because you wanted to arrange my end-of-life care. But that's my job, and I'll do it myself, Martine, with or without your help. And as this will be the last family holiday we'll have, let's forget the histrionics and dramatics and make some memories, for Joya most of all. I want to see pleasant faces, both of you, and a happy manner until we get home. And that's when we'll discuss things further.'

Joya's mouth went dry and she scuttled back into the bedroom, pulling the bathroom door shut behind her. The last holiday? And what did 'end-of-life care' mean? Was Grandma Vee's life going to end after all?

Joya sat on her bed, picking a rough bit on her thumb. Now she knew why people thought Switzerland was scary.

Chapter Fourteen

Friday, 18th July – Monday, 21st July

L eo stared into the blackness of the tunnel as the train rattled round the underground circuit. Work had been exhausting today. Thank God it was Friday, and he and Ashley were meeting at The Black Bear, one of their favourite pubs.

The train arrived at Hillhead and Leo jogged upstairs and turned right into Byres Road, the hub of the west end in Glasgow. Sand-coloured tenements stretched along both sides of the street, with roomy flats on the upper floors and small shops and businesses below. Happy Friday-after-work commuters were thronging the pavements, shopping or sitting outside with coffee and wine, chatting about the approaching weekend. The place had an almost continental flavour in the warmth of the summer sun.

The Black Bear was in a lane behind Byres Road, and Leo saw Ashley at one of the outside tables as soon as he turned the corner. She was glaring into the distance, and Leo's afternoon turned a little cooler. She'd asked a lot of leading questions this week, about his business and the money he'd borrowed from Eleanor, so she obviously wasn't convinced he was being straight with her. But he was, now. She was getting impatient about his failure to find a flat for Eleanor, too, but even with his inside knowledge it wasn't easy tracking down what Eleanor might consider an unmissable bargain in a place like Glasgow.

The other problem was, Eleanor was still being nice. These days, talking to Ashley's mother was like having a conversation with a Stepford Wife – courteous, superficial, and meaningless, and it was driving Ashley to distraction. Leo didn't know what was going on, and it wasn't a pleasant sensation. A leopard wouldn't change its spots, and neither would Ash's mother turn into the fairy godmother.

Leo's feet slowed as he approached The Black Bear, but Ashley smiled as soon as she saw him.

'TGIF,' she said, as he dropped a kiss on her head.

Leo squeezed into the chair opposite her. Ten tiny tables were crammed onto a splinter of decking outside the pub; he could eavesdrop four separate conversations without turning his head. Ashley's phone buzzed in her bag, and Leo stood up. 'I'll get the drinks. The usual?'

She nodded, and Leo joined the queue at the bar. When he arrived back with their G&Ts on a tray with a tub of olives and feta, Ashley was sitting with the sun streaming out of her face.

Leo didn't need to ask who had called. 'Anna?'

'Yes! Harry's back home, so she'll be speaking to him soon. She'll be in touch when she has an answer for us.'

Leo felt his grin stretch to match hers. Thinking about Harry was going to make Ash the happiest person in Glasgow – and it would give him a bit of time to work out how to sort the Eleanor situation. They hadn't done anything about Ash's 'tiny little bad things' idea yet.

His happy moment didn't last long.

'Leo, we have to get my mother out of the annexe. I'd like

to be ready for Harry if – when he comes to visit.'

She frowned across the table, and a lump rose in Leo's throat. How very much simpler his life would have been if only he'd never accepted Eleanor's proposition. Leo squinted heavenwards. Dark clouds were rolling in from the west. They matched his mood exactly.

Martine left the cases on the upstairs landing for Stu to put back in the loft, and trudged downstairs, arms full of post-holiday washing. Sunday evening, back home, and nothing had changed. Joya was outside with Ashley, transferring Snowball and his belongings to their own garden. There was a lot of giggling going on out there, and the familiar twinge of jealousy pierced Martine's heart. She and Joya had been together all week, and they hadn't giggled like that once.

Stu came up behind her as she filled the washing machine. 'Let's send for pizzas – what would you like?'

Martine shrugged. 'Whatever. Get three. Mum won't eat a whole one and neither will Joya.' And neither would she. Her appetite had vanished along with her peace of mind.

Vee's voice trembled out of the living room. 'Pizza Hawaii for me – Joya likes that too!

Stu put the order through, and Martine went to sit with Vee, who seemed a lot more cheerful now she was home. Pity, resentment, and fear rose simultaneously in Martine.

Vee's eyes were shrewd. 'Not such a great week, was it? You're a nervous wreck, Martine.'

Martine leafed through the pile of post Stu had already organised, because then she didn't have to meet Vee's eyes.

'I'm fine, Mum. I let things get on top of me for a while, but everything'll be better now we're home.'

'Not until you know if you've got it, they won't. Martine, you're in bits. Get that appointment with the psychologist behind you.'

'Listen to Vee, she's right,' said Stu, coming in and perching on the arm of the sofa. 'I'll come with you, don't worry. Concentrate on the positive – your life'll be one hundred per cent better when you know you don't have it. And even if you did have it – it'd be years away.'

Martine closed her eyes. Her head would explode if she had to take much more of this. It was her life they were talking about, and they both thought they knew better than she did. But bide your time, Martine. Say what they need to hear.

She made herself smile briefly. 'I know. Don't rush me. I know what I need to do, and I'll do it.'

Stu and Vee both drew breath to continue their advice session. It was a relief when Joya burst into the room.

'Ashley loved the Swiss tea towel and chocolate I brought her! And Snowball's got fat!'

Martine seized her chance. 'We'd better get him a nice low-calorie tea, then. Come on – we'll have time before the pizzas arrive.' She hustled Joya from the room. Chopping carrots while Joya raved about Ashley was infinitely preferable to listening to her way-too-upbeat husband and her dying mother.

The following afternoon Martine drove to Braehead, one of the big shopping centres on the edge of the city. It was good to be here on a weekday when it was marginally less busy than the weekend, and good to be out on her own. It was a while since that had happened. She collected Vee's prescription drugs at the chemist's, and wandered round a few boutiques before treating herself to a solitary coffee upstairs.

When she could put it off no longer, she went down to the supermarket and trundled round with a trolley, collecting enough to keep them going until the end of the week. Stu was still on holiday too, so they'd need a bit more than usual. And now it was time to go home. A brief respite, but it had done her good.

The kitchen was deserted when she went in the back door, but the TV was on so Vee must be in the living room. Joya was at Gill's with Stevie, and where Stu was, she had no idea. Martine called hello and filled the cupboards, fridge, and freezer, then took a sippy cup of grape juice through to Vee.

'Here you go. Would you like a biscuit?'

Vee looked up from the sofa, and Martine saw at once that she was pleased with herself.

'Thanks, love. Oh, I made you an appointment. Stu found me the number.'

Martine's head began to buzz. 'What number?'

'The psychologist. You can go on Thursday at ten; he had a cancellation.'

Martine sank into the easy chair. Her legs were shaking. 'What made you think I needed you and Stu to make my appointment for me? I'll make my own when I'm ready!'

Vee was shaking her head. 'You'd only keep putting it off. This way, Stu can go with you without taking time off work.'

The strength of sheer rage found its way into Martine's legs and she bounded out of the chair. 'I. Do. Not. Need. You – or Stu – to decide when I should see a doctor! Oh, for God's sake…' She broke off, not trusting herself not to burst into floods of helpless tears, and stormed to the door.

'Mummy?' Joya was standing in the hallway, her Little Princess rucksack in her arms and fear on her face.

Chapter Fifteen

Tuesday, 22nd July

'Leo? Be a love and pick some strawbs for me? I'm running late and I want to take some in for the team.' Ashley plopped her handbag on the breakfast bar and stood tapping her fingers while the machine hissed the first coffee of the day into her mug.

Leo glanced out to the strawberry patch, a metre or two away from the house. This unaccustomedly hot and sunny summer was perfect for the strawberry plants, no matter what it was doing to the rest of the garden. He dropped a kiss on Ashley's neck on the way to grab the colander. He was working from home this morning, and picking a bowl of strawberries seemed like an easy way to keep in Ash's good books. He'd managed to postpone the threatened 'good talk' over the weekend, but he couldn't do that forever.

Joya was sitting on the rabbit's hutch next door, Snowball cuddled in her arms, her face buried in soft fur.

'Is he glad you're home again?' called Leo, pulling red berries from the plants.

Joya put the rabbit down in the run, and ran to the fence. 'He had a nice time with you and Ashley but I think he knows I'm his mum. Ooh, what a lot of strawberries!'

Ashley appeared, car keys and a punnet for the strawberries

in one hand, and work bag in the other. 'Hi, Joya. You'll be missing all that lovely Swiss sunshine, I expect.'

Joya shrugged and shook her head, and Leo's eyes met Ashley's. Hell, poor kiddy. Heaven knows how long her little world was going to stay happy. Leo had no idea what had been decided in Switzerland, but Huntington's Disease didn't get better. Vee was doomed and Martine – and Joya – might be too. He stood up and presented Ashley with the full colander.

Ashley waved the colander at Joya. 'Half for us and half for you, okay? To share with your mum and dad and Grandma Vee.'

Joya's eyes lit up and Leo fell in love with Ashley all over again. What a great mum she'd be, and to think she'd missed all this with Harry. He held the punnet while Ashley shook half the berries into it then handed the colander to Joya.

Joya accepted, and bit into a large strawberry. 'We're all going to the seaside for a picnic today. Grandma Vee's going to stay with Eleanor.'

Leo smiled encouragingly. 'That's nice. Where are you going?'

'Near Seamill. We always go there. My mum wants to go swimming and my dad and me are going to build a sand boat.'

She kicked the fence and Leo and Ashley exchanged another look. Joya was frowning; it sounded as if tears weren't far away.

'I'm glad my dad's coming too because my mum's a bit sick, I think. Grandma Vee made her an appointment with a new doctor, but Mummy was cross about it. I don't think she wants to go.'

Ashley leaned over the fence and hugged Joya. 'Try not

to worry, Joya. Doctors are clever people nowadays, and anytime you want to talk, you can come over. I'm home every evening.'

A smile flickered through the uncertainty on Joya's face. 'Okay. I should go in, we're leaving soon.' She started towards the kitchen door, the colander hugged to her chest in much the same way the rabbit had been, then turned. 'I'm glad you came to live here.' She trailed towards the house.

'Oh, Leo. That poor little soul.' Ashley stared after the child, and Leo kissed her.

He waved, first to Joya and then to Ashley before she vanished around the corner to her car. And now he had his own problems to worry about.

'Good job we brought the windbreak, isn't it?'

Joya unpacked the towels while her dad unrolled the stripy canvas and stuck the poles into the sand. He was right – it was a whole lot windier here than beside the lake in Switzerland. It was colder, too. But here there were waves and seashells, and they could get a 99 when it was time for ice cream. They hadn't had those in Switzerland. Joya tossed her rucksack down inside the windbreak and went to look for a good place to build the sand boat.

The beach had lovely sand and it was quiet, too. Her dad said sensible people went to Spain on beach holidays, but Joya liked it here where they could play all day and then get chips. Proper chips, not pommes frites. There was a good chip shop on the rocky bit of land that stuck out into the sea further along the beach, and her dad had said they'd get some before they went home. Joya turned back to the windbreak. Her mum was sitting on a towel, staring across the water to Arran. Everyone said the island looked like The Sleeping Warrior from here, but Joya thought it just looked like an island. They might see the ferry soon, going across from Ardrossan.

Her dad was pouring coffee from the flask. 'Be with you in a minute, Joya. Start making the pile.'

Joya set to work. You had to find a place where the sand was damp but not wet, and make a big pile, then you shaped it into a boat, and if you bashed it down hard enough you could sit in it and wait for the tide to come in and wash it all away again. When she had a big pile of sand Joya jumped up and down and waved, and her dad ran down the beach. It was good he was still on holiday, because her mum was crying inside today. But she'd been happy in the real boat in Switzerland, so maybe she'd come and sit in the sand boat and be happy again.

Her dad was a good boat-builder. Joya helped pat the sand smooth, and when the boat was nearly finished she started to collect shells to decorate the front part. And a stick for a flag pole... When the shells were in place on the boat Joya ran back to the windbreak and her mum. She'd put some lovely tissues with rosebuds on them into her rucksack, especially for the flag.

'My boat's nearly ready – come and sit in it!'

Her mum put her book down, and Joya almost grabbed her hand to pull like she would have before. But maybe better not.

'That was quick. Is it a good boat?'

'I put fourteen shells on the front and I'm making a flag, too.' Joya rummaged for the tissues. She danced back to the boat and watched as her mum sat down carefully – you had to be even more careful in a sand boat than you did in a real one.

But oh... the happy face from the motor boat in Switzerland, the time when her mum had been lit up inside like a candle – it wasn't here today. Her mum didn't even answer when her dad made a joke about rocking the boat, and Joya felt like crying, but then her dad scooped her up and sat her across his shoulders while he was sitting beside her mum in the boat.

'You couldn't do this in a real boat, could you, Joya?'

Joya shrieked, and for a few minutes they played at sailing to Arran, then she fixed the squashed boat seat while her mum and dad went back to the windbreak. The beach was busier now, and the snack bar in a van in the lay-by had arrived.

Her dad pulled out his wallet. 'Who's for a sausage roll for lunch? Then we'll have ice cream later.'

A little shock zinged through Joya. Sausage rolls, and ice cream, and chips all on one day didn't ever happen, even at the beach. Her dad was like one of those TV presenters, all bright and happy, except he wasn't really and neither was her mum.

'Get me a sandwich. I'm – going for a swim first.' Joya's mum took off her t-shirt, and her dad nodded and jogged up towards the lay-by.

Joya plonked down in the warm sand. Her mum took off her jeans too and folded them up, then put them into a plastic bag .

'Joya, I – I've seen someone I know over there. We can go for a swim together. Off you go and tell your dad to buy you something to drink, too. I forgot your bottle. I'm sure you can choose something better than juice, anyway.'

She gave Joya an extra-big hug and pushed her towards

the lay-by. Joya ran. This was the oddest day ever, but if she asked nicely, her dad might buy her a Coke.

The queue at the snack bar was long and her dad was only in the middle. He grinned when Joya explained.

'Coke, eh? Why not? Come and have a look.'

And whoops, she was up on his shoulders again, looking into the high snack bar, and there was Coke and all the usual things, and a lovely blue drink too. 'Can I have the blue one?'

'You certainly can. And if your mum's gone swimming you'd better keep an eye on our stuff – can you see it from up there?'

Joya turned her head to see the beach. The windbreak was deserted. Out at sea, six or seven heads were bobbing in the water. Nobody seemed to be with anyone else, though – but that might be her mum right at the end of the beach talking to someone.

Back at the windbreak, Joya had a competition with her dad about who could make the least crumbs eating their sausage roll. Afterwards, her dad lay down with his book.

'Time for a read till your mum gets back. She shouldn't be long – it won't be much fun in the water all by herself.'

'She saw a lady she knows to go with.' Joya sipped the blue drink. It wasn't very nice after all.

'That's good.'

Her dad settled down on his towel, and Joya sat waiting.

It was lunchtime when the text from Anna came. *Are you and Ashley free for a 7.00 meeting at your place tonight?*

Leo's first thought was that she'd texted him by mistake. But no – *'you and Ashley'* – so it was meant for him. He texted back: *Yes – does Ashley know?* No reply appeared, though, and Leo drummed his fingers on his desk. This meeting would be about Harry – so why was Anna texting him? Possibly she hadn't wanted to get stuck in conversation with Ashley on her lunch break. Ash would want all the details, right there and then, and maybe Anna didn't have time for that. Or maybe…

Maybe the news wasn't good. Leo's thumb hovered over his mobile. Should he text Ashley? No, a call might be best. 'Hi love. Anna's coming round at seven – I said that was okay.'

'Oh wow – this is it, the first information about Harry! This is going to be so great!' Her elation was immediately followed by fear. 'Oh God, Leo – what if he doesn't like me? I couldn't stand that. Or – maybe he lives in Cornwall, or Shetland. I'd never see him. Do you suppose he wants to meet up straightaway?'

Leo's throat was dry but he managed to sound encouraging. 'Hope so, baby. Not long to wait now, huh?'

'One afternoon. Oh, Leo – it's so odd – I don't even know his name but I love him to bits.'

For the life of him, Leo couldn't think what to say to this. But he didn't need to say anything, because Ashley was completely fired up.

'My God – Anna might have a photo. I will never, ever forgive my mother for keeping us apart all this time. Eighteen effing years. And Leo – I've had a great idea for the annexe.'

The sudden change of subject made him blink. 'What's that?'

'We'll turn it into a holiday let. That way, it would bring in some cash if we need any after paying Mum back, and it would be there for Harry when he comes to visit. Good, huh?'

'Brilliant. I have to go, Ash, but I'll see you tonight. Love you.'

Leo ended the call and head-banged the desk. As if a holiday let would go anywhere near compensating for the potential loss of Eleanor's eight hundred grand. And heaven help her, Ashley was going to be devastated if Anna's news wasn't what she wanted to hear.

The sound of Eleanor's elderly Golf leaving from the side of the house droned through the afternoon air. There she went, the cause of all their grief and aggro. Leo hurried out to the path by the annexe front door, where Eleanor's tubs and pots were overflowing with begonias and carnations. Bloody woman. It was a pity he couldn't mix weed killer into her wretched rhubarb crumble. Or better still, some of the dodgy Ecstasy Davey at work had heard about from a mate last week. But the tubs would do for starters. He would get her out of here. He would. And if she never spoke to him again, well, it would be worth it.

A few quick stamps of his foot had the blooms in tatters and several pots in pieces. Leo crept back indoors, satisfied. A little vandalism might go a long way towards persuading Eleanor that Langside wasn't a nice place to live.

Martine looked back along the beach, the plastic bag of clothes swinging against her legs in the stiff sea breeze. Stu and Joya were nowhere in sight, presumably still in the queue for the snack van, or else tucked inside the windbreak. She turned to stare at the pathway leading up to the road. This was it. Decision-time. She could walk up here, go to Luss, and have a few days to herself. Find herself. Her cousin Fiona in Cornwall had a holiday cottage in Luss, but she kept it for family use in summer, and as no one had called to say they were in Scotland this week, Martine could assume the cottage was empty.

Luss… Or – she could leave the bag on the beach while she had a swim, collect it again afterwards, and go back to Joya and Stu. Back to playing happy families having fun, while all the time she was screaming inside and no-one was paying attention.

And back to Vee. Infuriating Vee, making her an appointment to start the test-procedure, as if she were a child with no say in if, or when, or what time. Oh, Vee had done it out of love, but still. It was yet another instance of Martine not being in control of her life, and how it stung.

An uncomfortable thought wormed its way into her head – this must be how Vee had felt about the trip to Switzerland and the doctor's appointment there. Martine shivered, then pulled her jeans from the bag. She would go to Luss. A few days on her own could only be an advantage. She would call Stu on the way; he would realise she meant what she said about needing some space, and hopefully he would realise too that he and Vee had to stop nagging her about the test.

What would Joya think? A picture rose in Martine's head, of Joya laughing with Ashley in the garden last night. It was crazy to be jealous of Joya's friendship with their neighbour – a mother-daughter relationship was – different.

And how she wished it wasn't.

Joya poked her head round the windbreak to see all the way along the beach. The tide had washed half the sand boat away and there was still no sign of her mum. Was that her, swimming a long way away by the rocky finger of land where the chip shop was? It might be, but if it was, she was alone. Not many people were in the sea now. What time was it, anyway? Joya looked at her dad. He had fallen asleep on his towel. After a minute she prodded his arm.

'Is it time to go for ice cream?' She didn't want any until her mum was back and they could all go together, but it was an excuse to wake him up. The day had gone funny, here on the narrowing beach. Hot tears gathered in Joya's eyes.

'Wha–' Her dad rubbed his face, then propped himself up on one elbow, scrabbling in his jeans for his phone. He flipped it open and winked at Joya.

'Ten to ice cream time! Where's your mum?'

Joya scooped up a handful of loose sand and let it trickle through her fingers. 'She's not back yet.'

'Huh?' Her dad scrambled to his feet, sliding in the sand and grabbing the windbreak pole to catch his balance. He shaded his eyes with one hand, and stared out to sea.

'I think that's her along near the chip shop.' Joya stood up too. But the only people in the water now were a family with three children splashing in the waves.

'Do you mean she hasn't been back since she went for her swim? Joya, that's over an hour ago – why the heck didn't you wake me up?'

Joya began to cry. She'd known something was wrong, but she'd been waiting for her mum and if she'd woken her dad then it would have been real, this something being wrong. And now it *was* real and her dad was mad and her mum wasn't here anymore. Her dad lifted her up and she could tell he was scared because he was panting. Joya clung round his neck, sobbing. He smelled of sun cream and sweat, and he was turning and turning, looking up and down the beach.

'Okay, she's not here. We'll check the snack bar and the loos.'

He ran up the beach with her still in his arms, and Joya held on tightly, hard bounces thudding all the way up her back as he rushed through the loose sand, groaning after just six steps.

'Mar – tine!' Her dad put Joya down and yelled across the lay-by, but no answer came, and people were looking.

Joya couldn't stop crying. Her dad ran right into the ladies and Joya ran after him. It was smelly.

'Martine?'

There was no one here.

'It's okay, Joya. She must be somewhere. She…'

His voice tailed off, and Joya felt thick tears pressing up in her eyes. Her dad's chin had gone all wobbly.

'I want my mum. I want to go home.'

They went back into the sunshine and her dad climbed up on a rock at the edge of the lay-by and yelled so loud Joya put her hands over her ears.

'Mar – ti – ine!'

'Can we help you, mate?'

It was a man holding a lady's hand, and in a minute it was Joya holding the lady's hand while the man ran along the beach in one direction and her dad in the other, both shouting 'Martine!' And no one was answering. Joya didn't stop watching her dad in case he disappeared too, and when he came back he was crying.

'I'll call the police for you.' The man stood with one hand on her dad's shoulder, and the lady was stroking Joya's hair, and Joya wished and wished it was Ashley with them, or Grandma Vee.

The police came very quickly, and Joya stayed with the

lady while her dad stood talking to them and waving up and down the beach. Then he pointed to the windbreak and one of the policemen walked towards it. The man from the snack bar brought Joya an ice cream, but it wasn't a 99 and she was shaking so hard she could hardly lick it. The lady wrapped a towel round her shoulders and that helped, but Joya's middle was so heavy she didn't have room for ice cream.

The policemen were looking out to sea now, and one of them was talking on his phone.

Joya turned to the lady, 'Is my mum still in the water?'

'I don't know. But the police have boats to find people, so don't worry,' said the lady.

One of the policemen and her dad came over.

'Hello, Joya.' The policeman sounded kind, and he crouched down so she didn't get sun in her eyes when she looked at him. 'We're going to look for your mum for you. Did she say where she wanted to swim to?'

'No. She said she saw someone she knew and they could go swimming together.'

'Do you know who it was?'

Joya shook her head.

'Did you see this someone?'

Joya shook again. There was something wrong about the someone.

'Did you see your mum go into the water?'

She managed to answer this time. 'No. I went to my dad at the snack bar.'

'And what your mum wearing then?'

'Her bikini. She took off her jeans and her t-shirt.'

'I see. But her clothes aren't there any longer, Joya. Your mum's probably just gone for a walk.'

'She wasn't – she was going for a swim?' Joya began to

cry. Why would her mum say she was going for a swim with a lady and then go for a walk? She pulled the policeman's sleeve. 'She was going for a swim, I know she was. She loves swimming.'

His face didn't tell her anything, and she only heard the words. 'We'll try our very best to find her soon.'

Chapter Sixteen

Tuesday, 22nd July

Martine clutched the plastic bag containing her purse and a sweatshirt, and stared out of the window as the bus rattled along towards Ardrossan. To her right was the sea, blue-green water sparkling in its usual picture-postcard way. What were they doing now, Stu and Joya, on that windy west coast beach? She could imagine only too well what Stu would think. When someone gets lost on the beach, people panic. Martine closed her eyes. Stupid, stupid. She had no way to contact them after all; she'd left her phone in the big rucksack. Stu would search for her, and he'd know within minutes that she was either in the sea, or… Would he realise she might be sitting in a bus? Joya, oh poor Joya – her little girl would be so scared. Misery swamped through Martine in a huge wave.

But she could still put it right. They'd be at Ardrossan in two minutes, she would find a call box and confess her sins, wait for Stu to come and pick her up, then take her punishment. And go back to the intolerableness that was her life. Why, why hadn't she thought to bring Joya with her?

The sun was still mocking down on her when they arrived at Ardrossan. Martine trudged into the train station, and what did you know, the solitary phone booth was stripped of its phone. Nobody used them nowadays, did they? Should she ask to borrow someone's mobile? Maybe on the train; it was leaving in three minutes.

Leo took his tool box from the hall cupboard and strode round the side of the house to Eleanor's front door. It was time to start reinforcing the idea that Langside wasn't a 'nice' place to live. The cracked and broken flower tubs still lay as he'd left them, pink and red begonias spilling over onto the gravel. Leo rang the bell, shaking his head when Eleanor yanked the door open.

'I've come to check your locks are secure – there've been several break-ins in the area since the weekend. I see the vandals have been doing their worst on your tubs.'

Eleanor tutted. 'Maniacs, more like. I was only gone for quarter of an hour. Do your check, then. I'm with Vee in the living room.'

Leo pretended to check the lock, then followed her through. Vee was sitting with the DVD case of *Charade* on her lap, and he peered over her shoulder.

'Ah, Cary Grant and Audrey Hepburn. Golden oldies.'

'They made a lovely couple,' said Vee. 'We've had a thoroughly nostalgic afternoon, in spite of the bad start with the tubs. I think Eleanor should report those yobs to the police, don't you?'

Leo could have kissed her. 'Unless she knows who it was, there's not much point. A lot of this happens around here, you know. Not much like your old district, huh?'

Vee nodded, dabbing her mouth with a tissue. 'Milngavie was such a nice area.'

Eleanor snorted. 'I'll put the kettle on. There'll just be

time for a cuppa before Martine and the others get back.'

Leo grinned. It sounded as if both he and Vee would be shot out of the door as soon as Stu's car appeared round the corner.

They were still drinking tea when Eleanor's landline trilled beside her chair. She barked her name into the receiver, then passed it to Vee.

'It's Stu.'

Vee jammed the phone against her ear, and her mouth, always slack, fell open as she listened. A whimper escaped from her throat. Leo's breath caught. Vee's eyes were wild; something was terribly wrong. She tried to speak, then dropped the receiver, waving to Leo that he should take it.

'Stu? Vee wants me to speak to you. What's up, mate?'

Stu's voice was flat. 'Martine's gone missing. She disappeared from the beach an hour or so ago, and it's not clear if she went into the water or if she's gone off somewhere. The police are here. Joya's in a real state.'

'Oh heck, no. Can I do anything?'

'Can someone stay with Vee in the meantime? We're on the way back.' The connection broke.

Eleanor's eyes were wide. 'What is it?'

Leo replaced the handset on its base. 'Martine. She's, um, disappeared.'

'Oh, my Lord. What could have happened?'

Leo shrugged, taking Vee's trembling hand and squeezing it. What, indeed? Surely there would be a simple reason for Martine's disappearance? But it was hard to think what that reason might be, apart from the obvious. Even a good swimmer could get into difficulties.

Eleanor poured more tea. and Vee sat nursing her mug without drinking any. Leo didn't like to leave them. Should he phone Ash to come home and help? For once, Eleanor had little to say, and Vee was wheezing away, her face white.

It was five o'clock before Stu's car drew up outside. Vee struggled to her feet, only to collapse back on the chair. Leo strode to the door.

'Grandma Vee, Grandma Vee, Mummy's lost!' Joya tore in and flung herself onto Vee's lap.

Stu stood in the doorway, and his expression told Leo everything. 'There's still no sign of her. But the police asked people along the beach, and someone saw a woman who might have been Martine getting changed at the far end of the beach.'

Joya shot to her feet. 'You didn't tell me that!'

Stu put a hand on her shoulder. 'It's… Try not to worry, Joya. The police are looking for your mum.'

Joya rubbed her cheeks with both hands, and a lump came into Leo's throat. It was such a despairing, old-lady gesture.

Stu pulled Leo to the side. His jaw was tight. 'The police are pretty sure she's just gone off somewhere – her clothes are gone. And you know the stress she's been under. But that's no excuse to up and off like that. What the hell was she thinking – and where the hell is she?' He turned back to Vee and Joya. 'Vee, I'll fill you in properly at home. The police'll be here soon.'

Vee allowed him to hoist her to her feet, then turned to Leo. 'Is Ashley home? Could she look after Joya for an hour until Stu and I get – organised?'

Leo reached for Joya's hand. 'She should be on her way. Come on, Joya. We'll wait for Ashley at ours.'

The small hand in his was hot and sweaty, and Leo didn't know what to say. What kind of mother left her child like that?

The answer popped straight into his head.

A desperate one.

She'd had her chances, and she hadn't taken either of them. She could have borrowed someone's mobile on the train. She could have got off at Glasgow Central and hopped on the next train to Langside. Instead, she'd ignored her fellow-passengers, and hot-footed it up to the bus station and jumped on the Balloch bus. Luss, here she came, and it might be the most monumental mistake of her life, with consequences even more far-reaching than her decision to offer Vee a home, or whether to take the Huntington's test. Martine clasped both hands round the purse on her lap. Her fingernails were picked raw. She shifted in her seat, aware of the stares she was getting, a windswept woman, clad in cropped jeans and a crumpled sweatshirt, clutching her purse and an empty plastic bag. All she needed to complete the misery was rain. She closed her eyes, thinking about the scene on the beach that morning, playing sand boats and trying to smile for Joya – oh, Joya – while all the time hopelessness was filling her gut. Pretend fun in her pretend happy family. She had seen her chance – no, she had *planned* her chance, and she had taken it. Plastic family life and fear of death by Huntington's were killing her – this was the only way to be real.

Ashley was home already. Joya heard her in the kitchen as soon as Leo opened his front door, and she ran straight through, unable to stop the sobs choking out of her throat. Ashley lifted her and held her tight, and she had a different perfume on today, a new one.

'Sweetheart – what's wrong?'

Leo explained while Joya snuffled into Ashley's pink t-shirt, feeling how Ashley's middle gave a funny jump.

'Oh poor darling Joya. How awful. Oh, Leo – Anna – will we have to delay her?'

'No, Joya won't be here long. Why don't we have something to drink?'

He poured Coke for them all, and Joya sat cuddled on Ashley's knee at the big dinner table, snuffling into her Coke and then drinking it so fast it made her burp. She hadn't had a drink since the nasty blue one at the beach. Leo was swirling his Coke in the glass and giving Ashley funny looks, but Joya couldn't see Ashley properly from here so she couldn't tell if Ashley was pulling faces back. And her mum had gone and her dad was scared and cross, and Grandma Vee had looked like a skinny old witch back there, even worse than Eleanor, so things must be really bad, because Grandma Vee was brave.

Leo's phone beeped, and he listened and said, 'Okay' three times, then clicked it off.

'That was your dad, Joya. He said the police are coming in twenty minutes, and he'll come and get you. He's helping Vee now.'

Joya's teeth began to chatter. She didn't know if she wanted to go back home. Ashley was much better at hugs than her dad and Grandma Vee. You didn't need to hold on when Ashley was hugging you, because she did it for you.

But then Ashley did let go, and Joya whimpered.

'Hot chocolate,' said Ashley firmly.

She sat Joya on a high stool at the breakfast bar and put a mug of milk into the microwave. The stool felt cold after being on Ashley's lap. Joya accepted the mug and a biscuit, and Ashley sat beside her rubbing her back until the doorbell went, and Leo went to get it. He and Joya's dad stood in the hallway talking, and it was as if Dad didn't care that Joya could hear everything. She'd never heard him so angry. This was worse than all the Grandma Vee fights put together.

'She's upped and bloody offed, Leo. She hasn't been herself for a while. All the bloody Huntington's stuff. We've had a few barneys about that, but this is working up to be the daddy of them all.'

Joya's thumb crept into her mouth and her head sank down on the breakfast bar. Ashley was listening too, because she didn't start talking about something else to hide whatever Joya wasn't supposed to hear, like most grown-ups did.

Leo sounded nice, not at all jokey like he usually did when he was talking to Joya's dad. 'We'll help all we can, Stu. I'm sure she'll come back soon.'

'I'll bloody kill…' Joya's dad stopped talking for half a second, and then started again. 'She didn't take her phone, so they can't track her with that. But her purse isn't anywhere. She's doing this deliberately.'

A huge wave of misery washed over Joya and a horrible, long wail escaped before she could stop it. Her mum never went anywhere without her phone. Maybe she didn't want to be found, ever.

Leo closed the door behind Stu and Joya, then went back to the kitchen, where Ashley was wiping biscuit crumbs from the breakfast bar. Her hands were shaking, and Leo hugged her from behind.

'What a mess, huh?'

She leaned against him. 'I'm scared, Leo. Poor Stu, and

poor little Joya. What if it all goes wrong for us and Harry too?'

'No reason why it should.' Leo crossed his fingers mentally. Ash must feel as if she was waiting for exam results, the kind when you thought you should have passed, but you didn't know for sure, and it was so important you did pass. But heck – Harry had been looking for Ash. It *would* be all right.

Anna was early, and took her place at the dining table, her face neutral. She didn't look like someone who was about to present them with the best news ever. Leo's throat was dry, and he could see doubt and fear replace the anticipation in Ash's eyes.

Anna squeezed Ashley's shoulder. 'Ashley, this isn't what you're wanting to hear, but remember it's just the beginning of a process for your son. He started to look for you a few weeks ago, but he isn't ready to meet you yet. I'm sorry. He knows he can call me if he changes his mind.'

Ashley clasped her hands under her chin, shaking Leo's hand off her arm. 'Oh no! Did you tell him I didn't have any choice about giving him up?'

'Yes. It's hard, but some kids react like this. He may come around to the idea quite quickly, but until he does, our hands are tied.'

Leo put his arm round Ashley. She was shivering; this was a real kick in the gut for her. He held her, his head touching hers while she fought tears, then he nodded at Anna. 'What happens now?'

Ashley spoke at the same time. 'Does he know where I am?'

'He knows you're in Glasgow. I spoke to him on the phone. He's a young lad, Ashley. I suggest we leave him for a week or two, and then I'll contact him again. That way, he'll have had time to process all this and decide what he really wants to do.'

Leo tried to sound encouraging. 'That sounds like a good idea, Ash. You know what kids are like at that age, up and down on a whim.'

Ashley bent over the table, sobbing. 'This is like losing him all over again, Leo.' She turned wet cheeks to Anna. 'Can't you tell me where he is?'

'I'm sorry. I'll leave you for today, Ashley, but I'll be in touch soon.'

Leo showed her out, and returned to find Ashley wiping her eyes. She thumped the table so hard Leo winced.

'That bloody woman! Who does she think she is?'

'Hey, it's not Anna's fault.'

'I'm not talking about Anna. I'm talking about my mother. She's ruined my life. And you haven't done much about your promise to get her out of our house but I'm telling you again, Leo, either she goes or I do.'

Leo could tell she meant every word, and his stomach began to churn. 'I – I'm working on it, Ash. A few more weeks.'

'I'm not waiting another few weeks, Leo. I want her out of here. We need to scare the shit out of her – force her to leave. If she's still here at the weekend, I'm leaving.'

She pushed him away and went to the drinks cupboard for the gin.

Leo fetched glasses. 'Ash, I'll fix it. I promise. I do have an idea but it's a mean one. You might not like it.'

'Oh, I'll love it. Look how she treated me. She's poison. So, what's the idea?'

Leo could hardly get the words out. This was desperation

talking now, and no mistake. 'Davey – you know, the builder – he knows someone who has some dodgy E tablets. They seem to make people really sick. We could give one to your mother and – and then afterwards, insinuate that bad things happen to bad people here. It might work…' His voice tailed off.

Ashley scowled, her mouth turned down as far as he'd ever seen it. 'Get some.'

Joya licked her lips. A different policeman was here now with a police lady, and another lady who was wearing jeans. The two ladies took her into the kitchen and shut the door. This was scary. Why were they taking her away from her dad and Grandma Vee – had she done something wrong? Joya sat at the table with her hands between her knees to stop them shaking. She didn't want to go to prison and she didn't want to be sent away like Ashley's baby, either.

The police lady was kind, though. 'Thank you for helping, Joya. We want to find your mum as quick as we can. My name's Susie, and this is Elaine. She's a social worker and she helps children. Okay?'

Joya didn't know what a social worker was, but she didn't like to say. Susie started asking about everything her mum had done and said at the beach, and Joya answered. When they got to the bit about her dad going to the snack bar and her mum going for a swim, Susie leaned forward and Joya leaned back.

'What exactly did your mum say, can you remember?'

Elaine was leaning forward now too and Joya couldn't help it. She started to cry.

'She said she wanted a sandwich and she took off her

clothes and she said she was going for a swim with someone along the beach, and she gave me a big hug and I went to my dad.'

Susie wasn't smiling any more. 'What happened then?'

'We bought sausage rolls and ate them and then my dad went to sleep and I made sand pies in the windbreak.'

'Did your dad leave you at all after your mum went for her swim?'

'Only to look for my mum. He ran all the way along the beach and I stayed with a lady in the lay-by. I want my mum.'

Susie patted her hand. 'I know, honey. We'll try hard to find her soon. Let's go back to your dad.'

'I want to go to Ashley,' said Joya, as soon as she went into the living room. Ashley would understand.

But her dad shook his head. 'It's time for bed. Up you go and get ready and I'll come and say night-night. Don't worry, chick. We'll find your mum. It'll be okay.'

It was all just words. Joya went to kiss Grandma Vee, who was sitting in her chair like an old, old lady. Even her face was shaking. Grandma Vee didn't say anything and she only hugged back a very little, and Joya fled upstairs. Sometimes things were so bad it nearly choked you.

Chapter Seventeen

Wednesday, 23rd July

'It's a migraine. I'm really sorry, but I don't think I'll be back.' Ashley ended the call and buried her head in her hands, elbows propped on the breakfast bar.

Leo stood by helplessly, twisting the key to the van in his hands. She didn't have a migraine, but what was happening with Harry was enough to make her a liability, typing important letters about people's medical conditions. Good job her current temp position ended this week. At the moment, she was still waiting for another, and hopefully the situation with Harry would have righted itself before her next placement started.

Leo cleared his throat. He was about to meet Davey's mate about the Ecstasy pills, but he wanted to be sure Ashley realised the enormity of what they were planning to do. Slipping E to Eleanor was crazy – and cruel – but then, Eleanor was cruel too. And if he didn't do something drastic, he'd lose Ashley. He could *not* let that happen.

'Get it,' said Ashley, when he stammered his question. 'I'll have no peace of mind until she's out of our lives. For all I care we can tell her afterwards we did it. What kind of mother virtually moves in with her daughter, after what she did to Harry and me?'

Leo shrugged. An over-confident, brash, insensitive one was the short answer. The long one would explore the realms of Eleanor having no idea what she had done to Ashley, who was now hurting as badly as she had at fourteen. The difference was, this time she was lashing out. Maybe the E plan was the best way forward after all. It was massive enough to make it clear to Eleanor that she had to go, without being actually dangerous. At least – Leo chewed his index finger. The people who'd taken the dodgy pills had all been kids. A woman in her sixties might react differently; they would have to be careful. And what came afterwards – blackmailing Eleanor into vacating the annexe while leaving her money in the business – wasn't exactly in a day's work either. Whichever way you looked at it, this was going to be awkward.

Leo checked his wallet. He could get hold of the pills, anyway. A movement in the garden next door attracted his attention, and he watched as Joya trotted across the grass clutching a bowl, which she deposited in Snowball's run before trooping back towards the house, her shoulders hunched.

Ashley was watching too, her expression contorted in sympathy. 'Poor kiddy, she looks like a little old woman. Martine can't have been found yet – I'll phone next door and see if Stu wants me to babysit for a while.'

The softness was back in her face again. Leo left.

It was up to Joya to make toast for Grandma Vee, because her dad had gone to the police station to find out what was going on. Joya waited to give the toast time to cool down after it popped up, then she fished it out of the toaster and spread it with margarine and Grandma Vee's marmalade. Marmalade was yukky, but Grandma Vee liked it.

'Will they find Mummy today?'

Grandma Vee gave a jerk, then smiled at Joya, but it wasn't a very good smile.

'I hope so, sweetheart. I think Mummy was very tired and went away to have a little rest. Try not to worry.'

Grandma Vee was croaking like a frog. She took a bite of toast and coughed and spluttered, and Joya jumped up to get a piece of kitchen paper. Grandma Vee wasn't very good at wiping her mouth any more. Joya poured some juice into the sippy cup and put it on the table. She wasn't allowed to make tea or coffee.

After breakfast Grandma Vee pushed her zimmer through to the living room and sat down on her chair with a loud 'ooff'. Joya stood at the window. There was still no sign of her dad.

'Do you want to go and play with somebody?' Grandma Vee didn't sound interested.

Joya shook her head. 'I want to wait for Mummy.' She wanted things to go back to normal, and that wouldn't happen until her mum came home to chivvy everyone around and make tea for Grandma Vee and – oh! She'd forgotten to change Snowball's water. Joya ran outside, and when she got back her dad was standing in the living room talking to Grandma Vee.

'The coastguards found nothing. They've called that search off, but they're worried about her state of mind. They might get in some CCTV images if she doesn't turn up. Oh God, Vee.'

Grandma Vee closed her eyes. 'Will there be an appeal?'

Joya's dad dropped onto the sofa and buried his head in

his hands, and Joya cuddled up to him.

'I don't know, Vee.'

Joya tugged his sleeve. 'What's an appeal?'

'It's when the police show a photo on TV of someone who's lost, in case anyone's seen them.'

Joya sniffed the tears back. 'Mummy always says it's wrong to tell lies, and she said she was going for a swim.' She swallowed, but the tears didn't go away.

Her dad kissed the top of her head, then staggered across the room when the house phone rang beside Grandma Vee's chair. 'Hello? Oh, Ashley…'

Leo got off the train, and walked across the station hall and down the steps to Union Street. He was meeting Davey's mate under the Highlandman's Umbrella, the long railway bridge that turned a section of Argyle Street into a dim and somewhat musty tunnel, full of snack bars and small shops.

He was early, which did nothing for his churning stomach. For the first time in his life, he was meeting a stranger for the purpose of acquiring drugs. Okay, according to Davey, this Mick wasn't a dealer, just the guy who'd bought the pills before he knew they were dodgy, but apparently he'd bought five so maybe he'd been going to sell them on anyway.

Leo turned the corner into Argyle Street and immediately saw the tall figure leaning against the wall at the start of the bridge. 'You can't miss him; he looks like a daddy-long-legs,' Davey'd said, and it was true. Lanky, dark hair and long, gangly legs – and now he'd seen Leo and was walking towards him.

'Leo?' He slid right up to Leo, whose heart was pattering away like he'd run up the hill at Langside.

156

Leo nodded, fingering the cash in his pocket. Mick opened his hand, and Leo saw the clear plastic bag with two pale blue pills inside.

'Twenty.'

It took Leo a second to realise the other man was talking about the price. 'What? Davey said you only paid a fiver each for them.' As soon as the words were out he regretted them.

Mick scowled, and made to move further into the dimness of the tunnel.

'No! Wait – I've got it.' Leo pulled out two ten pound notes, and Mick snatched them and dropped the pills into Leo's hand before moving away.

Leo grabbed his arm. 'Wait – do they dissolve okay?'

'How the shit would I know? They should. Now for Christ's sake go away.' He shook Leo off and strode under the bridge.

Leo turned and walked back towards Central, his heart rate slowly returning to normal. He fingered the little bag in his pocket. Would he really have the guts – or should that be the stupidity – to slip them to Eleanor?

Joya sat on the swing seat on the deck, listening to Ashley making iced tea in the kitchen. The radio was on and happy summer music was floating into the garden, and today was even more horrible than yesterday.

'Here we go.' Ashley put two tall glasses on the patio table.

Joya went over to the table. Ashley had given them four ice cubes and two straws and a sprig of mint each, but that still wasn't enough to make the day better. Joya stirred her iced tea, making the ice cubes chink against the glass, then fished the mint out to nibble.

'We can pick some strawbs if you like,' said Ashley. 'There are loads. Leo said we should get an ice cream maker and make strawberry ice cream, but I don't know. They're so nice to eat as they are, or with vanilla from the good ice cream shop. What do you think?'

Ashley was trying hard to be nice, but it made Joya feel worse. 'S'pose. You could try and see.'

'Tell you what. Let's make just a few scoops. You pick some berries, and I'll go online and find a recipe that doesn't need an ice cream machine.'

Joya filled a bowl with ripe strawberries, then ate two of them, but even lovely strawberries didn't make her feel good today. She picked two more to replace the ones she'd eaten, and sniffed into the bowl. Would this be enough?

Ashley wasn't in the kitchen to ask, and Joya hesitated. It might be rude to go looking for her. Then she heard Leo's voice in the living room.

'That'll give the old witch something to think about, huh? Pity we can't put her in stocks and chuck water over her like they used to.'

'They used to burn witches. Let's have a look – I've never seen Ecstasy in real life. And for heaven's sake keep your voice down, Leo. Joya's in the garden. You don't want her hearing our murderous plans for Mum, do you?'

Ashley was laughing, but it didn't sound funny to Joya. Surely they weren't going to murder Eleanor? Leo made a funny noise in his throat and now they were kissing, Joya could tell, and suddenly it was all too much. It was every bit as horrible here as it was at home today. Screwing her eyes up to keep the tears in, she tiptoed back outside.

Eleanor's pots were still lying in a big mess on the side path. Joya stared at them – they were completely spoiled. The poor little pink flowers were dying. She poked at them with one foot just as Eleanor came out her front door. Joya froze. There was no time to run away.

'Joya! Leave these, please.'

Joya couldn't say a word, and Eleanor made a 'huh' sound in her throat.

'I hope it wasn't you who vandalised them.' She turned her back and flounced off to her car.

Joya stood still as the car backed into the road and drove off. A big sob rose up in her throat, and she almost tripped in her hurry to get away. Everything was wrong here. She would go to Stevie's gran's – Stevie might be there too, and his gran always had time and she'd know what to do. Quick, quick, to Gill's. Joya tiptoed until she was out on the pavement, and then she ran like the wind.

At the corner, she turned and looked back. She wasn't supposed to go anywhere without telling someone. Everything was quiet, though – no one had missed her. Nobody cared. Joya ran on towards Gill's, going so fast the tears on her face ran into her ears. Along to the main road, across the bridge over the river, then instead of going up the hill you went around the corner, and there was Gill's house. But the car wasn't there, and no one answered when she rang the bell. Joya slid down on the doorstep and buried her head in her knees.

She would never get away from it.

Martine walked to the end of the lane and sat on the grey stone wall overlooking Loch Lomond. She had called

Fiona from the phone box at Luss library after looking up the number there – of course she hadn't said that she was already in Luss, just that she needed some alone-time. Fiona asked no questions. That was the one advantage of having Huntington's in the family; if conversation veered too close to anything embarrassingly intimate or distressing, people tended to let you have what you wanted. And oh, oh – she had started to phone Stu, too, but she'd disconnected before it rang. They must know by now what she'd done; she'd be on CCTV at Ardrossan, wouldn't she? And Glasgow. They might even find her soon; a policeman could come knocking at the cottage door any minute. Well, right now no one was home.

The loch was choppy today. Waves were slapping against the wall where Martine sat, and two sailing boats near the opposite bank were scudding along at a fair old pace. But even on a windy morning like this, the view was spectacular. Every bit as good as the ones in Switzerland. Scotland was wilder, and the colours were different – hazy greens and greys, today. It was chilly. Unable to stop the tears, Martine rose and wandered along the path by the water, thrusting cold hands into Fiona's coat pockets. That was another reason to come here – she could use the collection of clothes and bits and pieces Fiona kept at the cottage. They were more or less the same size, apart from their feet. Martine was stuck with plastic beach shoes and a pair of Fiona's flip-flops.

This wasn't how she'd thought she would feel. She'd wanted to leave all the problems, the frustrations, the awful, awful *dreariness* behind her, but it had all come with her. Martine closed her eyes and the usual swirl descended. The test, the awful test – or no test. She wrenched her eyes open and stumbled on, her cheeks tightening as the tears dried.

Her footsteps slowed as she rounded a bend and a cold summer wind hit her. This mess wasn't going to go away, and it wasn't going to change for the better, either. So, she had to be the one to change. She stopped, chin down. How logical it was, really. She had to accept that Huntington's was in her life. That bit was easy, because it was true and it wasn't something she could change. Right. All she had to decide was whether to take the test. Or not.

A conversation from years ago slid into her mind. Martine had been fifteen and she and Vee were having one of those excruciating mother-daughter talks about sex. *How will I know it's the right time?* Vee had given the only possible answer. *When the time's right, you'll know.* It was the only answer to the question about the Huntington's test too.

Martine lifted her head and gazed unseeingly across the loch. She didn't know. She didn't know if it was the right time to have the test – so it wasn't the right time.

It seemed so reasonable now. Why on earth had she considered taking it? Not knowing was better.

Leo pulled away from Ashley and patted the pocket where the pills were. 'I got two, in case one doesn't work. All we have to do is get it into her.'

Ashley lifted the iPad. 'Later. I've got strawberry ice cream to make.'

Leo followed her through to the kitchen and slid a cup under the coffee machine.

Ashley bounded out the back door. 'Joya? Let's have those strawbs!'

Leo was stirring his coffee when she burst back inside clutching a bowl of strawberries.

'She's not there – did you see her? Joya!' She set the bowl on the breakfast bar and ran to the downstairs loo, but it was empty.

Leo licked his spoon. 'Upstairs?'

Ashley ran up, and he heard her hurrying through the bedrooms before thundering back down. Her face was drawn. 'She's not here, Leo.'

'She must have gone back home. Come on.' He ran along the pavement and pushed the bell next door, Ashley at his heels.

Stu was pale, and Leo cursed silently. He might be about to make the other man's day a whole lot worse.

'We can't find Joya – did she come back here?'

Stu's already drawn face became even paler. 'Hell. Joya! Are you here?'

Leaving Stu to search the house, Leo ran up their garden. No Joya. Ashley was wringing her hands beside Vee in Stu's living room when he returned. 'Nothing.'

Stu crashed down the stairs and into the room. 'She's not here. Christ – how did you lose her – where was she?'

Ashley burst into tears. 'In the garden. I left her for two seconds. She seemed – well, she was down, but she was talking and she was picking berries when I went in.'

Leo put his arms round her. This was as much his fault as Ashley's. What had gone through Joya's poor little head to make her run off? He racked his brains. 'Where would she go? Could she have gone to a friend's place? Vee?'

'She might have gone to Gill,' said Vee thickly. '62 Bowers Road.'

Leo touched Stu's shoulder. 'You phone her, I'll go. Ash, you go home, she might come back there.' Leaving Stu searching the landline phone for Gill's number, Leo ran to his car and reversed into the road. Around the corner, over the bridge, turn right, quick...

She was huddled on the doorstep, arms round her knees. Leo double parked and shot up the path, connecting to Ashley on his mobile as he went. 'She's here, tell Stu. We'll be right back. You okay, Joya? Let's get you home – your dad's worried.'

She allowed him to pull her to her feet and back to the car, but as soon as he drove off she began to cry. 'I want my mum.'

Leo swallowed the lump in his throat. 'I know. I'm sure the police will find her soon.'

As soon as he stopped the car Stu had the door open. He lifted the little girl and hugged her close, and Leo joined Ashley on the pavement.

'Stu, I'm sorry,' said Ashley. 'I should never have left her alone.'

Stu was standing with his eyes closed, Joya clutched in his arms. She was snuffling into his neck, and Ashley reached out and rubbed the little girl's shoulder. A lump came into Leo's throat. It wasn't fair. Ash's child had been taken away, and Martine had left hers... Some people didn't deserve kids. But that was unfair too; Martine was a poor soul.

Stu opened his eyes and gave Ashley a shaky smile. 'Don't worry. It wasn't your fault. Joya, let's go back in and let Grandma Vee see you're okay, huh?'

Joya nodded, peeking out at Ashley and Leo. 'Am I going back to Ashley's afterwards?'

'Whatever you like, Joya. I'll make the ice cream, and it'll be waiting for you in the freezer whenever you come.' Ashley was still close to tears.

Leo hugged her, and she clutched his hand as if it was her

child who'd gone missing.

Back home, he and Ashley sat looking at each other. 'They're falling apart over there,' said Leo. 'Did you see Vee's face?'

Ashley grimaced. 'If they're falling apart it's because Martine's not there to hold them together. Stu's a lightweight and Vee's too ill to cope. Poor little Joya.'

Leo reached into his pocket, and tossed the tiny bag with two blue pills on the breakfast bar between them. 'What do you want to do with these?'

Ashley fingered the packet. 'Mum always has coffee after dinner. We could put the pill into her cup. Does it dissolve okay?'

'Davey's mate says yes, but I'll crush it anyway. We'll need to arrange things so that no one can prove we were involved. Have a think – we can plan more later. It doesn't have to be today – in fact after all this it would be better to wait.'

Ashley looked as if she was thinking, the sooner the better, but she said nothing, and Leo put the pills into the cutlery drawer beside the teaspoons. How unreal was this? With the pills in their kitchen, the plan had taken on a fantastic kind of reality, like a film, but he wasn't at all sure he was made of Hollywood material. The two blue pills danced in front of Leo's eyes. Okay, Eleanor was overbearing – a grandmother who gave her grandchild away because she was too – ashamed? lazy? disinterested? – to help a teenager mother the child. But was this really the way? And would it actually help shift Eleanor?

'Ash, supposing she goes to the police?'

'She won't. They'd find out what a bitch she is. Okay, this is huge, but it'll take something massive to get her out of this place. And Leo, I meant what I said. Either she goes, or I do.'

Leo was silent. This wasn't the Ashley he'd fallen for, but then that one had never existed, had she? At the age of fourteen, the real Ashley had been hurt more than most people were in a lifetime. By her mother. He went back to the breakfast bar.

'We'll do it. It can't be too dangerous. Davey said the kids who took these pills were sick as dogs, but they were okay the next day. We'll give one to Eleanor, then afterwards we'll make some remark about how bad things happen, especially to people living in flimsy annexes – and that's when I'll produce details of a nice little flat.'

'Supposing she doesn't bite?'

'Then we get a bit more obvious. But my guess is she'll pack her things. Trust me, babes.'

Martine hurried along the path. A night of cold, hard thoughts spiraling through her head, followed by a morning of the same had convinced her this wasn't the way. She was being horribly unfair to her family. There was a call box at the pier; she would phone Stu, apologise, and go home. They'd have a lot to work through together, but they'd manage because they had to. She would start things by taking responsibility for her own stupid actions.

The phone was ancient, and obviously hadn't been used – or cleaned – for years. Martine shuddered as she lifted the receiver. And thank heavens, someone was answering.

'Hello?'

It was a frail, shaky old voice, and for a second Martine didn't recognise it as Vee's. Oh, no. 'Mum, it's me. I'm sorry. Is Stu there?' She heard Vee draw breath to reply, but then

Stu boomed in her ear.

'Where the bloody hell are you? Are you all right?'

Vee was agitating in the background to speak to her again, but Stu must have been walking with the phone. A door banged shut and Martine could hear the sound of a distant lawnmower. The receiver slid in her hand. He was furious, and no wonder. She had behaved like a three-year-old in a strop.

'I'm okay. I just snapped, Stu, but I've done some thinking, and—'

He had never sounded colder. 'Where are you?'

'Luss, in Fiona's cottage. I—'

'Listen to me, Martine. I know you've been under a big strain, but this can't go on. Your mother and Joya are distraught – Joya ran off this afternoon, she was so upset. This hysterical to-ing and fro-ing stops here. We can go to counselling, family therapy, whatever. But we get help, and you get the test. End of.'

Martine leaned forward over the sticky grey phone, her heart beating wildly. 'No – Stu –that's what I want to talk to you about. I don't want the test. I want to—'

'It's not about what you want. It's about family stability for Joya. We can't have this happening again.'

Martine gripped the phone. It was as if he was the head teacher talking to a naughty pupil, and horror grew. He wasn't going to back down. 'We can have stability without the test, Stu.'

'We can't. Maybe you should stay in Luss another day or two until you've thought it through properly. Joya deserves better.'

The connection broke and Martine slammed the receiver back on the sticky, disgusting base. Who was he to order her about? Of all the unreasonable…

But it wasn't unreasonable, was it, given her behavior? Martine buried her face in her hands and leaned against the phone box wall, tears trickling through her fingers. What had she done? And what was she going to do?

Leo lifted the tray with three bowls of strawberry ice cream and strawberries, and started towards the back door. 'Oh, spoons. Joya, could you get some from the drawer?'

Joya opened the cutlery drawer, and too late Leo remembered the pills.

Fortunately, Ashley was onto it. She abandoned the coffee machine and whipped the plastic envelope from under Joya's nose. 'Oh, my headache pills. I won't need them again today.' She stuffed them into a high cupboard, her eyes meeting Leo's.

Outside, Joya spooned up her dessert, her little face sober. Leo and Ashley kept up what was supposed to be a comforting conversation about Snowball and holidays, but the child said little. Leo stretched his legs under the patio table. This was the oddest day ever. Wednesday, midweek, and he hadn't been near work. Good job none of his projects were at critical phases at the moment. And Ashley, who was so gutted about Harry she was pulling a sickie, had ended up caring for another woman's child.

Leo looked up to see Stu standing at the side fence, his entire posture rigid. 'Joya! Your mum phoned, and she's fine. Having a little break like we thought, so everything's all right.'

Leo glanced at Ashley. Whatever was going on next door was still a long way from being 'all right'.

Joya leapt to her feet, her expression a mixture of Santa Claus and birthdays. 'Mummy phoned! Where is she? When's she coming home? Can I phone her back?' She ran to the fence.

'Good news, mate,' said Leo, as Stu bent to hug Joya.

'Very good news, isn't it, Joya? Mummy's in Luss, at Fiona's cottage, but she was calling from a phone box so you can't call her back. She'll be home in a few days, I hope. Why don't you finish your ice cream, and I'll come and get you when I've finished telling the police your mum's okay?'

Joya beamed up at Stu, then skipped back to the table, a different child. Leo saw tears in Ashley's eyes as she watched the little girl with her ice cream.

By four o'clock, Joya had gone home and Leo was slumped on the swing sofa, too bushed to move. The sound of Eleanor's car door made him jump, and of course the first thing she did was come round the back to examine the bloody rhubarb.

'Finished work already, Leo?'

He sat straight. 'No. I'll be out again later.'

'Good. I hope you're making good use of my money. By the way, I have a job at the charity shop near the church – they were looking for long-term volunteers.' She swept back down the path to her front door.

Leo wilted into the sofa. That had been a jibe. The sooner they did something to eject Eleanor, the happier he and Ash would be. Maybe tomorrow would be a good day to put plan E into action.

Ashley glared at him when he went back to the kitchen. 'I heard that, Leo, and I'll say it again. It's her or me.'

Chapter Eighteen

Thursday, 24th July

Stu's words were haunting her. 'Distraught' was a terrible word to use to describe an eight-year-old. Fear twisted in Martine's gut. How could she have left Joya? She hadn't been thinking straight; Stu was dead right about that.

On the other hand, what he'd said about getting the test meaning family security, that was a load of rubbish, and when he'd calmed down she'd do her very best to convince him that she was right. She was right, wasn't she?

Martine wandered round Fiona's small garden, where early-afternoon sunshine glinting through trees in next-door's garden was casting flickering shadows across the small patch of grass. There was so little to do here, except think. She'd dead-headed the roses, but she didn't feel like weeding, and there were so many tourists milling around the loch path today she didn't want to go for a walk either. Martine sank down on an uncomfortable garden chair. She would have to talk to Stu again, make him agree to her coming home. And she should do it immediately, while she was feeling brave.

Her pockets filled with coins for the phone, Martine strode down the lane. This was such a pretty place; hazy, rolling hills beyond the loch, the wide sky blue against the green.

But she couldn't enjoy it. The guilt was eating into her soul – her sanity needed this break, but she'd been selfish. What was best for her wasn't best for her child or her mother, and Stu'd been left to pick up the pieces.

The phone box was free. Martine grasped the receiver – she should have brought some wipes. This time, she keyed in Stu's mobile number.

'Martine. How are things?' His voice was completely neutral and Martine's fragile confidence wavered.

'Okay, thanks. Can we talk?'

'Talk away, but I think I said everything yesterday, so unless you've changed your mind…'

'Stu. Listen. I want to concentrate on Mum – and Joya too, of course – for the moment, and worry about me later. Dealing with Mum, *and* thinking about what might happen to me in the future – it's too much. The only way I can manage is not to have the test until later.'

It sounded reasonable in her ears. For a moment he was silent, and hope flared inside Martine. She could go home this afternoon, be there in time for tea. But the brief hope plummeted when he spoke again.

'You can't ignore what's going on with you – for Joya's sake. Now, I'll help you, but you obviously need more time to think. I'll come and see you tomorrow after lunch, and we'll plan your test and the counselling together.'

'No, Stu, I—'

The line was dead. Martine crashed the receiver down. Who the *hell*, just who the hell did he think he was, talking to her like that? *Now, I'll help you* – as if she was a silly child who'd got into a pickle with her homework. *You obviously need more time to think…* What a sanctimonious git he could be.

On the other hand, she had left him looking after their child and her terminally ill mother.

Thinking about Joya and Vee deepened Martine's misery tenfold. He hadn't given her time to ask about them. Was Joya missing her? Or had Ashley stepped in to help? That seemed likely, and Joya would enjoy it, too. But who was helping Vee? Oh, Lord, she had to see them. She would go today, no matter what Stu had said.

Martine dragged her feet back up the lane. If she turned up unannounced she might make things worse. But she had to see Joya, at least. She'd been mad enough to leave her child, now she was sane enough to need reassurance that Joya was okay.

The first thing to do was hire a car; thank heavens she had her credit card in her purse. She would see her daughter no matter what Stu said.

Ashley's parking space in front of the house was empty, so she must have gone out somewhere. Leo pulled up in front of the cheerful display of begonias in the blue ceramic window box, and glared at Eleanor's Golf by the annexe. Hopefully, she'd leave them alone tonight. He was fumbling for his door key when a green Clio crawled down the road, almost stopping as it drew level before kangarooing forward to pull into a space on the other side of the street. Someone taking their kid for a driving lesson, perhaps. You saw a lot of that around here – the streets were nice and quiet for learners to make their first parking attempts, and four o'clock was early enough to have spaces available. Cars were bumper-to-bumper after six. Leo glanced over to see if the car had L-plates, then stood still. That was no learner; it was

Martine behind the wheel. Had she come home? But she was behaving oddly, sunk down in the driver's seat as if she was trying not to be seen.

At that moment she saw him, and Leo raised a hand. She hesitated, then beckoned him over.

Leo jogged across the road, sliding into the passenger seat when she opened the door for him. 'Hi there. Home again? You okay?'

She was pale, and she wasn't returning his smile. Leo's heart sank. He was sorry for her – for all of them – but he had enough drama in his own life at the moment without getting involved in the neighbours'.

'Stu doesn't want me home until I agree to taking the Huntington's test,' she said, pushing her hair back with both hands. 'I came to see Joya, and Vee if possible. I don't suppose you know if they're inside? I don't want Stu to know I'm here.'

Leo stared at the house across the road. 'I've only just arrived, sorry. Would you like me to go and see?'

She nodded, and he loped across to ring their doorbell. But nothing was stirring inside the house, and he returned to the Clio where Martine was dabbing her eyes with a scrunched-up tissue.

'Joya was really happy yesterday when Stu told her you'd been in touch,' he said, trying to sound encouraging. 'They'll manage until you're back, Martine. I think Stu's got community nurses or something in to help Vee, and probably Joya'll be at her friend's this afternoon.'

'Oh, heck. I want to come back, but Stu...' She twisted in the seat to stare at him. 'Will you do something for me? Tell Joya you met me in town, and give her these.' She fumbled in her handbag and produced a packet of jelly babies and one

172

of chocolate raisins. 'Please, Leo. This is doing my head in. I could do with some of Vee's happy pills to take the edge off.'

Leo took the sweets, the germ of an idea floating into his head. Vee had a lot of pills, didn't she? And they might be even more effective inside Eleanor than a dodgy E, and safer, too. He could work this to his advantage, but it needed a bit of thought first. He stalled for time. 'Sure. Why don't you go back for now, and come again tomorrow when I'll have had a chance to see Joya?'

Fortunately, she didn't think to ask if she could come into their place until Joya came home, and Leo returned to the house as the Clio vanished round one corner and Ashley's Smart arrived round the other. He hurried to open the car door for her.

'Hi, gorgeous. Where were you?'

'I popped up to the library. My books were due back yesterday.' Ashley brushed past him into the house. 'Let's chuck a pizza in the oven – unless you can be bothered cooking?'

'Pizza's fine.' But what was all this about library books? He hadn't known she had any – heck, that could be an excuse. She might have been out looking for somewhere else to live. Depressed, Leo opened the back door and stepped onto the decking. Snowball was hopping about in his run next door, looking hungry, and Leo remembered Martine's sweets. He would catch Joya when she took the rabbit his food. Meantime, he could butter Ash up a bit.

'Guess who I met today,' he said, going back in to grab cutlery and glasses. They could eat outside; it was a beautiful evening. Would Ashley approve of his offer to help Martine?

'Dunno.'

Ashley wasn't in the mood for guessing games. Leo was

drawing breath to tell her about Martine's visit when the landline phone shrilled in the living room. He and Ashley frowned at each other. No one had ever called them on it.

'I'll go.' Ashley abandoned the packet of grated carrot salad she was about to open, and vanished into the hallway.

Leo went out to set the table. He put the sweets for Joya on the swing seat where he could grab them as soon as the kid appeared, then went back to the kitchen and spilled some salad into two individual bowls. He was a French dressing guy, Ash preferred Italian. Pizza plates, and–

'Leo? I think that might have been Harry.' Tears shone on Ashley's eyelashes, and her face was white.

Leo gaped. 'Harry?'

'I said hello, but there was no answer and I was going to hang up, and then he – it sounded like a kid – he said, 'Is that Ashley Frew?' and I said, 'Yes,' and then he didn't say anything, and then he hung up. If it was Harry, that means he knows where I am and he wants to get in touch!' She flung herself into his arms. 'Oh God, Leo, why didn't he talk to me?'

Leo hugged her. 'I guess he still needs time, Ash. You'll have to give him that. I wonder how he got our number.'

Ashley pulled back to stare at him. 'Aren't we in the online phone book?'

Leo almost laughed. The simplest explanation. 'Well, baby – sounds like good news to me. He'll be in touch again, you'll see. We can toast him tonight.' He pulled a bottle of cider from the fridge. They would save the bubbly for more definite news.

They were onto their second cider when Joya appeared in

the garden next door, Snowball's bowl in one hand and a bag of hay in the other. Ashley jumped up, and Leo grabbed the packets of sweets. Hell. Ash had yakked on about Harry all through the meal; he hadn't had the chance to tell her about his meeting with Martine.

'Hi, Joya, sweetheart! How's things?' Ashley leaned on the fence, and Leo put his arm round her.

Joya abandoned the rabbit food in the middle of the lawn and came over. 'I was at Stevie's today and Grandma Vee was at therapy. So I don't know if my mum phoned again or not.'

Leo waved the sweets. 'I can help you there – I met her today, and she said to give you these.' He handed the packets over the fence.

Joya and Ashley spoke together. 'Where did you meet her?' They looked at each other and giggled, and Leo relaxed. He could work this.

'This afternoon, in town.' Langside was 'in town' in that it was in Glasgow, wasn't it? 'She said to give you her love, and she wants to come home in a day or two.'

Joya stared at the jelly babies. 'I want her to come home too.'

'I'm sure she will soon,' said Ashley. 'You didn't tell me, Leo.'

'Well, you didn't give me a chance, did you?'

'I suppose not. Joya – I think Harry phoned! My baby who's a big boy now.'

Leo twitched impatiently. It wasn't the kind of news he'd have shared with an eight-year-old who was having her own problems, but Ash was bubbling over.

Joya heaved a great sigh. 'Will you still be my friend when you've found your baby?'

'Oh, sweetie, of course! And Harry's a boy, don't forget – I'll still need my girlfriends!'

Joya gave her a very small smile, and turned away to give the rabbit its food.

Ashley was frowning now. 'Poor little thing. What did Martine say, exactly?'

They went back to the table, and Leo launched into his explanation, telling her the truth this time, only omitting the bit about the drugs idea that he hadn't had time to consider properly yet. They were sitting in silence when Eleanor marched round the side of the house.

'Leo, I have some new tubs from the garden centre in my car, could you unload them, please, and help me fill them? They're too heavy for me.' She raised her eyebrows at Ashley. 'Better again, I see. I'll need to watch your little friend next door when my tubs are planted again. I caught her kicking them yesterday.' She made a smart about-turn and disappeared around the corner.

Leo forced himself to his feet. 'I suppose I'd–'

Ashley yanked him back down, her face livid. 'Wait half an hour at least. Poisonous cow. And don't forget – it's her or me.'

Chapter Nineteen

Friday, 25th July

Joya packed her rain jacket into her rucksack and added a banana from the fruit bowl. Bananas weren't as good as strawbs, but maybe they'd have some of those tonight. She was spending the morning with Stevie at his gran's, then after lunch she was going to Ashley's. Her dad was going to Luss to talk to her mum, and then to his office, even though it was still his holidays. Joya was hoping he'd bring her mum home, but he said that might not happen yet. Joya sighed. The house felt lonely without her mum. And the lovely perfume smell in the bathroom was gone.

Grandma Vee was in the living room in her nightie, waiting for Shona, the lady the doctor had organised to come and help Grandma Vee in the shower. This morning, Shona was going to take Grandma Vee to the big hospital to see what more help she needed. Except Grandma Vee didn't want help. The doorbell rang and Joya opened the door – Stevie's mum had come to take her and Stevie to his gran's.

Grandma Vee gave Joya a big hug. 'You be a good girl, and I'll see you tonight. I'm going to Eleanor's when I get back; you can come and get me later.'

That didn't sound like a good idea to Joya. She hurried into the kitchen to kiss her dad goodbye. 'Will you come with me to get Grandma Vee from Eleanor's tonight?'

'Sure, Joya. You have a lovely day.'

Joya clambered into the back seat beside Stevie. It wouldn't be a lovely day until her mum was back home.

'I don't know why you came here. You haven't said anything new and you're ignoring my feelings about not taking the test.' Martine glared across Fiona's tiny kitchen table.

Stu's mouth was a tight slash. 'I was hoping that after a night to sleep on it, you'd see sense.' He stood up.

Martine pressed a hand on her chest, only just managing not to snap back. That would bring them no closer to an agreement; she had to concentrate on what mattered. 'I want to come home. And I'm sure Joya wants me to.' Oh God, surely Joya wanted that, despite having Ashley next door? 'Not to mention my mother needing me, Stu, and the fact that your life would be a whole lot easier if I was back home. I wanted a few days out, and I've had them. Let's get back to what passes for status quo in our family.'

'I'm sorry you feel like that. You're putting your own selfish wishes before everyone else. Joya needs to know about the Huntington's, and it would be so much better if we can tell her she hasn't got it.' He turned abruptly and left her alone in the cottage. The car engine roared as he drove away.

Martine tapped cold fingertips against her cheekbones. Was he right? Was she being selfish? In a way, yes, but – Joya didn't have to be told yet that Huntington's was hereditary. It should be enough for Stu that she'd agreed to go for counselling.

Martine hunted round for change for the call box. Joya. She had to see her little girl, and Leo was the only person who could help with that.

There was no sign of Stu's car an hour later when Martine pulled up twenty metres from the house. She killed the engine and waited. She'd called Leo when she set off; he'd be watching out for her.

Five minutes later he opened the car door, and Martine gathered her courage. She needed a favour here, and there was no guarantee that he'd help her, knowing that she was going against Stu's wishes.

'I'd be really grateful, Leo. Stu won't hear of me coming home until I take the Huntington's test, and I can't do that. But I – I really need to see Joya. And Vee.'

'Vee's at OT.' Leo tapped his fingers on his knees, frowning.

Martine's heart sank. It didn't look as if he was going to help. Would she have to drive all the way back to Luss without having seen her little girl? Tears welled up in her eyes and to her horror she started sobbing. She couldn't help it.

Leo rubbed her back. 'Martine. Of course I'll help you. Come on, don't cry. You'll only frighten Joya if she sees you all blotchy.'

He was hugging her now, and something snapped inside Martine. She reached up and pulled his face to hers. For a second their lips met, then she broke off, horrified.

'Leo, I'm sorry. I shouldn't have—'

'Bloody right you shouldn't have. What if Ash had seen that? Or Stu? Or Joya?'

Martine mopped her eyes. 'I know, I'm sorry. It was just…'

It was just he was the only person who'd given her a hug for oh, so long, and she needed a hug.

He was staring at her now and his eyes were glittering. 'Forget it – it's okay. No harm done and all that, and I'll help you see Joya. And – you could return a favour, maybe.'

Martine shoved her tissue up her sleeve. 'Okay. What can I do?'

'I need drugs.'

Martine's breath caught. Whatever she'd been expecting, it wasn't this. 'What drugs?'

'Painkillers. Strong ones. I've, ah, done my back in, but I can't get a GP appointment until next week and I don't want to go to A&E. I guess Vee must have something I could – borrow.'

Martine's heart was beating hard. He was asking a bigger favour than she was, and it sounded pretty iffy to her.

Leo looked out of the window towards the houses, then turned back to her. 'Martine – Stu mustn't find out you came on to me. The mood he's in now, he wouldn't forgive you.'

Bile rose in Martine's throat. Dear God in heaven. Was he blackmailing her?

Leo touched her arm. 'Joya's at our place. I'll swap you a handful of drugs for a visit with your daughter.'

Martine drummed her fingers on the steering wheel. He might just as well have said, '…a visit with your daughter, and my silence.' But did she have any choice, after what she'd just done?

'Vee doesn't have anything like that, just antispasmodics and so on. But Stu still has some from a year or so ago when he broke a bone in his foot. How many do you need?'

'As many as you can spare. I'll go and check no one's home at yours, shall I?'

Martine shrugged. She was selling her soul here, but what the hell. Leo ran along the pavement and rang the doorbell. A moment later he beckoned her over, and Martine waited on the doorstep while he fetched the emergency key he and Ashley had. Inside, she winced. Her few days' absence had been enough to give the place a dusty, neglected look. Toys were strewn here, there, and everywhere, and judging by the smell in the kitchen, no one had emptied the bin since she'd left.

Leo pulled a face but said nothing, and Martine was grateful for so much at least. She had to get back here to make a home for her girl.

Stu's pills were in the bathroom cabinet. He hadn't used many. Martine pondered, then extracted two full blister packs. 'Twenty,' she said to Leo. 'But I'm not sure we should be doing this.'

'Don't worry. Wait here. I'll bring Joya over.'

Martine flopped onto a kitchen chair. *Had* he been blackmailing her? She wasn't sure any longer.

Leo jogged to his front door then hesitated, one hand on the handle. Talk about taking advantage of someone – but she'd fallen for it. The merest hint that he'd tell Stu had been enough. Hot shame coursed through Leo. But he had the pills now; he would make things right with Martine. He pushed the door open, and the first thing he saw was Ashley's suitcase in the hallway. Shit and hell, what was going on?

Ashley sat hunched over the laptop at the dining table, and Joya was perched at the breakfast bar, drawing. Leo blinked at them both. First job, get the kid next door. He went to look over her shoulder. An asymmetric vase containing a selection of garishly-coloured flowers was taking shape on a sheet of his planning paper.

'Looking good, Joya.'

'It's for my mum when she comes home.'

'You can give it to her right now; she's come to collect something. Off you pop for a quick visit. Tell her I'll join you in ten minutes.'

Joya gasped, her eyes as round as saucers, then she jumped from her stool and ran.

Leo turned to Ashley. 'Ash, I—'

She clasped her hands under her chin, her lips quivering.

Leo pointed to the hallway. 'What's going on?'

'I can't do this, Leo. Mum called earlier and ordered us both over for dinner on Sunday. It's hopeless. I'm out of here.' Defiance and despair were fighting for possession of her face.

Leo sat down opposite her. This was turning into the biggest possible nightmare. But he could fix it.

'No, babes. We get her out. It's Operation Eleanor tonight – we'll give her the fright of her life. She won't be thinking about cooking us dinner any time soon, believe me.'

Ashley took a deep, shaky breath, her eyes wide, and he could see how much she wanted to believe him. He pressed home his advantage. 'Anyway, you can't leave now Harry has this number – you don't know when he might phone again.'

She slumped in her chair. 'I didn't think of that.'

Leo walked round the table and hugged her from behind. 'Leave it to me. I'll go and collect Joya again.' He kissed her head and left before she had time to object.

Brilliant. Just how, exactly, was he going to work the drugs and Eleanor thing at such short notice? But he'd have to.

Martine and Joya were in the living room, but Martine brought the little girl into the hallway the moment he appeared.

'You scoot back to Ashley, Joya, and don't worry. I'll be home for good before you know it.'

Joya held up a hand, her fingers spread. 'Five more sleeps?'

'At the very most. But shh! – I want to surprise your dad, so not a word.'

Joya's lips trembled, and she hugged her mother tightly before allowing herself to be ushered out. Martine stood waving as the child trailed along the pavement, then turned to Leo. She looked nothing if not determined.

'Leo, in the car back there—'

He put a hand on her shoulder. 'We were both wrong and we're going to forget anything ever happened. You did nothing, and I said nothing. Okay?'

She sniffed. 'Okay.'

She walked to the door with him, her eyes brighter, then to his surprise grabbed him again for a hug on the doorstep. Leo patted her back awkwardly.

'Um… Martine…' What was he supposed to do here? Hell on earth – did she fancy him?

She stepped back, tears in her eyes. 'Sorry, sorry. It was – sometimes you need a hug, and apart from Joya… You give good hugs, Leo.'

He touched her shoulder. 'Ashley's waiting so it's time I wasn't here. You take care, Martine.'

He fled next door. Life was getting more complicated by the hour.

And now he had to get the pills into Eleanor.

Martine moved round Fiona's cottage, straightening the kitchen and putting the living area back the way she'd found it. This would be her last night here. Tomorrow, she'd take the hired car back first thing, and get the train down to Glasgow. No matter what Stu said, she was going home to stay. And talking about Stu, she should start her plan.

Fiona's old-fashioned mantelpiece clock was ticking the time away. 5.35 p.m. Stu usually arrived home around half past, so she would give him a moment and then call – he'd be surprised to get a call from her mobile.

She used the time to wipe out the microwave, then connected.

'You've got your mobile?' He sounded surprised but not angry, and actually, why would he be angry? She had every right to take her own possessions from the house.

'I collected it and my bag earlier this afternoon. Stu, I'm coming home tomorrow.'

He sounded tired. 'I want you to get the test, Martine.'

'I will. When I'm ready.'

Silence. Then – 'I suppose I can't stop you, and Joya and Vee need you. But we can't go on the way we were.'

'We'll talk soon.'

He disconnected, and Martine slumped. Would talking change anything?

The good thing was, she still had another week's holiday coming up. She'd be able to get her life and her family organised, and as Stu would be back at his desk on Monday, she'd have peace and quiet all day, every day to do it.

Leo slid the bubble packs of Stu's meds into a bag, and put it in the cupboard beside the Ecstasy. He would use some of them to start Plan Eleanor tonight. He was ashamed of how he'd got them, but the main thing was, he had them. They were capsules, which were easily emptied and better to stir into Eleanor's coffee than chunks of crushed E. But – how could he know how many would be enough just to give her a fright? Sweat broke out on his brow. Hell. But he had no choice; if he didn't get Eleanor out, he would lose Ashley. Three or four wouldn't kill her, surely.

Ashley came in and murmured in his ear. 'Joya's watching cartoons. I could murder Martine, leaving the poor kid like this.'

Leo answered carefully. He hadn't told Ash about the new pills yet. 'Remember the Huntington's. Martine's in a bad place too.'

Ashley sniffed. 'Was that why the two of you were canoodling so fondly on her doorstep? I saw you, Leo. What's going on?'

Leo cast his eyes heavenwards. 'Do you think Martine and I are having a torrid affair, and decided to show the world by snogging on the doorstep? She was grateful for the chance to see Joya, that's all. Let's plan Eleanor's bad trip tonight. We have the pills – I've got something safer than the E to start off with. So how can we best get them into her? I thought in her coffee.'

Ashley glared at him. 'Don't change the subject. That looked like more than a 'thank you' hug to me, on her part, anyway. Be careful, Leo.'

Leo felt the sweat soak into his t-shirt. 'It wasn't. Ash – Eleanor. We want her out, don't we?'

Ashley's face was sulky. 'She always has coffee after

dinner. You'd need to sneak into hers and doctor it while–'

'While you keep her talking at the front door. Yes, that would work.'

'Except Joya's here for dinner.'

'Perfect. She can be our alibi. We'll have dinner and then go into the living room to watch telly or play a game, then you can pretend to go to the loo, and I'll go to the kitchen to – to get dessert ready. You ring Eleanor's bell and get her outside – I'll only need a minute to nip through the connecting door and put the meds in her coffee.'

'How can we know what time she'll be making it?'

It was a fair point. Leo felt his confidence drain away. 'Well – she always eats at six, doesn't she? So, if we try at half-past there's a goodish chance she'll be at the coffee stage, and if it doesn't work today we can try again.'

Ashley shrugged, and Leo breathed out. So tonight might be a long shot, but his plan would work eventually. The other problem, of course, was to persuade Eleanor to go after her tummy upset or whatever, and keep her on side at the same time. He literally couldn't afford to fall out with Ashley's mother.

He stroked Ashley's hair back, and kissed her. 'You're gorgeous and I love you.'

Flattery got you everywhere, didn't it? And now to empty some capsules.

Joya pushed pasta shells around her plate, blinking to keep the tears in and not daring to look at Ashley. Dinner was lovely, but she wasn't hungry today. It might be another five sleeps till her mum was back home, and Grandma Vee was getting worse every day, and now Leo had given her too

186

much dinner.

Luckily, Ashley noticed she was having problems. 'Joya, sweetie, you can leave the rest if you've had enough – there's a very yummy pud and you want to have space for that, don't you?'

Leo took her plate away, and Joya heaved a sigh. Five sleeps weren't a lot, were they? Ashley squeezed her hand, but Joya noticed the big smile wasn't the one Ashley usually wore. All the grown-ups were pretending today, even Ashley.

'Let's go through to the living room for pud,' said Leo. 'Then we can watch telly, or, um, sing something before you have to go home, Joya.'

Joya blinked at him. What did he mean, sing something? But Ashley had jumped up and was clearing stuff away, and Leo swung Joya right up into the air and back to the floor. She followed him through, and sat on the floor in front of the coffee table while Ashley searched through a pile of DVDs. Maybe they always had pudding in the living room.

Leo sat on the chair and poked her. 'Why was six afraid of seven?'

Joya could feel the corners of her mouth starting to twitch.

Leo wiggled his eyebrows. 'Because seven ate nine, of course!'

At first Joya didn't understand, but then she did and giggled, and Ashley waved a library DVD in the air.

'This is a good one, Joya – it's children's songs. We got it specially for you visiting.'

Leo rubbed his hands together and spoke in a very jolly voice. 'Tell you what. I'll make dessert while you ladies are getting square eyes.' He winked at Joya as he passed, and she clambered up on the sofa and cuddled up to Ashley. If only all this was real – a funny DVD and having a lovely time, but Leo was pretending and so was Ashley. But they were doing it so that she would be happy, so it might be best if she pretended to be happy.

Ashley started the DVD. 'Let's have a sing-song. It's *Ten Green Bottles* first.'

A group of children on the TV screen began to sing, and to Joya's astonishment Ashley immediately joined in, and then Leo did too, from the kitchen.

'Come on, Joya – you know the words, don't you?' Ashley gave her a big smile, so Joya sang too.

Eventually the song finished and Ashley clapped.

'I'll just go to the loo and then help Leo while you sing the next one. It's *The Wheels on the Bus*. Sing nice and loud so we'll hear you.'

Joya lifted the DVD case. It was different to the song one she had at home because it wasn't a cartoon, but the children were funny anyway. *The Wheels on the Bus* was better than *Ten Green Bottles* because it was louder – Ashley had turned the sound right up. Joya bounced on the sofa. She wasn't usually allowed to have songs on this loud. And Ashley and Leo were making her a yummy pud and her mum would be home before five more sleeps. So maybe she was having a good time after all.

Leo stood close to Ashley and muttered in her ear. 'Okay. On you go and ring her bell. Keep her talking outside. If there's no coffee lying around I'll come straight back here, and we'll try again tomorrow.'

Ashley went out without a word. Leo crept into the hallway and put his ear against the connecting door to the annexe. Eleanor's doorbell chimed, and he heard her footsteps pass by on her way to the door.

'Ashley! Come in—'

'I can't this time, Mum, but I noticed a scratch on your car this afternoon – is it a new one? Come and look.'

Leo grinned. The scratch idea was his, and it was a good one. He didn't hear Eleanor's tut, but he could well imagine it. Her voice, complaining bitterly about vandals, faded as she and Ashley moved away. Right. Quick, quick, while Eleanor was still outside with Ashley.

Holding his breath, Leo slid into the annexe. A quick glance into the kitchen revealed no sign of a coffee cup, so he slunk along the hallway and – yes! An almost-full cup was there on the coffee table. Hands shaking, Leo opened his bag of pill-powder, upended it into the cup, and gave a quick stir.

He was passing the bathroom on his way back to the connecting door when the toilet flushed.

Leo jerked to a halt. Eleanor was still outside, so who the hell was in the loo? A clacking noise from the bathroom gave him the answer. That was Vee's zimmer, shit, she must be visiting Eleanor and *holy* shit – whose coffee cup had he doctored? Sweat cold all over his body, Leo about-turned swiftly, grabbed the coffee cup and emptied the contents into Eleanor's avocado plant. No, no – you could still see powder in the cup. He lifted the saucer too and ran back through the connecting door.

The Wheels on the Bus was still blaring in the living room, and Leo thrust Eleanor's cup and saucer into the cupboard until he had time to deal with them. He leaned against the sink, panting. Jesus, that had been close. Too close. How terrible – and how ironic – it would have been if he'd poisoned Vee with Stu's pills.

'Where's Ashley?'

The Animal Fair was trilling from the television now, and Joya was staring at him from the door.

Leo fanned himself with the tea towel. 'She's popped out for a word with Eleanor. Okay – are you ready for a lovely meringue with a cherry on top?' He barely managed to get the meringues safely onto the plates, his hands were shaking so much. Joya accepted hers and took it back through to the living room. Leo collapsed on a stool and laid his head on the breakfast bar.

'What on earth are you doing? Leo! Did it work?' Ashley came in and shook his arm.

'Oh, it worked. Until I realised Vee was in the bloody loo and I didn't know if I'd put the meds in her cup or Eleanor's.'

'There were two cups? What did you do?'

'If there'd been two, I'd have known from the outset someone was there, wouldn't I? I tipped the coffee into a plant and hot-footed it.'

Ashley thumped the breakfast bar. 'Vee uses a mug. It would be on the little table beside the other chair and you didn't notice it. Oh, God, Leo. So we're back to trying again tomorrow.'

Leo got to his feet. 'Yes.' If he didn't die of delayed shock in the meantime. 'Take those bloody meringues through and stay with Joya. I need a drink.' He needed a fag, too, but no way could he have one without Ash half-killing him.

Joya stamped her foot. 'You said you'd come with me!'

Her dad glared. 'For heaven's sake, Joya, you're only going next door – and Grandma Vee's there. You've had a lovely day, even dinner with Leo and Ashley, but I'm shattered. There's no reason you can't go alone. Scoot.'

Joya stuck her chin up and left the kitchen. Her dad had no idea what a horrible day this had been. Eleanor thought Joya had broken the flower pots. Now she had to go and ring the bell, and then it would be just her and Eleanor all the way into the living room, and Grandma Vee had gone with her zimmer so it would take ages to escape from the annexe. Joya hesitated by Grandma Vee's room, where the wheelchair was parked. Should she take it with her? Yes, she would. It would help them get away quicker.

Eleanor had lots of new pots with little tiny pink flowers on both sides of her door. Joya steered the wheelchair past them, taking care to go nowhere near touching distance. She angled the chair at the front door all ready for Grandma Vee to sit down on when she came out, rang the bell, then rushed back round behind the wheelchair.

Eleanor opened the door and it really did look as if she was peering down her nose at Joya.

'I've come for Grandma Vee.' Thank goodness she had thought to bring the wheelchair.

Eleanor stepped out and glared at her new tubs. 'I hope you didn't scrape these when you pushed that chair past. I'll be keeping an eye on you, Joya.'

Joya's mouth was so dry it was difficult to speak. 'I didn't touch your pots. I like flowers.'

'I saw you kick them yesterday. Don't make it worse by telling lies. Wait there.' She turned into the annexe.

Joya was hot and cold with being angry and scared at the same time. She should put a spell on Eleanor, like Wanda the Witch did when the imps from the Black Cloud came to steal her magic spurtle.

'Abracadabra!' she whispered, waving her hand into the

annexe. 'Zuzipzu cam doh – and go!'

There. If she was Wanda, that would be enough to get rid of Eleanor forever. Eleanor was the nastiest person Joya had ever met and it would serve her right if she was banished to Zuzipzuland – why did Grandma Vee like coming here?

'Here we are. Your chariot's waiting. I'll see you tomorrow, I expect.'

Eleanor was back, so the spell hadn't worked. Joya held the wheelchair while Grandma Vee sat down and Eleanor fussed over arranging the zimmer so Grandma Vee could hold it in front without dropping her handbag. Grandma Vee was oofing and ahing, but then they were ready, and Joya inched the wheelchair past the flower tubs again without saying goodbye to Eleanor. Grandma Vee didn't even notice, and she would have done – before.

Five more sleeps.

Chapter Twenty

Saturday, 26th July

Thank God it was Saturday. Leo lay in bed, listening to Ashley moving around in the kitchen downstairs. The washing machine was on, and the smell of coffee was wafting up the stairs – would she bring him a cup? Dream on, scoffed his cynical self. Ash had never been one to make romantic gestures, though she wasn't averse to being on the receiving end.

He stretched, feeling the tightness in his shoulders, then relaxed into the mattress. 'Knackered' didn't begin to describe how he felt this morning. The thought of what might have happened if Vee had somehow drunk the medicated coffee was – scary. Someone in her condition might not have survived an overdose. Though – life didn't get more macabre – wasn't that what Vee wanted? To die? Leo blinked at the ceiling. Maybe it was, but she didn't want to die at the hands of one neighbour, in another's living room. And if she'd been taken to hospital, they'd have found the meds in her system. And then what?

Leo struggled into a vertical position, and sat on the edge of the bed, grinning wryly. What was Eleanor making of the missing coffee cup? Only one thing was clear about the whole sorry mess – Ashley was even less impressed by his performance yesterday evening than she had been before. He was in real danger of losing her. So, today's tasks were a) get into Ashley's good books again, by b) coming up with the perfect Eleanor plan. Both of which were going to be easier said than done.

At that moment the landline rang, and he heard Ashley rush to the living room to answer it. Leo's stomach churned nauseatingly. Something was screaming at him that the day was going to get a whole lot more complicated. He lurched to the top of the stairs and listened.

He could barely hear her at first. 'Ashley Frew here … hello? … Oh! Oh my God – I'm so glad you've called, I–'

Leo reached for his jeans, his heart pounding. That was Harry. It had to be.

Martine double-locked the cottage and took the key back to Fiona's neighbour. She stood in the lane, looking down to the loch side. They should come back soon, as a family. Depression sank heavily into her gut – that was unlikely to happen as long as Vee was around. With its tiny rooms and odd stairs all over the place, the cottage wasn't exactly zimmer-friendly.

She drove to Balloch and returned the hired car, then caught a train for Glasgow, staring out unseeingly as the stop-start service meandered towards the city. What was happening in her life was scary. And now she had supplied Leo with strong, prescription drugs. What if they didn't agree with him? Martine twisted her hands together. She had to get these pills back.

Central Station was full of happy Saturday shoppers en route for an afternoon in town. Martine hurried towards platform eight and the train to Langside. At ten past twelve she was turning the corner into their street, her steps quickening as she approached the house. Please let them be home. And they were.

Joya spotted her from the window, and burst through the front door before Martine was halfway up the path. 'Mummy! Are you back for good?'

Martine dropped her bag to hug Joya, lifting the child into her arms and twirling round to make the little girl laugh. 'Hiya, sweetheart! I certainly am. What did you do this morning?'

Joya held on for a moment longer than she usually did, and Martine brushed tangled wisps of fair hair back from the small face, warmth and power flowing through her. Joya loved her, of course she did, how could she ever have doubted that she was an integral part of her child's world?

'We went to Braehead and did all the shopping. Now Grandma Vee's sleeping and Daddy's on the laptop and I'm watching my new Wanda DVD. Come and see it.'

Joya ran back inside, and Martine followed on. Stu was coming down the hallway, and he was frowning.

'Joya, off you go back to Wanda while your mum and I have a talk.'

Joya's face fell. 'Promise you won't fight, and promise you won't go away again, Mummy.'

Stu ushered Joya back into the living room. 'Don't worry, Joya. We'll come and get you in a few minutes, but stay here until we do, huh?'

Martine walked into the kitchen ahead of him and went to make coffee. Take charge, Martine. 'Stu. What we're doing is plain wrong. I was wrong to leave, and you were wrong to try and blackmail me into having the test. And it's Joya who's suffering. I'm moving back in, like I said.'

To her surprise he didn't reply at once. She put his coffee on the table in front of him, and started the machine again for her own. When she was sitting opposite, he raised his eyes and stared straight into hers.

'Okay. You're moving back in. But I'm agreeing for your mother. The past few days have been hard on her. I think it would be best if I left you to sort yourself – and Vee – out. I'll bunk down with Graeme for the weekend, and come back after work on Monday.'

Martine was lost for words. So much for having a good talk. She could see what was going to happen here – Stu would go to his brother's, then come home on Monday. He'd be sniffy for a day or two and then revert to his usual self – pleasant, having-a-good-time, superficial Stu. But for the moment, she'd take it.

Her mouth was dry. 'Mum isn't ill, is she?'

He gave a short laugh. 'Apart from the Huntington's? No. But she's not happy, and who can blame her? I'll tell Joya what's going on.' He drained his cup and strode from the room.

Martine left her coffee untouched on the table and went to ease Vee's bedroom door open. Her mother was lying on top of the bed, eyes closed and breathing loudly. Her arms and chest were covered by a cardigan pulled roughly over her. Martine gripped the door. Vee's cheeks had sunk; in four days, she had aged ten years. Still gaping at her mother, Martine listened as Stu talked to Joya. Joya's shriek woke Vee, and Martine moved into the room.

'Mum – I'm back. I'm so sorry you've been worried.'

Vee rolled to her side and, with an effort, pushed up to a sitting position, not meeting Martine's eyes.

'Grandma Vee! Mummy's home!' Joya danced in.

'Your mum and Grandma Vee need to talk, Joya. Why don't you come and help me pack?'

Stu led Joya away, and Martine sank onto the edge of Vee's bedroom armchair. All she felt now was remorse.

'Mum. How are you?'

Vee scowled, a thin dribble of spit inching down her chin. 'Been a tough few days. I hate what I'm doing to you all, and I hate that you were selfish enough to leave us thinking you could have drowned. I'm getting worse, Martine. I want to have the summer and then go.'

Hot shame spread through Martine's middle and her head reeled. 'Go where?' She clamped her hands between her knees to stop them shaking.

Vee was calm. She'd obviously thought it through. 'I want to die right here, in this bed. I'll do it all myself, and I'll take enough pills to kill me, don't worry.'

Martine closed her eyes. What was she supposed to say to that? 'You might be sick. And would you manage to get all the pills out of the packaging? Wait up a bit, please, Mum. Have more time with—'

'I would love more time with Joya, but it wouldn't be the kind of time I want to be her last memories of me. My mind's made up, Martine.'

There was nothing Martine could think of to say. She left her chair and sat beside Vee on the bed, hugging her mother to her side. Would this have happened if she hadn't swanned off on Tuesday?

Joya watched from the window until her dad's car turned the corner, then she ran back to the kitchen where her mum was making scones and Grandma Vee was sitting in her wheelchair. Grandma Vee must like her wheelchair, because she sat in it a lot now, and Joya could see why. It was black, with a nice squishy blue cushion to sit on, and the spokes and the rests for Grandma Vee's feet were shiny silver. It was nice that Grandma Vee had such a lovely wheelchair, but... Joya hesitated, leaning on the table top and kicking both feet in the air. Was the chair for keeps?

'Look, Joya – you can take this out to Snowball.' Her mum handed over the colander with some lettuce left over from lunchtime.

Joya stroked Snowball's back as he scoffed his snack, then she waved to Ashley, who was standing near an upstairs window in her house. But Ashley didn't see her, and Joya pouted. Something about yesterday's dinner with Ashley and Leo was making her feel odd today. And oh no – what had she done to Eleanor?

Joya ducked her head as she remembered. It was awful. Yesterday she'd put a spell on Eleanor, and today she hadn't seen Ashley's mother yet. Had the spell worked after all? It was worrying, because Wanda often got her spells wrong and things disappeared forever. If Eleanor disappeared, Ashley might call the police and they might find out about the spell. But then spells and witches weren't real – were they? Joya ran to the front garden and peered along the street. Eleanor's car had been in the same place all day.

At that moment, Eleanor hurried round the side of their house and got into her car. Joya clasped her hands under her chin, then hopped back to the kitchen. Her mum was home, Eleanor wasn't magicked away, and they were having afternoon tea with scones and jam. Three good things all at once.

Leo closed the laptop and glanced outside to see Eleanor's car exiting the driveway. He'd spent the past hour trying – and failing – to work out how he could get hold of enough cash to repay her. The only thing that would work in a useful time frame was to sign over property, and even if Eleanor agreed, which seemed unlikely, that would affect his business. Leo drummed his fingers on the breakfast bar.

At least Ash was happy – for the moment. Harry's call had lifted her into something like euphoria; she was so elated that anyone could be forgiven for thinking she was drunk. Harry's name was Tom now, and he lived with his adoptive parents in Dumfries. After the summer, he was going to Dundee University to study law. They hadn't talked for long, according to Ash, but at least the boy had made contact, and Ash had talked him into going on Skype that evening. She had gone to Braehead to buy a mum-like top to wear. All of which was distracting her very nicely from yesterday's failed attempt to scare Eleanor off, but Leo knew that wouldn't last. Ash would want the annexe freed up and ready for Tom if he wanted to visit.

His mobile buzzed in his pocket. It was Martine.

'Leo, are you at home? Can I come over?'

The last thing Leo wanted was a complicated conversation with Martine, but under the circumstances he couldn't say no. Two minutes later she was sitting opposite him at the breakfast bar, telling him about Stu going off for the weekend. There was a new determination in the set of her chin, and despair clouded over Leo. This might be heading in a seriously wrong direction.

It was.

'Leo, I've been thinking, and I'm not happy about giving you those pills. If you don't mind, I'd like them back.'

Little did she know he'd already tipped a whole load of them into Eleanor's avocado plant. Leo tried to stall. 'They're really helping my back, Martine. I'll try to make sure the doc gives me the same kind so I can replace them next week, okay? Hey, did you hear Ashley's found the baby she gave up to be adopted?'

'That's wonderful for her. But Leo, the pills–'

His eyes slewed round to the window as he tried to think of a reason she couldn't possibly have them back. 'It's a bit embarrassing – I'm not sure where they are, offhand. I'll get them to you.'

'You're not sure – I don't believe you. Where did you see them last?'

'Ah – in the cutlery drawer, I think.'

'For God's sake, you can't leave those pills lying around for people to come across and swallow instead of paracetamol or whatever. You may not have kids yet, but Joya's in and out of here.'

Leo pushed his stool back and stood over her. 'Get off my back, Martine. You're not being fair.'

'Fair? When was anything ever fair? You're being irresponsible with strong meds while my life and my marriage are falling apart, and my mother wants to top herself and I don't know what to do next, Leo, I–'

'Hey, hey. Come on.' He pulled her into his arms and held her while she sobbed. Hell, this was dire. All he needed to perfect the chaos was for Ashley to burst back in and find them like this. He stood there patting Martine's back, and cursing Stu – the man didn't deserve a family. And now they seemed to be hugging all the time, him and Martine, and it was not what he wanted.

He pushed her back onto her stool. 'Okay. Uncle Leo is prescribing a stiff drink. Scotch or brandy?'

Martine fumbled a tissue from her pocket and blew her nose. 'I shouldn't. Scotch, please.'

Leo poured two generous measures of Glenmorangie and added ice. 'To fewer complications, and family peace,' he said, raising his glass.

They clinked, and Martine tossed the whisky down her throat and shuddered. 'I needed that. Sorry, Leo, and thanks. I should get back. Will you bring the pills over when you find them?'

'Don't worry about it.' He took her to the door, then poured another two fingers of whisky into his glass. Martine wasn't the only one who needed a drink.

Joya stood on her swing and swung as high as she could. It was lovely, the whoosh you got when the swing was going forwards. And you could see into all the gardens, too, especially Ashley's. Lots more strawbs were ripe; the luscious red was shining through the nets Leo had put up to keep the birds off. This could be a good time to go and tell Ashley that everything – well, most things – were all right again. Joya jumped from the swing and hopped down the path and out to the pavement. Ashley's car wasn't here, but you never knew…

The front door took a long time to open when she rang the bell, but then it did, and Leo was standing there. He gave her a big smile and it was a funny one, like Stevie's grandad when he came back from the betting shop on Saturdays. Today was Saturday.

Joya smiled back carefully. 'Is Ashley here?'

Leo winked. 'No – she's gone clothes shopping, so she could be a while yet. Want some juice? I could do with a drink too.'

Joya jumped over the doorstep. Maybe Ashley would be back before she'd finished her juice. In the kitchen, Leo poured out whisky first, and Joya wrinkled her nose. Her dad drank whisky sometimes and it smelled awful.

'Juice for Joya now.' Leo winked again, and opened the cupboard where the glasses were. 'Ah! Eleanor's cup – must get that back to her.'

He gave Joya a glass of juice and she stood at the breakfast bar sipping slowly to give Ashley more time. 'Why is Eleanor's cup here?'

Leo made a funny face. 'It's not here really. Let's put it back while she's out.'

He gave the cup a quick wash then finished his whisky, so Joya drained her glass too, and skipped along behind him as he walked round the side of the house with the cup and saucer. He was walking like Stevie's grandad, too.

'Have you been to the betting shop?'

'Eh? No, but I'm going to Eleanor's and I'm betting she won't know what happened to her cup.'

'What happened?'

But he only laughed. Joya was glad to see Eleanor's car was still gone. Leo went right through to Eleanor's kitchen and put the cup and saucer into the dishwasher. The cup clinked against something else in there and Leo made a loud oosh noise through his teeth, then laughed again in a funny high voice.

'All sorted, Joya. Let's go while she's still away.'

Joya didn't need to be told twice. 'Why don't you go

through this door?' She touched the connecting door as they passed.

'Ah! I'm glad you said that; I nearly forgot. Look, it opens over the new carpet here and it made a bit of a mess yesterday. We'll clear that up right now.' He thumped down on his knees and gathered up some fluff the door had scraped from the carpet. 'There! She'll never know. I don't know when Ashley'll be back, Joya, and she has plans for tonight. I'll tell her to look out for you tomorrow, okay?'

Joya gave up on Ashley. It didn't matter. Her mum was making spaghetti bolognese for tea. It was still a lovely day.

The whisky bottle was on the breakfast bar, and Leo slid it back into the cabinet. He should eat something to mop up all that booze. And – great idea – he could pre-empt any disapproval of his slightly pissed state by having grub ready for Ashley when she arrived home. Ash and Harry – no, *Tom* were skyping at half six, so if he aimed the meal for six it should work.

Ashley's favourite saffron risotto was soon bubbling on the cooker, and Leo was laying the dining table when he heard her key in the door. He went into the hallway to kiss her.

'Pooh, you stink of whisky. Where's Mum?'

'Charity shop, I imagine. She's been gone all afternoon.'

Ashley glared. 'And you spent all afternoon getting pissed. For pity's sake, Leo – it's barely six o'clock.'

'I spent the afternoon clearing up the aftermath of yesterday's attempt. I deserved a small whisky. By the way, Martine's back.'

'Good. Let's eat. I don't want to be late for Tom.'

Leo made a show of seating her at the table, then served his risotto. So far, so good.

Tom wasn't how Leo had pictured him. He'd been expecting a strapping teenager with Ashley's dark hair and wide forehead. The boy looking at them was slight, mousy-brown hair falling into his eyes, and a flushed, ill-at-ease expression.

'Oh! Tom…'

Ashley couldn't get another word out and Tom wasn't speaking either, so Leo leapt in. He and Ash had arranged that he'd say hello, then leave them to it. He squeezed Ashley's hand and grinned at Tom. 'Great to see you, mate. Ashley's been wanting to find you forever.'

'I never wanted to lose you,' said Ashley, reaching out to touch Tom's head on the screen.

The boy looked away. 'You were a kid. My mum said it wasn't your fault.'

Leo stood up. It wasn't the best of beginnings, but three was definitely a crowd here. He should leave them to it.

He sat in the living room watching the day's events according to the BBC, the occasional buzz of voices from the kitchen in the background. It was mostly Ashley's voice; Tom didn't appear to have much to say. Heck. If this went the wrong way, it would be hell for Ash. He would get the blame, and of course, now that Tom had made contact there was no need for Ash to stay for the landline. Leo slumped, wishing he'd thought to bring a drink with him.

It was nearly seven before Ashley came through. She flopped into an armchair, her face pale.

'Oh, that was hard. I could hardly get a word out of him, and when he did speak it was all about his mum and dad and his older sister. She was adopted too, and has contact with her birth mother now, and she encouraged Tom to find me.'

Leo tried to sound upbeat. 'It's a start, Ash. Tom's a teenager. It's not an easy age.'

'I just got the feeling he didn't really want to talk to me. He wanted to know who I am, and now he does know.' Two tears trickled down her cheeks.

'Give him time, love. Wait a few days and then text him. Take things slowly.'

Ashley shrugged. 'I want to see him sitting right here, Leo.'

She stared out of the window, and Leo flinched as Eleanor's car turned into the driveway and came to a halt in her space. Not the best timing, Eleanor.

Ashley leaned forward, her expression savage. 'And I want *her* gone, do you hear? You got her in here, Leo. You get her out.'

Leo rubbed damp hands down the legs of his jeans. 'I will, baby, but—'

'I'm not your baby! Harry – Tom was my baby, but I missed all that and I might miss all the rest of his life too. But I want the annexe ready if he does come here.'

'Ash, it's complicated. Eleanor's put a lot of money into the business. I can't repay her just like that, and even if I could she might not—'

It was the wrong thing to say. Ashley banged both hands on the coffee table.

'This isn't about money! This is about family, Leo – the family I lost because of that interfering old cow. So, you can borrow some bloody money and while you're working out how best to do that, I'm out of here. I can't be with someone who prioritises money over me and my son.'

'I'm not! But I do need time.' It sounded pathetic even in Leo's ears.

'You take all the time you want. I won't be here to complain.' She glared straight ahead.

Eleanor's matchstick figure appeared outside, tapping down the path and turning left onto the pavement.

Ashley almost spat. 'Look at her. Off to play bloody bridge, no doubt. While I've had to wait eighteen years to find my son. Do it, Leo.'

She stamped off upstairs and Leo buried his face in both hands. Christ. She had packed yesterday – she could be gone in ten minutes, and what could he do? Another whisky seemed like a good idea. He staggered through to the kitchen and stood sipping, feeling the amber liquid warm its way down his gut. He and Ash were so great together, and now she was leaving and it was all bloody Eleanor's fault.

He set the glass down by the fridge, and some of the whisky sloshed over the edge. Leo dabbed his finger on the drips and licked. Right. He had reached his limit. Eleanor had to go, and he had the pills. Ashley was all that mattered. He would doctor Eleanor's milk, then when she'd recovered from her bad trip he'd tell her, yes, that was it – he'd tell her it was all Ashley's work, and Eleanor could expect the same again only worse, if she didn't move out. Ashley could be bad guy. He would find Eleanor a nice flat, be the good guy, but she would see that living in the same house as the daughter who hated her was never going to work.

And there was no better time to act than now, while the old cow was out. Leo pulled out the packet of pills. Should he use more of Stu's meds, or one – or both – of the E tablets? The meds, he decided, popping the capsules from their plastic bubbles. That way, he definitely couldn't give them back to Martine no matter what she said, and he'd still have the E in reserve.

His hands were shaking as he opened capsules and shook out their contents, and it wasn't all down to the drink. The thought of Eleanor's self-righteous face sipping her spiked cocoa made him want to throw up and laugh at the same time. Leo giggled, and took another slug of whisky. This had to work, it had to.

He shovelled his pill powder into the plastic bag, leaving the two Ecstasy tablets in an eggcup on the work surface in the meantime, then drained his glass for max Dutch courage and lurched towards the connecting door. It took him a moment to get the key into the lock, but then it was turning, and he was back in Eleanor's small home.

Now to do his worst.

Vee had barely spoken since Martine's arrival. It wasn't so noticeable when Joya was around too, because the little girl chattered enough for them all. Martine smiled grimly. It was wonderful to see Joya happy, and she would do her utmost not to let things get out of hand again, but – her life here hadn't improved in her absence. Heaven knows how long she'd be able to be convincing about 'getting the test soon', which was a major factor in Stu agreeing to her return.

But the first thing was to get Vee on a more even keel.

'Let's watch a film,' she suggested after dinner. '*Pollyanna* was on Channel 5 last night – we could get it on catch-up.'

Vee looked up, a spark of interest in her eyes. 'An old one?'

'Hayley Mills is Pollyanna, so it's probably from the sixties. Joya, you can be in charge of making popcorn.'

'Ooh, yes!' Joya took the bait immediately, and ran for the kitchen.

God bless microwave popcorn, thought Martine, as the microwave hummed into action. Okay, she would switch her phone off and give her mother and daughter her undivided attention for a couple of hours.

She was plugging the phone into the charger in the corner of the kitchen when she noticed the ring with the spare keys wasn't hanging on its hook. Odd. Or had Stu needed them at some point?

'Have you seen the spare key ring?'

Joya was sprinkling salt over the popcorn, now in a glass salad bowl. She shook her head energetically, and Martine frowned. It wasn't only their own keys; her set of emergency keys for next door was on the same ring, so it wouldn't do to lose it.

Joya carried the popcorn through to the living room, and Martine dropped onto the sofa and slipped her arm through Vee's. 'Let's have some nostalgia, ladies.'

Missing keys could wait.

Easy does it, into the kitchen. Leo tossed his bag of pill powder onto the work surface, and opened Eleanor's fridge. Okay – the carton of milk was unopened, but there were two glass bottles of fruit juice, one with orange and one with orange and mango. Both were well in date, the orange with about a glassful remaining, the other a little fuller. Leo tipped some orange and mango down the sink, then added half his powder to each bottle, and shook. There! Eleanor was bound to drink one of these today or tomorrow, and if it didn't give her a case of the heaving, nasty vomits or the runs, well, he still had the E. Leo giggled as he gave the work surface a quick wipe with the tea towel. Lord, he hadn't been this bevvied for a while. Time for another.

Back home, Ashley was still moving about upstairs, and Leo sat nursing his glass at the dining table. Could he persuade her to stay? No, now that he was planning to blame Ashley for putting the pills in Eleanor's OJ, it would be much better to let her go, then make sure he had Eleanor agreeing to move out by the beginning of the week. He and Ash could have a grand reconciliation as soon as her mother was gone.

Outside, Eleanor's car door slammed, and Leo giggled again. Home already, so she couldn't have been playing cards with the other OAPs. Or maybe Eleanor had lost all her money, ha. So now she'd either make some cocoa, in which case the juice wouldn't come into operation until tomorrow, or she'd pour a stiff vodka to drown her sorrows and add a slosh of meds. Heck – would that be a lethal combination? No, no. Leo swigged more whisky. Vodka would only help his cause. Wouldn't it?

Thumps on the stair heralded the descent of Ashley and her suitcase, but Leo remained in his chair. If he stood up, he might not stay upright.

She came into the kitchen and poured a glass of water from the fridge. 'I'm going to Noelle's in Sanquhar.'

Leo laid his head on his arms. 'Ah. Nice and near Dumfries and Harry-Tom. Good thinking.'

'God, you are so drunk. It's pathetic.' She moved towards the window. 'Good – Mum's back. You know what, I'm going to tell her exactly what I think. You'll never get her out of here, but you're welcome to my mother, this house and the annexe. Good luck, Leo. You're going to need it.'

Leo didn't look up when she banged her glass onto the

worktop and marched out. A moment later the boot of the Smart slammed shut, and Ashley's indignant footsteps were stomping along the side path. Leo groaned as he swayed towards the sideboard and the whisky. Ashley had gone, and she was good and mad and no mistake. Not like his Ashley at all. But who could blame her?

Tears welled up in his eyes as he emptied the bottle of Glenmorangie into his glass.

PART THREE
NO ESCAPE

Chapter Twenty-One

Vee's early morning routine had changed in Martine's absence. Shona, the community carer, arrived at eight, and helped Vee in and out of the shower while Martine hovered in the background, feeling redundant and helpless. The downstairs loo was too small to hold three people; it might be worth the expense of turning it into a wet room. Assuming that Vee agreed to extend her life beyond the summer, that is. What a mess this was. Now she had to look on as another woman did something she could have done today – but on the other hand, what would happen when she was back at work? Vee and Joya home alone sounded like an even less good idea than it had been a week or two ago. The carers only came morning and evening. Martine accepted a damp towel and Vee's nightdress from Shona, and took them through to the washing machine.

Leafing through the care service brochure, she saw that a variety of arrangements could be made, including lunch. Well, she had a week to get things organised. Vee was on the waiting list for a place in a day care centre, too, but whether that would happen in a useful time frame was anyone's guess.

The positive thing about the care arrangement was, Shona's chatter about her sister's baby and the dog next door had given Vee something new to think about, and she said goodbye to the girl with pink cheeks and a smile.

'What would you like to do this morning, ladies?' said Martine, standing by as Joya chopped a carrot into Snowball's bowl. 'It's a lovely day. Shall we drive across to Victoria Park?'

Vee shook her head. 'In the afternoon, then. I'm having morning coffee with Eleanor in five minutes. You can push me there, Joya.'

Joya's face fell a mile and a half at this, then she ducked her head and scurried out with Snowball's bowl. Martine stared after her. What on earth was going on there? Well, with Vee next door there'd be time for a mother-daughter chat. And oh, dear, if Vee wanted to go with the wheelchair she must be feeling weak and wobbly again today.

'It's okay, Mum, I'll take you.'

Martine called to Joya that she'd be back in two minutes, then pushed Vee along the pavement. The path up to Eleanor's door was tricky; the paving slabs were laid on gravel and they were narrower than the wheel base of Vee's chair, and the flower tubs were in the way too. And the zimmer that Vee was clutching in front of her catching in the lilac bush made things no easier, but at last they were at Eleanor's door.

Vee struggled to her feet and pressed the bell. 'I'll manage now. I'll call when I'm ready, shall I?'

'Okay.' Martine sighed, then turned it into a cough in case her mother noticed. A few short weeks ago, Vee would have been mortified to be so dependent on outside help.

Martine wandered down the path with the wheelchair, inspecting Eleanor's new tubs as she went, then turned to look back. Vee was still leaning on her zimmer at the door. Martine hesitated. Maybe Eleanor had popped up to the shops. Or gone to see Ashley.

Vee reached out and tried the door, which swung inwards. 'Okay!' she called, manoeuvring her zimmer over the doorstep.

Martine waved, and waited while Vee lifted first one foot and then the other over the threshold. Good. Home. She and Joya could scrub out Snowball's hutch. That needed to be done, and it would make for a good opportunity to talk. And—

A faint, strangled scream came to Martine's ears and she stopped, half way home. Had that been—? Oh no, had Vee fallen? Abandoning the wheelchair on the pavement, she sped back up the path.

Leo awoke with the hangover from hell, and three coffees and two paracetamols did little to shift it. Jungle drums were pulsating around in his head and his mouth felt – and tasted – like the bottom of a budgie's cage. He sat at the breakfast bar, jabbing half-heartedly at the laptop, but trying to read from the screen added nausea to the general misery, and he gave up. It was Sunday, business emails could wait.

Thinking about the business made his stomach churn ten times harder. Eleanor's money – it would have to be extracted somehow. But he could find the old cow the best flat in Scotland and if she still wouldn't leave, Ash would never come back. He tried to text Ashley, but his fingers were incapable of getting even a quick, *hi, hope all's well in Sanquhar* into his phone. He would never, ever drink so much whisky again.

And – Eleanor. Leo groaned. The previous evening had vanished from his memory, leaving more than vague

214

uneasiness. What the shit had he done? He'd wanted to give Eleanor the pills – hadn't he? If he had, she must be feeling every bit as bad as he was, and serve her bloody well right. She was to blame for the state of his life right now.

One hand clutching his heaving stomach, Leo shuffled across the kitchen.

'Mum? Are you okay?' Eleanor's front door was open, and Martine ran straight in. She could hear Vee's breathing from the hallway.

Her mother was standing by the sofa, leaning heavily on her zimmer and whimpering between breaths, and a faint but definite smell of faeces was hanging in the air. Martine's head reeled, and for long seconds she saw stars. Oh, no no no. Eleanor lay on the sofa, twisted on her side, one foot on the floor beside an upturned coffee cup, the other leg stretched along the seat. Both arms were hugged across her thin chest, and – oh dear God. That terrible face.

Martine's fists clenched so tightly her fingernails spiked into her palms. It wasn't so much the scowl and the half-open mouth, it was the colour. The uppermost side of Eleanor's head was waxy white, while the lower was a ghastly purplish hue. Something unidentifiable had dribbled from her mouth and dried down her chin and neck. Martine gagged. She stretched a shaking fingertip towards Eleanor's wrist, then withdrew it. No need to check. Those eyes were empty; the chest was motionless.

Vee swayed beside her, and Martine seized her mother's shoulders and supported her the few steps to the armchair. Vee plumped down and lay back, eyes closed, reaching for Martine's hand. Martine grabbed hold, forcing the panic back, her own hand shaking almost as much as Vee's. She had to do something, take charge. An ambulance – no, the police … Ashley. Hell, she'd left her mobile at home. The landline…

Vee moaned, panting, and Martine swallowed the saliva that had rushed to her mouth. Her first duty was to her mother; all help was too late for the woman on the sofa. It must have been a heart attack.

'She's gone, Mum. Let's get you home. Hold on.' Her own heart pounding, Martine ran into the kitchen and yanked the window open. Thank God, Joya was still in their garden. 'Joya! Come round to Eleanor's door and bring the wheelchair; it's on the pavement. Quickly, Joya!'

For a second, she thought the little girl was going to refuse, but then Joya skipped down the side of their own house. Martine ran into the hallway and rattled the connecting door, but it was locked. She thumped as hard as she could with her closed fist. 'Leo! Ashley! Come to Eleanor's!' Heck, they might still be in bed.

'What is it?' Joya was manhandling the wheelchair through the front door.

'Don't come inside, sweetheart. Eleanor's very ill. I need you to take Grandma Vee home and stay with her. I'll be there as quick as I can.'

Joya blanched, and shot back outside. Martine grabbed the wheelchair, shoving it into the living room as the connecting door opened and Leo stumbled in.

He clapped both hands over his mouth, staring wide-eyed at Martine. 'What's going on? Smells like shit in here.'

By the look of him he hadn't been anywhere near the shower that morning. Martine touched his shoulder. 'I'm so sorry, Leo. It's Eleanor. You have to get Ashley.'

He followed her into the living room. 'Shit. Oh shit. She's gone.' He began to sob into his clasped hands.

'Yes. Did she have heart trouble? We have to phone for help, Leo.'

He gripped her wrist. 'No. Ashley. Ashley's gone.'

Joya stood waiting at Eleanor's front door, but all she wanted was to run and run and never stop. She'd never seen her mum look like that, not even when things were scary in Switzerland, or when Frosty died. Eleanor must be really ill. And oh – Leo was crying. Men never cried. Joya leaned on the door frame because her tummy hurt and she couldn't breathe properly. It was like when her mum had vanished on the beach and her dad was so scared he'd made Joya scared too.

This was her fault, wasn't it? She had put a spell on Eleanor, and it had worked, because Eleanor was ill. The spell was supposed to make things vanish, not get ill. But Wanda's spells often went wrong too.

Her mum came into in the hallway, pushing Grandma Vee in her chair, and they both looked sick as sick. Leo was behind her with Grandma Vee's zimmer, and he looked terrible too. Joya blinked back hot tears. Had she magicked everyone in the house sick?

Her mum pushed the chair out to the path, and patted Joya's shoulder. 'Joya – take your grandma home, and go straight in the kitchen door with the wheelchair and sit there for a few minutes until I come. Give Grandma Vee some water. She's upset because Eleanor is so ill.' She patted Grandma Vee's shoulder too. 'Okay, Mum? I need to help Leo for a minute, but I'll be home before you know.'

Grandma Vee was covering her cheek with one hand, but she had to uncover it to hold her zimmer and Joya saw the way her mouth was drooping. She pushed the wheelchair all the way down the path to the pavement, very slowly because it was difficult, and then headed for home as fast as she could for the pain in her middle. When they were safe in the kitchen, she poured water into Grandma Vee's sippy cup, and they both sat at the table.

'What has Eleanor got?'

Grandma Vee's face was closed like she was trying hard not to think about something terrible, and a nasty trembly feeling started in Joya's middle beside the pain. She had done this.

'I don't know, Joya. I expect they'll get the doctor in.'

Joya nodded. But doctors couldn't always help, could they – at least Grandma Vee's doctors couldn't. All Joya wanted was for her mum to come in and say, 'Eleanor's fine now'. Except it didn't look like anyone was thinking Eleanor would be fine soon.

'You're a good girl, Joya. Thank you for helping me.'

But she wasn't a good girl. Joya was crying inside but she didn't want to let Grandma Vee see because Grandma Vee was sick too, and this was the most horrible anything had ever been.

'I – I'm going to the bathroom.' Joya sped upstairs and shut herself into the bathroom where she could cry for a minute. But her mum had said to sit with Grandma Vee, so she couldn't have a big cry. She wiped her face with the hand towel, then opened the dirty clothes basket to put the towel in because it had snot on it now – and there were the spare keys, half-hidden between a bra and her dad's trousers. Joya fished them out and ran downstairs. The hook the keys had in the kitchen cupboard was too high for her to reach, so she put them in her crayon box where they wouldn't get lost, and sat down beside Grandma Vee just as her mum came in the back door.

Joya jumped up again. 'Is Eleanor better yet?'

Martine pulled out the chair opposite Vee and sat down, hugging Joya to her side. She had to tell the truth; Joya looked stricken and that was wrong. The child could see that Vee was beside herself with anxiety – her poor mother, what a shock that must have been, especially for someone unable to run and get help. Thank goodness she'd heard Vee cry out.

'Sweetheart, poor Eleanor's dead. She must have been taken ill very suddenly. You know that can happen with – old people.' No way did Martine want Joya to start worrying about her and Stu dying without warning.

Joya went sheet-white. 'No!'

Dismayed, Martine pulled the little girl onto her lap and sat cuddling her. Another upset in what had turned into an over-eventful summer for Joya. They would have to do something about this, or the child would be traumatised for life. Joya hadn't been fond of Eleanor; she shouldn't be so upset.

'Leo'll need to get the doctor in, but I expect it was a heart attack. Older people sometimes have them.'

She stroked Joya's hair, but the little face remained as bleak as her grandmother's. Vee's cheeks had sunk even further, and her mouth was trembling.

'Want to go for a lie down, Mum?'

Vee nodded, and Martine put Joya down before wheeling Vee into her room and helping her onto the bed. She bent to murmur in Vee's ear. 'Leo's in bits over there and Ashley isn't answering her phone. Can I bring Joya to rest with you while I go back and help him? I'll be as quick as I can.'

Vee seemed to rally at this. 'Bring her through. We'll lie here and have a cuddle. That'll do us both good.'

Martine hurried back to the kitchen. It had helped Vee to feel needed. She should remember that.

Joya was on the chair Martine had vacated, her small blonde head on its side on the table top, eyes unblinking.

Martine sat beside her and rubbed her back. 'Sweetie, don't worry about Eleanor. These thinks happen when people get, um, old. It's sad, but mostly for Ashley and Leo.'

Joya's voice was a whisper. 'It's all my fault.' She scrubbed her face with one hand.

'No, no. It was an illness Eleanor couldn't have known she had. Why do you think it was your fault, lovey?' Martine leaned her head close to Joya's, but the child closed her eyes.

'It *was* all my fault.' Her lips were trembling.

Martine thought fast. Joya must have had some dealing with Eleanor they didn't know about, something unpleasant. 'Joya, listen. *You didn't hurt Eleanor.* You didn't even see her this morning, did you?'

The blue eyes were open again, and Joya shook her head.

'Well, then. It wasn't your fault. I promise. People get ill sometimes. Okay?'

A silent nod. Martine stood, and lifted Joya in her arms. Probably Eleanor had ticked the poor kid off recently, and said something along the lines of 'You frightened me to death there'. Hopefully, Joya would be ready to talk about it later.

'Tell you what – we'll pop you into bed with Grandma Vee for a good rest while I help Leo. Ashley's visiting a friend but he'll get her home soon. When you get up again, you'll feel much better. How's that?'

Joya gave a tiny smile, and Martine kissed her. Two minutes later the child was snuggling up to Vee, her thumb in her mouth. Well. They hadn't seen that for a long time. Martine closed the door, then sped back along the road to Eleanor's.

There was no sign of Leo in the annexe. Martine glanced into each room, averting her eyes from the body on the sofa. Should they cover her? But it would make no difference to Eleanor, so it might be best to wait for the doctor.

She went through the open connecting door. Leo was cowering over the breakfast bar, his breath still coming in unsteady pants. Martine put a hand on his shoulder.

'Did you get hold of a doctor?' She had no idea what happened when someone was found dead like this. It wasn't as if a doctor could help. But then, they'd need a death certificate.

Leo's mouth was tight. 'I want – I should talk to Ashley first. Her phone's still off. She's in bloody Sanquhar and I can't remember the surname of the friend she's with.'

Martine hesitated. They needed to call for help, Ashley or no Ashley. 'Phone the doctor, Leo. And let's make coffee. You've had a shock.'

He shrugged, and Martine slid a cup under the machine. Leo brought the milk from the fridge and set it on the work surface.

'Fuck!' He reached past Martine and grabbed a little plastic bag, the kind you could seal by pressing the top together.

Martine nearly jumped out of her skin. 'What is it? What's that?'

He glared, his mouth working in a way that made Martine think that more tears weren't far off. 'It's where the bloody powder was – from the pills.'

Martine gaped at him. She had almost forgotten about the pills. 'Stu's pills? What were they doing in there – you opened the capsules?' Sick dread wormed through her middle. Something was very wrong, and it wasn't just – just! – the fact that Eleanor had died.

He made a grunting sound in his throat, then slammed the packet down on the work surface. 'Christ almighty. What *happened* here?'

'I don't understand. Why did you open the capsules?'

He wasn't looking at her. 'I've – never been able to swallow pills.' His face was colourless.

'Maybe Ashley did something with them?' Martine's head was reeling.

'Why the hell would she?'

'Someone else, then?'

'The only other person in here yesterday was your Joya.'

Martine's lips began to tingle, and Leo's kitchen swayed around her. That dreary, hopeless little voice... *It was all my fault...* Bile rose in Martine's throat and she swallowed painfully, feeling it burn its way down again. Oh no, oh Joya. Those pills had been lying around, waiting for a peeved and fanciful eight-year-old to pick them up and–

What had her little girl done?

Leo closed his eyes. Martine was gawping at him, clueless that she was looking at a man who didn't remember poisoning his partner's mother. He motioned towards the coffee machine, more to get her doing something instead

Chapter Twenty-Two

Sunday, 27th July: afternoon

He had killed Eleanor. He must have. Instead of getting the fright he'd intended, Ashley's mother had swallowed an overdose and exited life, and the fact that Leo had no recollection of doing it would be no help at all when it came to a court case.

He paced up and down between the kitchen and the front door, hands clasped under his chin. If he called the police, or the doctor, it would all come out. He had plenty of motive to want Eleanor out of the way. And he'd been aiming for that, but he'd wanted her safely in Clarkston or Pollokshaws, not bloody dead. He thumped the connecting door as he passed – he hadn't meant any of this to happen, but there was no way out of the mess. With Martine knowing, he couldn't make out he'd been away for the past twelve hours and found Eleanor dead on his return. Even if Martine totally fancied him, she was hardly likely to give him an alibi for Eleanor's murder. Anyway, Vee and Joya had seen him too. Leo sobbed into his fists.

And Ashley, his beautiful, hurt, angry Ashley, who only wanted a life in a lovely house and her son coming to visit. Not much to ask, was it – but how impossible it sounded now – and hell, he was basically hiding from the police. Leo tried Ashley's number again, with the same non-result, then flung himself onto a chair at the dining table.

He had to think; he had to be active. Save them all. What he had with Ashley was worth saving, no matter what. So he could either up and off, in which case he would be a wanted man, so that wasn't an option, or – he could face what had happened, and try to minimise the damage. He needed to know what Martine was planning. She wasn't quite blameless here; she had given him the pills. Maybe he could sweet-talk her into helping him.

In your dreams, scoffed his head. Leo pulled up Martine's number anyway. It was all he could think of.

'I'll come over,' she said, and disconnected before he had a chance to open his mouth.

Leo went into the hall and checked that the connecting door to Eleanor's body on the sofa was firmly closed. When had she died? Last night? This morning? He rubbed his churning stomach. Her body would be decomposing all the time…

Martine rang the bell, and Leo let her in. She was much paler than this morning, and her eyes were shifting all over the place. She was nervous, hell – had she called the police already?

Leo took her into the living room and she sat in Ashley's corner of the sofa. He flopped down beside her, half-turning so that he could look at her while they talked. 'How's Vee?'

Her eyebrows shot up. 'Vee? Pretty shocked, but she'll be okay. She had a sleep but she's up again. Keeping Joya occupied playing dominoes.'

'That's good. Martine. What have – what do you think is the best thing to do here?'

To his astonishment, tears welled up in her eyes and she

reached for his hand. So she was on his side, at least. Leo gasped aloud in sheer relief. There was no way they could make any of this unhappen, but at least she wasn't yelling for the police. Yet. He took her hand in both his own, and squeezed.

'Oh Leo, I don't know. I can't think straight. Have you called the doctor?'

Leo blinked. 'No. Ash still isn't answering. I – we – have to do something soon, though. Eleanor can't stay there much longer. I wish to God we could spirit her away and pretend it never happened.'

She didn't let go of his hand. 'Me too. Thanks.'

He wasn't sure why she was thanking him, but he was glad they were agreeing. 'I'd do it in a second, but I don't see how it's possible. Unless you have a bloody magic wand.'

'I wish I had. Leo. I don't want – anyone's – life ruined because of this.'

Leo let go her hand and hugged her shoulders, feeling her slump against him. Christ. Maybe she *would* help him hide what had happened. 'How about we say we were all away, and then I came home this morning just after you found her? Or something.' But that wouldn't work either, would it?

Martine sobbed loudly. 'We couldn't depend on Vee being able to keep any kind of lie upright. The police would come, and they'd interview Joya too. She feels so bad she'd be bound to blab everything out.'

Leo leaned to the side while she wriggled a tissue from her jeans and wiped her eyes.

'My little girl, Leo. It's unbearable. If only I hadn't been so occupied worrying about the stupid Huntington's test.'

Hope flared in Leo. She was taking part of the blame. 'Let's think. We'd need to hide Eleanor somewhere.'

'Oh, for heaven's sake. You can't hide a body in real life. Someone would find out and it'd be discovered and we'd all end up in prison.' She pulled away from him and buried her face in both hands.

Leo sat motionless, his brain working like fury. 'Not if we make it seem she's gone away. Listen. Let's say we hide her in the meantime. We'll work out where later. Then I can get rid of some of her things, and say she's gone to visit a friend in – Spain, or somewhere. Without leaving an address, because she's fallen out with Ashley. And that bit's true, by the way. All you'd need to do then would be to make Vee stay schtum. She'd never have to talk to police about it, and nor would Joya. You could…' He thought, the idea expanding in his head. 'You could tell Joya the doctor came and saved Eleanor, and she's gone away to recuperate.'

Martine stared at him, and he could almost see her brain whirring. And hell, it was a good idea; there was every chance they'd pull it off. If she co-operated. He reached for her hand again.

Two tears trickled down her cheeks. 'I don't know what's going on with Ashley, Leo, but you are one great guy.'

Mentally, he punched the air. This was going to work.

Martine sank down on Vee's bed, the folder with Shona's contact details in her hand and sick dread in her heart. This was the pits; much worse than the prospect of watching Vee die, or having the Huntington's test. Her child had killed. But she didn't have time to throw a wobbly, no, she had to act, save Joya, and the first thing was to cancel the nursing service for the next few days. The fewer people who were in and out of the place talking to Vee, the better. This was the craziest thing she'd ever been involved in, but if she could get Joya's life back to what passed as normal in this family, she'd have done the best thing for her girl. And that was all that mattered.

The call made, she went through to the kitchen, where Vee and Joya were still playing dominoes. Martine stood behind Vee, massaging the thin shoulders, and gave Joya what she hoped was a reassuring smile. The child gaped.

'The doctor's on his way. Ashley's not home yet, so I'm going back to help Leo for ten minutes – will you two be okay here?'

Vee's voice was slurred, but she nodded firmly. 'Course we will. Don't worry.'

'You're stars, both of you.'

Martine started back next door. The sun was warm on her back, a summer breeze was chasing cotton wool clouds across the sky, and – how unreal it all was. She wasn't even sure she was doing the right thing. But if Leo was prepared to put himself out like this for Joya, she would do all she could to help. Martine felt sick just thinking about it – poor little Joya, the child whose mother had gone AWOL because she was too bloody selfish to cope with the possibility of having Huntington's Disease, whose grandmother wanted to end it all, whose father was as supportive as a stick of boiled spaghetti. The child who had done – what? If the authorities became involved, they might well remove Joya from her dysfunctional family. That mustn't happen.

Leo called from the back of his van. 'Give me a hand with this, will you?'

He was heaving tools and various other pieces of equipment from a large metal container and flinging them to the side of the van. Martine's middle jolted. She knew what would end up in that container. Leo banged the lid shut and jumped down, and between them they manhandled the box up the path to Leo's front door. Martine sniffed bitterly. There was no sign of his bad back now, was there, so it couldn't have been that bad in the first place. She glanced over her shoulder as she went inside. The street was quiet, but supposing someone had seen them? But there was no reason for anyone to connect Eleanor's holiday in Spain to a metal box going into Leo's home.

'Straight through to Eleanor's,' said Leo, as Martine made to put the box down in the hallway.

The smell in the annexe was now definitely bad; sweet and sickly with something indefinable pervading it. Martine's stomach lurched. She'd never smelled a rotting corpse before. Leo was in front, pulling her and the container into Eleanor's living room. Martine dropped her end, gagging.

Leo shoved the coffee table to one side and slid the box in front of the sofa. He straightened up, shuddering. 'See if you can find us some rubber gloves in the kitchen, huh?'

Martine was glad to get away from Eleanor even for a minute. It wasn't easy not looking at the woman's face, but it was infinitely worse when you did look. Like a waxwork with a sheen of reality shining through. There was a pair of gloves in the sink along with a plate and an empty glass, and she found a new pair in a cupboard, then trailed back through.

Leo had opened the box. He gloved up. 'She'll fit in here if we ball her up. Take hold of her legs.'

Retching, Martine did as she was told, wishing she'd tied something round her mouth and nose. Oh God, would they really get Eleanor in there? It didn't look big enough. As soon as they moved Eleanor the smell multiplied by about a hundred, and they struggled to get her into the box on her side. One leg was sticking out stiffly, and Martine moved to the head end while Leo forced the knee and hip to bend. There was a nasty crack as Eleanor folded into the container, her head sliding down Martine's front as she did so. Nausea burned through Martine, and she breathed in short pants for a moment, then gave up and dived into the bathroom where she hung over the toilet bowl, her stomach heaving.

'Rigor mortis,' said Leo when she returned. 'But we did it, Martine. Well done.'

The crate lid was shut, thank God. Martine peeled off her rubber gloves and dropped them onto the coffee table. 'What next?'

Leo tightened the catch on the container, looking as sick as she felt. 'We leave it here in the meantime. This thing was originally used to ship chemicals and it's supposed to be airtight, so the smell should dissipate soon.'

One hand over his mouth, he pulled Martine through to the kitchen, where he flung the window open. Martine took a few deep, grateful breaths of garden air. Her stomach was still churning like mad, and the sour taste of vomit was lingering in her mouth.

Leo leaned on the worktop. He was breathing heavily too. 'Okay, that was the worst bit. Now we have to make the place look as if Eleanor's gone on holiday, but I'm going for a shower first. You should do the same.' He gestured towards Martine's t-shirt, where a dark stain was still wet.

Martine shuddered. 'I'll come back in half an hour, then.' She touched his shoulder on the way out, gratitude almost choking her. He must be wishing he'd never started this. He was no relation to Joya and he hadn't known them long, but oh, he was doing more for her little girl than anyone ever had.

Leo stood for long minutes while boiling hot water rained on his shoulders, feeling the slow release of tension. That was better. Now to plan more. For better or for worse, he was committed to concealing Eleanor's body. He grimaced wryly – for the rest of his life he'd need to be the most law-abiding citizen in Scotland. He couldn't afford the police snooping round after anything at all, ever. Leo stepped from the shower and buried his face in one of Ashley's fluffy soft bath towels. Hell, oh hell, oh hell. This time yesterday he'd been a normal guy in the middle of a slightly dodgy deal and a relationship crisis. It seemed like a lifetime ago.

He pulled on old clothes – there was still Eleanor's living room to deal with as well as the container – and ran downstairs. He would allow himself a very small whisky. Oh.

Leo lifted the empty bottle from the cabinet. Hell, he'd finished the Glenmorangie; no wonder he couldn't remember what happened last night. That had been over half full. He poured a small brandy instead, breathing deeply as it warmed its way down.

Right. He had a sofa to clean. Not to mention a coffee-stained carpet.

The air in the living room was definitely fresher now, in spite of the presence of the crate and its contents. He raided the cleaning cupboard and set to work. Martine reappeared while he was still sponging the sofa cushion.

Leo stood back to inspect his work. 'Do you think the stain's gone?'

'You won't see until it's dry.' She kicked at some crumbs of plaster that had come in with the crate. 'Want me to vacuum clean?'

Leo draped his rubber gloves over the side of the bucket. 'Nah, come and help me pack her case. You'll know better what a woman would take on a long trip to Spain. We don't want Ash getting suspicious.'

Martine stared at him, wide-eyed, then followed him into the bedroom, where he pulled Eleanor's case from the top of the wardrobe and dumped it on the bed.

'She'd put her shoes in first,' said Martine, and Leo grabbed Eleanor's favourite black sandals from under the chair. Martine opened a drawer and began to extract underwear.

Leo found a pair of shoes and another pair of sandals, and threw them into the case. He gathered a selection of miscellaneous items – Eleanor's alarm clock, her netbook and her phone, and turned to find Martine folding blouses.

He almost laughed. 'Martine, honey – just stuff them in. She isn't really going to Spain.'

Martine sniffed, and he saw the tears in her eyes. She was hating this, and she must have real feelings for him to be helping to this extent. Leo's heart thudded dismally. Thank God Ashley wasn't here. He yanked Eleanor's drawers open and added a couple of cardigans to the case. He tried to give Martine an encouraging smile, but heck, they were packing for a dead woman's holiday. Life didn't get more grotesque.

'She'd take a handbag, too, for her phone and her purse and so on,' said Martine, when the case was full. 'And don't forget her meds, if she had any.'

Leo strode into the living room and grabbed Eleanor's handbag, and her enamel pill box on the coffee table. Now her pills and potions; they were in the kitchen. He stuffed everything into the bag and went back to Martine.

She helped him close the case when the handbag was in. 'What are you going to do with it?'

Leo sank down on the bed and ran his fingers through his hair, still damp from the shower. This was where plan A ended and plan B didn't exist yet. 'Never mind the case. I'm more worried about what we should do with Eleanor.'

It didn't seem to have occurred to Martine that he might not have everything planned, because she went white and dropped down on the chair by the wardrobe. 'You – we could bury them.'

'Dig a hole in the strawberry bed at midnight? No way.'

'Or – drop them in the river? The sea?'

Her voice was wobbling again and he hurried to reassure her. 'Too risky. But don't worry. I'll think of something. The important thing today is to get them well-hidden, if not disposed-of.' He slid the case to the floor beside the bed.

Back in the living room, Glasgow summer air was flowing in through the window, and the smell had changed to a mixture of city, Sainsbury's upholstery cleaner – and Eleanor. But it was heading in the right direction. Encouraged, Leo grasped one of the container handles.

'Help me pull it over to the window.'

Martine complied, and they arranged the crate under the window. Leo crossed to the sideboard and rummaged in the middle drawer. 'How's this?' He draped a tablecloth over the crate and its contents.

Martine's expression was bleak. 'Not funny. Who are you disguising it from?'

He bit back a sharp retort. 'In case Ash comes back unexpectedly. But you're right. Let's put it in the space between the wardrobe and the wall in her room.'

Covered by a blanket, and with a selection of handbags

and a box of paper piled on top, the crate all but disappeared in Eleanor's bedroom.

Leo swung the case into the hallway. 'This can go in the back of my van for the moment.'

Martine's expression was dismal, so he joined her on the bed and hugged her. She wasn't cuddling up to him this time.

'Well done, and thank you for helping,' he said, but she shrugged his arm away. Leo rushed on. 'Okay. Eleanor is going to Spain. She can't fly there, that's much too traceable, and she wouldn't drive all that way alone. So it's the train. She was planning to go to London, stay a day or two with a friend, perhaps, and then on down to Spain. That's what I'll tell Ash.'

Martine shook her head. 'You should assume Eleanor would tell Ashley. Even if they weren't on good terms, would Eleanor really go for a prolonged stay abroad without saying anything? There would be stuff Ashley might have to look after for her, bank business and so on.'

'Good point.' And it was. As next of kin, Ashley was the one who'd be dealing with the banks and so on – maybe he'd have to tell her what had really happened. But think about that later, Leo. He turned back to Martine. 'Okay. Now all we have to do is work out where to hide the evidence.'

Martine stood up. 'I'll do my thinking at home, if that's okay. I need to get back to Joya and Vee.'

This was stupid. Joya gathered the dominoes together and reached for the box. They'd played about ten games of dominoes because Grandma Vee couldn't play most games any more – she couldn't throw dice or hold cards properly, and even pushing dominoes over the table was getting hard.

And they were only pretending to play anyway, and that wasn't like Grandma Vee. Everything was wrong today, and what if the doctor was over there now, with Leo and Mum and dead Eleanor? Would he notice that Eleanor had a spell on her? Joya's middle shivered at the thought. Maybe the doctor would rush in here and shout at her. They might send her to prison. Making someone dead was the worst thing you could do, ever.

The front door banged shut and her mum called out from the hallway. 'Be with you in a minute!'

Joya felt a tiny bit better – the doctor hadn't come to shout, because her mum was going upstairs. But what was happening?

Joya pushed her chair back from the table. 'I'm going to Mummy.' She ran off while Grandma Vee was too busy breathing in to reply.

Upstairs, water was running in the bathroom, and the door was locked. Joya banged on it. 'Can I come in?'

The lock slid back, and Joya squeezed in and sat on the bathroom stool. Her mum was drying her face, but she gave Joya one of those funny half-smiles that meant something was wrong but Joya wasn't to worry about it.

'Has the doctor been?'

To Joya's astonishment her mum's smile changed to a big bright one, and she sat down on the edge of the bath. 'Yes – and oh, Joya, he saved Eleanor's life! She wasn't dead at all, just unconscious. She'd taken too many sleeping pills by mistake, but the doctor gave her an injection to wake her up again, so everything's all right! What a fright she gave us, eh? Silly Eleanor!'

Joya could feel her mouth and eyes making a big round Os. Her spell hadn't killed Eleanor after all, she'd been sleeping all the time! 'Like the Sleeping Beauty?'

'Something like that. So there's nothing you need to worry about. And Eleanor's going to Spain for a long holiday now, so we won't see her for a while. Okay?'

Joya jumped to her feet. 'Can I tell Grandma Vee?'

Her mum grabbed her wrist. 'No, I want to do that. Grandma Vee had a big fright this morning too. We don't want to give her another, even if it is a nice one this time, do we?'

Joya didn't see how a nice fright could be a bad thing, but she let her mum hold her hand all the way downstairs and out the front door so Joya couldn't even give Grandma Vee a big smile, and round to Snowball in the garden.

'You stay here until I come for you, and then we'll have ice cream. You can tell Snowball we'll get him a new little friend very soon. Maybe even tomorrow.'

Joya clapped her hands, warm happiness spreading all the way from her toes to the top of her head. She sank down on the grass beside the run. All she had to worry about now was finding a good name for Snowball's new friend.

Chapter Twenty-Three

Sunday, 27th July: evening

Vee was completely silent while Martine explained the plan.

'It's the best way, Mum. Joya can't have known what she was doing, and the entire situation here this summer has upset her. It's time for you and me to forget our own woes and concentrate on getting Joya back on track.' She finished, and waited for Vee to respond.

'What are you going to tell Stu?'

'The same as Leo's telling Ashley. That Eleanor's gone to Spain. Stu won't be home until tomorrow night; we'll have things planned properly by then.'

Minutes passed, and the grey eyes staring into Martine's were bleak. At last Vee spoke, her voice thick. 'This is all your fault. Giving Leo pills, indeed. I don't want any part of your cover-up. I want to die, Martine. If you leave the meds in a bowl for me, I'll manage to take them. No one would know I need help to get them out of the packaging.'

Martine choked. 'Joya knows, and Stu knows too. And for heaven's sake, Mum – you don't want Joya to go through all the grief about your death after everything I've put her through this summer. Please.'

Vee was silent, shaking visibly, her hands gripping the

arm rests of her wheelchair.

Martine waited. What wouldn't she give to be able to turn the clock back? Two months would do. 'I'm not asking for me, you know that. I promise I'll help you. Next year, if you like.'

More silence. Vee's eyes were fixed on the middle distance, almost as unblinking as Eleanor's dead eyes had been. Martine shuddered. What would she do if Vee didn't cooperate? Quite possibly her mother, who'd had more dealings with psychologists than most people, would think the best way forward was to bring Joya's actions out into the open and get her professional help. Dear heavens, no.

She was still contemplating the awfulness of this when Vee looked up again.

'We'll make a deal. I think you're doing the wrong thing, hiding this. But get the test done, Martine. I want to know. Then I'll say nothing, and next year I'll go to Switzerland to die.' She pushed with her feet on the floor and the wheelchair moved back from the table.

Bitterness swelled inside Martine, leaving a sour taste in her mouth as her mother propelled her chair out to the hallway. This wasn't fair, but what was, today? And she was Joya's mother. If Vee required her to take the test in return for silence, she would.

The solution came to her as she stood by the window watching Joya play with the rabbit. She would take the test, but she wouldn't open the results. Vee could do that, and take her blackmailed knowledge to her grave.

It was impossible to sit still. All Leo could do was clutch a cold pack to his head as he paced the ground floor of the home that wasn't home any more, with no Ashley. The headache, dulled by paracetamol that morning, was back in full force. *What could he do with Eleanor?*

For the fourth time, at least, he went for a prowl round the annexe. The bedroom was tidy, and no Eleanor-smell was coming from the container in the corner. Good. The suitcase was in the van, hidden under a tarpaulin. The kitchen was cleared, and he had run the dishwasher and emptied it, and – hell, he'd forgotten the fridge.

He dropped his cold pack on the table and yanked the fridge door open. Eleanor would be away for weeks; she wouldn't leave anything in her fridge, in fact she'd switch it off, wouldn't she? A litre of milk, down the sink with that. A piece of cheddar, wrapped in cling film – out. Half-empty tubes of mayo and mustard – out. He tossed butter, jam, a carton of eggs and a jar of mixed pickles into the bin too, then started on the contents of the fridge door.

Fruit juice. Orange. Mango. Hell.

Legs shaking, Leo collapsed onto a stool, the bottle of orange juice clutched in both hands. Yes. Oh yes. The memory was dim, but – he had put his pill powder in here, hadn't he? Or in the other bottle – or in both? He twisted round to look at the fridge door. There wasn't much mango juice left either. Leo twisted the top from the bottle in his hand and sniffed. Cold orange juice in a glass bottle. He took it to the sink and tipped, slowly, and a thread of orange liquid spattered on shiny stainless steel, then trickled down the plughole. When the bottle was empty Leo held it up. Was that some kind of residue in there? Or just the remains of the juice? He rinsed the bottle three times, filling it with fresh water and shaking vigorously, then binned it too. No recycling for this one. Or for its mate, which he put through the same procedure.

Okay, a wipe round the empty fridge, and – power off. It was a mere fridge in waiting now. Sorted. Leo left the bin bag by the front door and continued his prowl.

The living room was perfect. TV unplugged, everything clean and nice. A stain-free sofa. Leo sank into Eleanor's armchair and closed his eyes, deliberately relaxing his shoulders. Wait – something was... He reached behind Eleanor's cream and brown velvet cushion, and pulled out a wallet. Typical. It was the kind of thing a man usually had, with compartments for credit cards and bank notes, and only a small section for change. Leo leafed through the cards. Eleanor would take some of these with her, her concession transport ticket, her credit cards, and a couple of the shopping cards too – she was spending time in London first, wasn't she? This should all go in her case.

He was cramming the cards back into the wallet when the landline shrilled out beside him. Leo leapt to his feet in fright, and the wallet and its contents scattered on the floor. Bloody hell – it was Ashley. Calling her mother. Should he lift it? Yes, yes, he should.

'Hello?'

'Leo? I'd like to speak to my mother.'

There was no friendliness in her voice, and Leo swallowed hard. This was where the real acting started.

'Didn't she tell you? She's en route for Spain.'

'*Spain*?' Ashley couldn't have sounded more incredulous, and Leo hurried to make it sound like the normal thing for Eleanor to be doing.

'She's gone to stay with some old friend on the Costa del whatever for a bit. I thought she'd let you know.'

For a long moment Ashley was silent. When she did speak,

she sounded shaky-pleased. 'Oh. That's fantastic news. She does know a couple of people who've retired there, now I think of it.'

'What did you want her for?' Leo held his breath.

'I met my son and his adoptive mother today. I wanted Mum to know that if she's still in the bloody annexe when I get back, I fully intend to kill her.'

'You've met him? How did you manage that?'

'I texted him I was in Sanquhar, and he agreed to meet up in Dumfries.'

'How did it go?'

'Not great. Better than the Skype call, but only because Doris was there too.'

'Oh, well, you—'

She interrupted him. 'I'll come back to Glasgow, shall I? We should clear the annexe while we have the chance, Leo. We can put her stuff in storage with the rest of her things from her house, and get the annexe ready to use ourselves. If and when Mum comes back you can find her a flat as far away as possible, but if she knows the annexe isn't available any more it might help her decide to stay in Spain. I'll let you know when I'm coming.' The connection broke.

Relief flooded through Leo, and he punched the air. Ashley was coming home. And she had given him an idea about what to do with Eleanor. He swept up the wallet and cards, and trotted back home.

Storage. The ideal solution.

Chapter Twenty-Four

Monday, 28th July

Joya skipped outside with a breakfast carrot for Snowball. It wasn't really his breakfast because it wasn't in his bowl and there were no rabbit pellets, but she wanted to give him something. Snowball was going to be so happy when he had a new little friend to talk to. Would the new rabbit be white too? Joya opened the hutch and waved the carrot, and Snowball hoppled out and began to munch. Joya knelt on the damp grass beside the run. Actually, a black rabbit might be better. She didn't want to get them mixed up all the time.

And oh, this was such a lovely morning. Joya lifted her face to the sky – blue, with big fluffy clouds. Everything was all right again. Grandma Vee was still sick, of course, but maybe she'd get better soon. Joya remembered the plans to give Grandma Vee a happy summer.

She ran back to the house and burst into the kitchen. 'Can we go to Largs and have ice cream today?'

Her mum was scraping toast. 'It's a great idea, sweetie, but I think we should have a quiet day today, after all the excitement yesterday. I've got washing to do, and Grandma Vee might still be feeling wobbly. How about a trip later this week? We could watch a DVD today.'

Joya pouted. It didn't sound very exciting. She trailed through to the living room to find a good DVD – but she'd watched them all so many times already. Maybe there was something in Grandma Vee's box.

Joya poked around in the box of DVDs Grandma Vee had brought with her, but they all looked boring. Or… here was one – *Houseboat*. It had children on the cover, and they seemed to be having a good time. Oh. There was no DVD inside. She searched around, but the *Houseboat* DVD wasn't here. In Grandma Vee's room? At Eleanor's? Grandma Vee had taken piles of DVDs to Eleanor's for their film afternoons. Joya ran to the door; she would go and see if Ashley was home yet, and they could look for the DVD at Eleanor's. It was quite safe, because Eleanor had gone to Spain.

Leo answered the doorbell, and the surprise on his face when he saw her made Joya surprised too.

'Oh, ah, Joya. I guess your mum doesn't know you're here?'

Joya wound one foot around the other leg. 'I won't be long. Can Ashley help me get a DVD Grandma Vee left at Eleanor's?'

For what felt like a very long time Leo stood staring at her, then he reached behind the door for Eleanor's key. 'O – kay. Ashley isn't back yet, but we can have a quick look. How's Grandma Vee today?'

'She isn't up yet.' Joya hurried along the side path to Eleanor's door. She stood to the side to let Leo put the key in the lock, but then he stood there without turning it. Joya gaped up at him. He was scowling and trying to smile at the same time.

'Give me two seconds to check it's, um, tidy.' He opened the door but only enough to squeeze in, then he closed it behind him.

Joya waited. Why was he worried about Eleanor's being tidy?

The door opened wide this time. 'Okay, in you come. Why don't you see if it's in the living room while I, ah, check in the bedroom?'

Joya dropped to her knees in the living room, and opened the drawer under Eleanor's TV where she kept her DVDs. They were all old ones like Grandma Vee's, but none of them looked as good as *Houseboat*, and – yes! Here was the DVD. Joya was about to stand up when she spotted something under the chair. A little card. She went to fish it out – oh, it was Eleanor's driving licence, but it wasn't a very good photo.

Leo's phone pinged in the other room.

'Hi, sweetheart!'

Joya stood still. It must be Ashley.

'Oh, that's fantastic. I'm really glad. We'll get things, um, sorted, no worries. I've started clearing Eleanor's kitchen already.'

He sounded all lovey, and Joya wished her dad talked to her mum like that. They only sounded lovey after they'd had a fight, and that didn't count.

'Okay. Bye, sweetheart.'

Leo came in wearing a big soppy smile. 'Ash'll be back tonight, isn't that great? She's met her son, too, you know. Sorry, I'm gabbling. Did you find your DVD?'

Joya shoved Eleanor's driving licence into her jeans pocket. She would give it to Ashley later. She showed Leo the DVD. 'Why are you clearing Eleanor's kitchen?'

He looked at the ceiling. 'Oh, we're going to turn the annexe into a flat for holiday people, now Eleanor's gone to

Spain.' He took Joya to the door. 'You should get back now, if your mum doesn't know where you are.'

Joya sped back along the pavement and crept inside. She hadn't meant to be this long. Her mum was helping Grandma Vee in the downstairs loo, so Shona wasn't coming today either. Joya put the DVD back in its box. Everything was all right again, and Eleanor must be staying a very long time in Spain, if Leo and Ashley were getting holiday people in Eleanor's house.

A few minutes later, Grandma Vee came back into the living room with her zimmer. She gave Joya a smile, but it turned into a cough when she started to speak.

Joya's mum came in with Grandma Vee's tea. 'Where were you, sweetie? I called you ages ago.'

'I was talking to Leo. Ashley's met her son and she's coming home today. Leo's getting Eleanor's place fixed up for visitors.'

Tea slopped out the spout of the sippy cup her mum was putting on the coffee table.

'Oh, for God's—'

Joya jumped in dismay. But before she could say anything, her mum rushed out to answer her phone in the kitchen. Joya sat frozen in her chair. Why was her mum so cross?

'For pity's sake, Leo—'

The kitchen door closed, and Joya couldn't hear any more.

'I'm going to my swing,' she said to Grandma Vee. It might be better to go out the front door to get there.

Martine jammed her phone into her bag on the worktop. Leo was infuriating. Here was Ashley coming home, and Leo was talking about big confession scenes and getting things out in the open so they could all move on. Martine could see where he was coming from – it was a big thing to have your partner arrive back unaware that her mother's body was in a chest in the corner, and bank stuff would be easier if Ashley knew everything – but if Leo told Ashley, Ashley might tell her son one day, and God knows what would happen to Joya. Martine wiped hot, angry tears on the tea towel. All she'd done this summer was destroy her child's safe little world. What a wimp Leo was – if she could keep this from Stu, he could keep it from Ashley. Of course, this wasn't his problem; he may well be regretting helping her and Joya.

Trying to behave as if this was just another day, Martine slapped butter and marmalade onto Vee's toast. Her poor mother was a shadow of her old self, and her chest was rattling again. But they couldn't have the doctor until – oh God, what a mess – until she was sure Vee would keep the Eleanor secret.

'Here we go. Breakfast in the comfort of the living room,' she said, handing Vee the slice of toast.

'I don't know how you can joke after what you did.'

Martine slumped onto the sofa. She didn't know either. 'We're doing this for Joya, don't forget. Where is she?'

'In the garden.'

Marmalade smeared over Vee's chin as she aimed the toast at her mouth, and Martine winced in sympathy. 'I'll get you a cloth.'

'Get me a bloody bib, why don't you.'

Martine retreated to the kitchen. She could understand that Vee was upset, but why wasn't her mother jumping at the chance to protect her granddaughter? It would ruin Joya's life if the child realised what she had done, and it wouldn't bring Eleanor back, either.

Leo was halfway through his cheese roll, and trying to ignore, just for the length of his tea break, what was happening in his life. He'd gone into the office partly to attend to some of the work that was piling up, but also because being home alone was unbearable. Ashley wouldn't arrive until tonight; impossible to wait all that time with dead Eleanor his sole companion.

But there was no peace here either, because his partner was constantly in and out, complaining about wrong estimates and slow plumbers. Leo's only comfort was that Eleanor's eight hundred grand had made a huge difference to the business, and now that she wouldn't be sharing the profits, they could look forward to a nice little increase in business by the end of the year. He leaned back in his chair and thrust both hands into his pockets. It was unbelievable, what was happening to him. He wasn't a bad person, how had he ended up like this? Plan, Leo, plan. You can fix things. You must.

The most immediate thing was to get rid of Eleanor. He could do that now, actually. Hopefully she had details of the storage place she was using on a piece of paper, because they'd packed her netbook and he didn't know the password anyway. Time to go home, Leo. He grabbed his jacket and ran, stumbling on the stairs in his hurry to get back to the van and the house and Eleanor.

Luck was on his side. A brief rummage in the sideboard in the annexe, and the storage details were in front of him, as well as the key to Eleanor's unit. Leo felt weak with relief. The storage place was in Paisley, half an hour's drive away. He could take the van with Eleanor and some small items over today, then organise help for the rest.

He called the storage firm, and was told he was free to access his unit any time. Good. Leo went through to the bedroom and tossed the items covering Eleanor onto the bed, then pulled the crate out of the corner and sniffed all the way round the lid. Nothing. It was a blessing he needed chemicals to get rid of stains and mould during renovations; theoretically the box *should* be airtight, but it was an old one. Still, it was nice to know that theory and practice could meet when you needed them to.

The strength of an almighty adrenaline surge enabled him to heave Eleanor in her container into the van. At least now she wasn't in the annexe, and Leo relaxed slightly. A macabre thought came to him as he slid sundry small items of furniture in after her. They'd need the annexe furnished if they wanted to let it to holiday people. It would actually be more sensible to keep everything here in the meantime. But it would look silly to unload it all again, and anyway, there was still the box to get rid of.

The man at the storage unit remembered Eleanor, and Leo was forced to grin as they walked along a container corridor to Eleanor's unit.

'Changed her mind about what she wants, has she? She wasn't too happy about leaving her stuff in the first place.' The man took the key from Leo and swung the unit door upwards, and Leo stepped in. Eleanor's furniture occupied over half the space, but there was still room for the entire contents of the annexe, if they wanted to leave it here.

'She's gone to Spain, planning to stay there,' he said. 'We're turning the granny flat into a holiday let. I might be back and forward a couple of times, getting it refurnished. No point wasting this lot.'

The man snorted. 'You want to save every penny you can,

mate, in these enlightened times. You can drive to the end of the row there, and we have wagons if you want to borrow one.'

Leo followed him back along the corridor, his footsteps light. At least one thing today was going well.

As soon as they turned into the entrance area he saw he'd relaxed too soon. A large Alsatian dog was sniffing round the back door of the van.

Joya sidled into the kitchen with Snowball's empty breakfast bowl. Her mum was doing a huge washing load and she was cross. All the bed things were lying in piles on the kitchen floor, and all the clothes she normally washed on Mondays too. She was even doing cushion covers and things from the living room.

'Times like this I wish I had a tumble dryer,' she snapped. 'Joya, go and sit with Grandma Vee for a while, huh? See if you can cheer her up a bit.'

Grandma Vee did look as if she needed cheering up. Her face was all droopy and she was dribbling, too. Maybe she was sad that Eleanor had gone to Spain and she couldn't?

Joya slid into the living room and sat on the armchair opposite Grandma Vee. 'Would you like to watch *Houseboat*?'

Grandma Vee did a jerk in her wheelchair, but then she smiled at Joya. So that was good, even if it wasn't a happy smile.

'Later, darling. Can you help me look for something on the iPad?'

'Ooh, yes!' Joya loved going on the iPad. She fetched it from the table by the bookshelf and knelt up in the corner of the sofa beside Grandma Vee's chair. Carefully, she switched the iPad on. She'd been allowed to choose the password – Snowball99. She tapped it in. 'What do you want to look for?'

Grandma Vee's hands were too shaky to tap the iPad now. She leaned forward. 'Respite care Glasgow. Can you spell that?'

It took Joya a couple of goes, but the iPad was good at correcting wrong spelling so it didn't matter too much if one of the letters was wrong. She held the screen where Grandma Vee could see it.

'Tap the second on the list.'

Grandma Vee's breathing was very loud today. Joya tapped, and what looked like a hotel appeared on the screen.

'See where it says *contact*? Tap there.'

A page with a map and an address came up.

'Good girl. Find a piece of paper and write down the phone number for me, please.'

Joya fetched the pad from beside the landline phone and copied the number from the screen, checking twice to make sure she'd got it right. 'Are you going for a holiday there?'

Grandma Vee was leaning back in her chair again, but she looked a lot more cheerful now. 'Maybe someday.' She tucked the piece of paper into her cardigan and smiled at Joya, and this time it was a lovely kind smile. 'Let's put *Houseboat* on now, shall we?'

Home again. Leo yanked the handbrake on then strode round to the back of the van. Chaos was much too mild a word for the state of his mind today. He hadn't been able to get the container and its grisly contents away from the storage unit quickly enough, after seeing how that dog had reacted. The storage guy had called it off, but it hadn't been at all keen to leave Leo's van in peace. Leo had covered his terror with a joke about yesterday's lunchtime sandwiches, but the bloody dog had barked its head off all the time he was unloading Eleanor's effing furniture. No way could he leave her there – everyone knew about dogs and their keen sense of smell. If the dog ever started barking around Eleanor's unit, the storage people would get suspicious and investigate. So here they were, him and Ashley's mother, back in Langside. Leo opened the back of the van and stared inside. What the shit was he supposed to do with her now?

Nothing came to mind, and Leo left the container where it was while he went inside to think. He couldn't leave Eleanor in the annexe long term, not if they were going to have Tom and holiday guests tripping in and out. Suppose someone brought a dog? Leo slapped his forehead. He *had* to find a safe final resting place for Eleanor. Deep in a cupboard at the office, or somewhere on a building site? A cupboard would be easy, but the same thing applied – someone could investigate the container. Hell. But surely at some point he'd find an opportunity to bury it safely at a renovation, yes, he would watch out for an opportunity. The property off Great Western Road might be a possibility, if they got it.

But could he really allow Eleanor to rest so completely out of sight? Leo's gut tightened. No way. He'd never have a moment's peace. He'd have to think of something better, and in the meantime, she would just have to stay in the van.

Martine put down her roll and pushed the plate away. Bacon rolls didn't sit well in your stomach when you were worried, and here it was, only lunchtime and she was bushed already.

Vee had hardly touched hers, either. Martine sipped iced tea and worried. Had Leo found a safe place for Eleanor? She would call in a moment and ask. Meantime, she had Joya and Vee to occupy.

'Can we go to Largs tomorrow, then?' Joya wiped her fingers on her Little Princess serviette, staring expectantly at Martine.

'I suppose we could. Mum? Lunch at Nardini's?' At least it would get them away from Langside for a few hours.

Joya's disappointment was palpable. 'I wanted to have big ice creams there, not lunch.'

Martine caught Vee's eye. Her mother was smiling, thank heavens. It was the first smile they'd seen since Eleanor's demise.

Vee reached an unsteady hand across to touch Joya's head. 'Lunch *and* ice creams … with my girls. Lovely.' She coughed.

'Yay! I'll tell Snowball!'

Martine pushed her chair back. With Vee's chest sounding the way it did, it was anyone's guess if they'd make it to Largs, but they could worry about that later. Her mother was still pale. She put a hand on Vee's shoulder on the way to the coffee machine, and felt the older woman flinch. Heck. 'You go on to the living room, Mum, I'll bring your coffee in there.'

The landline phone on the worktop rang as she was sloshing milk into a mug and Vee's sippy cup, and Martine grabbed it before Vee struggled to reach the one in the living room and fell.

A strange voice greeted her. 'Hello, this is Moira Woods from Hartford House respite care – I'm calling about Verena Kelly's request this morning for an emergency place.'

Martine stood still. 'I'm her daughter. I didn't know she'd made a request, I—'

'Can I speak to Verena?'

Dazed, Martine took the phone to the living room, where Vee was manoeuvring her chair into the space beside the sofa.

'Moira Woods for you.'

Vee gave her and then the door a significant look, and Martine went back to the kitchen. What was going on? Obviously, Vee wanted away from them for a bit, which was understandable in view of what was going on, but to put in a request like this without saying anything wasn't like Vee. She must have called while Martine and Joya had gone for fresh rolls.

A succession of 'yes', 'I see' and 'thank you' from the living room told Martine little about what was going on. When the call ended, she went back, taking their coffee with her.

'Mum? What was that about? Have you applied for respite care?'

Vee's chin jutted into the air. 'Yes. Two reasons. First, you and Stu and Joya need some time on your own to work things out. Second, it was a mistake, coming here to live. I want to find a home or a hospice, and come to you for visits. It would be better, Martine.'

The words were jerky and the breathing laboured, but Martine could tell her mother meant every word.

'Oh, Mum.' She paused. There was truth in both Vee's reasons. 'Okay, let's not rush into any major decisions. Do they have a respite place for you?'

'Monday, for two weeks. I've put my name down for a permanent place there too.'

Martine stood still. 'Let's wait up before we argue about that. And Mum, about Joya and all this here—'

Vee's index finger zig-zagged towards her mouth. 'My lips are sealed.'

'Okay. I'll keep my promise too, about the test.'

Martine sipped her coffee, feeling as if she'd run a marathon since lunchtime. But the prospect of not having Vee here 24/7 was – restful. Did that make her a bad daughter? Leaving Vee watching *The Antiques Roadshow*, Martine went back to the kitchen.

Yes, she would take the test. Time enough to tell Vee she didn't want to know the result.

Martine looked round for her mobile, and connected to Leo's.

Joya skipped across the grass to the back door. Nardini's ice creams were the best. And lunch too – this was way better than Switzerland, even if the grown-ups were being funny. She heard her mum talking in the kitchen, and hesitated outside the door. Then she heard her mum swear, and it was a word her mum never used, not ever.

'For *fuck's* sake, Leo, you can't leave it in the effing van. Supposing you get stopped for speeding or something and the police…'

Fear chilled through Joya. Why were they talking about the police?

'Leo. We're talking about a bloody dead body – it would mean a prison sentence.'

Joya stuffed her fingers into her mouth, terrible questions whirling through her head. What dead body? And – blood? And – *prison*? Joya held her breath to stop herself crying.

Was Eleanor dead after all? Had her mum found out about the spell? *Was Leo going to tell the police?*

Joya crept round the house and ran down the path to the gate. Away, away, and quick.

Martine slammed her phone down on the table, then checked to see she hadn't damaged the screen. Losing her temper was no help to anyone, least of all Leo, who was, after all, helping her conceal what Joya had done. Martine thought for a moment. Maybe she could send Joya to Gill's this afternoon, and help Leo with… Eleanor. She glanced outside. The garden was empty, the swing motionless. Martine returned to Vee, and peered out the front window. No Joya.

'Where did Joya go?'

'I don't know.' A spasm of coughing shook Vee in her chair, and Martine looked on, concerned. That sounded painful. She handed Vee the sippy cup. 'I'll get your pills.' Lord. If Vee went on like this, there would be no choice about getting the doctor. Sick dread rose in Martine's throat.

Back in the kitchen, she yelled out of the back door for Joya, but no answer came. Martine slid Vee's lunchtime pills into a bowl and left them on her mother's lap. 'I'm going to look for Joya. Won't be a minute.'

The garden was quickly searched, and Joya wasn't there. Martine rang Leo's bell, but next door was deserted too, and so was the street. Had Joya gone to see if Stevie was at his gran's? That wasn't impossible. She dived back indoors and ran through every room in the house, just in case – no Joya – then lifted her phone. And of course, Gill's mobile went straight to voicemail. Heck. Her landline? Martine let it ring fifteen times, then dropped to her knees on the floor, gasping for breath. Joya had seemed fine earlier on – what could have happened to make her run off?

Martine's fingers slid on the phone in her hand. Oh no, no – but it must be. Joya had overheard her call with Leo.

Stevie's gran wasn't in. Blinking hard, Joya turned away from the door and dragged her feet towards the zebra crossing. When the green man came on she ran across. Gill was usually home in the afternoons because she didn't go to work any longer, and usually Stevie was there too. Maybe they were away doing something nice together. Or maybe they'd gone to the little shop near the park; she would look there. Joya wrapped her arms round her middle and started up the hill.

It was a very steep hill – her mum called it 'the killer hill' and for the first time Joya understood why. She trudged to the top, watching out in case Gill's car came from the opposite direction. But it didn't.

The top of the hill was still a long way from the little shop, and Joya stopped, her heart thumping. If her mum came looking for her, she'd drive this way, so she should change to one of the littler roads. She crossed over and trotted along, her breath loud in her ears. She didn't want her mum to find her, and she didn't want to know if Eleanor was a bloody body or in Spain and she didn't want to know that Grandma Vee was sick, either.

It was better, away from the main road. Not many people were around, and Joya was careful not to look at the people she passed. Too late, she realised this new street didn't go past the shop. This was the one that went past the library. Should she go in there and look at the books for a while? The library ladies were nice. But they might ask a lot of questions if she went in all alone. Joya's feet dragged for a moment, but then the library was behind her and she was standing at the corner. Downhill to the hospital, or uphill again to the little shop, and the park? Joya sniffed. She had taken too long. If Stevie and his gran had been in the shop, they'd be gone again by this time.

The park was a better idea. She could go for a swing.

Leo's mobile buzzed on the desk – hell, it was Martine. Surely she wasn't going to pick another argument. As soon as he'd had time to think about it halfway rationally, he'd seen that telling Ashley was the best way forward – she was Eleanor's next of kin, so they'd need her to deal with the authorities. Leo hefted the phone, frowning. On the other hand – it might be best just to report Eleanor missing, in a month or two. Maybe Ash *didn't* have to know the truth; he would think about that. He pressed connect.

Martine didn't even say hello. 'Have you seen Joya?'

'Not since she came for her DVD this morning. Why?'

'She's disappeared, and I'm worried she could have overheard us on the phone.'

Leo wracked his brains to remember the details of the call. 'She wouldn't have heard what I said.'

'But I mentioned dead bodies and the police. I'm worried, Leo. Where are you?'

He stood up. He wasn't doing anything useful here anyway. 'At the office, but I'll drive around the area now. Do you want to take Eleanor's car to look for Joya? The key's hanging behind our front door.'

'Oh. But thanks, I will.'

She hung up, and Leo grabbed his jacket. It was hard to know if an eight-year-old listening to half a telephone conversation would realise that Eleanor was dead after all – but it wasn't impossible. And it must be pretty obvious even to a small girl that something odd was going on. What if Joya worked out that he had killed Ashley's mother?

Darker still was the next thought flashing through his head, and Leo's hands shook as he pointed the key at the van to unlock it. Joya was out and about all alone, in Glasgow. Supposing… But no. She'd be all right – wouldn't she? If she wasn't…

If she wasn't, he could have two deaths on his conscience.

'Have you tried Gill's? That's where she went last time.'

Martine held the phone further from her ear. Stu was angry, and she couldn't blame him. 'Gill's not at home and she isn't answering her mobile. Leo's driving around now.'

'I'll – Martine, I'm up to my neck in work, after the so-called holiday we've just enjoyed. Call me if Joya hasn't turned up in half an hour.'

The connection broke, and Martine leaned a hot head on the back door. Please come home, Joya baby. We'll work this out. Where would the child have gone? If she'd been at Gill's and found no one there, she'd probably go on in the same direction, and land at the library. Of course. Joya loved going there.

Vee's cough from the living room turned into a major struggle to breathe, and Martine rushed through with water.

'You need something for that cough, Mum. Let's see if Doctor Shepherd can fit you in today.'

Vee glared. 'Have you … found Joya yet?'

'Leo's out looking and I'll go too, when we've got you sorted. She must have gone to the library. I can't think of anywhere else.'

'Don't want you … to sort me. Give me … the phone. I'll make … my own appointment.'

Martine passed over the landline. Vee had managed to call Moira Woods this morning, so it was odds-on she'd manage another call this afternoon. Right now, she had to find her girl.

She grabbed the spare keys and ran from the kitchen, shutting from her mind the horror of sitting in a dead woman's car, looking for the child who had killed her.

Twenty minutes later she pulled up opposite the supermarket and burst into tears. She'd driven along every street in the district, and checked the Italian ice cream shop and the library, but found no small girl out alone. Oh, Joya baby, where are you? Martine wiped her eyes on her sleeve. Leo couldn't have found her or he'd have called, and if Joya had gone home, Vee would have called too. Her little girl was missing, thinking heaven knows what. They would have to get the police in. Martine gripped the steering wheel, staring straight ahead as raindrops spattered over the windscreen.

There weren't many people in the park. Everyone had rushed off when the rain came on, and she had climbed up into the playhouse. Joya felt her lips trembling as she looked out the window. A sick pain was squeezing her tummy, and she sat hugging her knees, head bent forward. She was going to get into bad trouble, and not just for running away. What had happened to Eleanor? First she was dead and then she wasn't and now she was a bloody body, so either Mum and Leo had made a mistake, or they were telling lies. And Leo had been crying at Eleanor's, and he wouldn't have done that unless something truly dreadful had happened. Like Eleanor dying. Joya sniffed, blinking hard as the hot sore lump in her throat grew. That spell. It was still all her fault. And she didn't have a tissue.

Someone was climbing up the rope ladder. Joya inched backwards into the corner, the rough wooden floor of the playhouse hard beneath her backside. She didn't want anyone to find her. A dark-haired boy crawled through the hole in the floor, closely followed by a girl. Both were younger than she was, and Joya stuck her chin in the air.

'This is my place! Leave me alone!'

The boy shrugged, and crawled to the other side of the playhouse where there was a slide down to ground level. Joya watched as the pair slid down and ran towards the climbing frame.

A few blinks of sunshine slanted through cracks in the playhouse wall, and she crawled over to the slide. It was sticky because of the rain, and the boy and the girl sliding down hadn't been enough to dry it off very well. Back at ground level, Joya wandered along the path, rubbing her tummy. She should go home. At least there were tissues there, and her mum might make her some hot chocolate. She started towards the park gates, but oh, no...

Big fat raindrops were plopping all around again. Joya scurried back to the playhouse and squeezed into her corner again, eyes shut tight.

Leo pulled up in front of the house and switched off the engine, staring next door where Stu's car was in the driveway. Should he ring their bell and see what was going on? He swung the car door open and forced himself to his feet, heavy reluctance laming his legs. No – he would phone Martine. That way, she could go out of the room to talk to him. He flipped the cover off his mobile, still leaning on the open car door.

She didn't take the call. Hell. Leo slammed the door, wincing as the sound echoed between the houses. He shouldn't be so conspicuous.

Martine's text pinged into his phone as he was unlocking the front door. *No J. Stay away. Have called police.* A pulse throbbed in Leo's neck, and he massaged his temples. That was all he needed, the police nosing around and talking to the neighbours. He glanced at the time on his phone. It was nearly three o'clock. He pictured Joya, lost in the city, and his throat closed. If she'd seen him do whatever with the pills, she could destroy his life with a few innocent words.

He sat down at the breakfast bar to answer the text. *Careful what you tell police. Make sure Vee's out the way.* He hesitated before sending it. Both these instructions sounded pretty impossible, but a woman who had helped hide a corpse should manage that. He added *It'll be ok. xx* Again he hesitated, then deleted the kisses. Enough was enough. Send. Leo dropped his phone into his pocket and tapped his fingertips together. He had to make some pretty good plans, and the sooner the better.

The sound of car doors slamming nearby had him rushing to the window. A police car was parked outside Martine's, and two officers, a man and a woman, were striding towards the house next door. Leo's heart began to pound. Eleanor was a mere five metres away from a police vehicle. Any moment those officers would be radioing for help to find

Joya, which meant that every policeman in the city would be on the lookout. So unless – God forbid – something had happened to Joya, she'd be found pretty quickly, and oh… Leo thumped the breakfast bar so hard he felt the vibration all the way to his shoulder. *What would Joya tell them?* A sob rose in his throat, and he forced it down.

Okay – don't panic, Leo. It was more than possible the cops would come by to ask about him seeing Joya this morning, so he should create a perfectly normal Monday, working from home. Leo opened the laptop on the dining table and pulled a folder of papers from his briefcase, scattering a couple over the table top. And a pen. Sorted. A cup of coffee would be an idea too.

He was staring at the screen and doing nothing when the doorbell rang ten minutes later, and Leo's heart leapt. Was that—?

It was. The two officers were standing in the rain.

The man spoke. 'Sorry to disturb you, sir. Joya next door's still missing and I believe you saw her today?'

Leo clutched the door, but that would look normal in the circumstances. The truth, the truth, and nothing but the truth… 'She came by for a few minutes early this morning looking for a DVD, but I haven't seen her since.'

'And she didn't say anything out of the ordinary?'

'Nothing at all.'

Evidently this confirmed whatever Martine had said, because both officers nodded. Leo waited until they'd driven off, then grabbed an umbrella from the stand. Now he had an excuse to go next door. He had to know what was happening.

Stu let him in, and Leo followed the other man into the living room, where Martine was hunched up in an armchair, her cheeks tearstained. Vee was nowhere to be seen.

'Thanks for helping Martine search,' said Stu, pacing up and down. 'Hell, if I'd known she was really missing I'd have come back straightaway.'

Leo perched on the arm of the sofa. 'What did the police say?'

'They're organising searches. I'll go out with them.' Stu thumped one fist into the other palm, his mouth tight. 'If anyone's hurt her, I'll—'

'They know she's upset because of Vee and our – problems,' said Martine, her eyes meeting Leo's. 'They said she's probably run off to somewhere she knows, but I can't think where she'd go in the rain. I checked the library…' She dabbed her eyes with a scrunched-up tissue.

Leo stood up. 'I'm on my way to, ah, take the van to, um, a site. I'll drive the long way through the district and keep an eye out as I go.' It was his turn to stare meaningfully, and Martine's face crumpled. 'I'll look in when I get back, but hopefully she'll be found by then.'

He almost ran from the room.

The rain had stopped pattering on the roof. Joya crawled across to the slide, then stopped. It was even wetter now, and where would she go, anyway?

'Home,' she whispered, and now she was sounding all throaty like Grandma Vee. 'I want my mum.' It was horrible crying when you were all alone.

She lowered her legs into the hole in the floor on the other side and clambered down the rope ladder. It was made of blue plastic and not proper rope like they had in the gym hall at school, and it was slippery and wet, but she reached the bottom safely and started along the path towards the gate.

Was she really the only person here this afternoon? Joya walked round a little group of trees, staring at the wrinkles their roots had made on the path and – oh no! Policemen and a whole lot of other people were walking along the path and across the grass towards her and they had seen her and they were coming, and oh – she couldn't escape. A police lady was running towards her. Would they send her to prison?

Head bowed, Joya stood still.

Leo stared at the text on his phone. Joya was found – thank God – but Martine and Stu were on their way to the police station. If Joya said anything at all to arouse suspicion, they'd have policemen poking around all over the place, and sooner or later everything would come out and both he and Martine would – what? The worst thing was, there was nothing he could do about any of it. He watched as Stu's car disappeared round the corner, then flung himself onto the sofa.

Ash would be back any time now. Act normally, Leo. The van was at the office, the annexe looked like an annexe, and he was a remorseful idiot waiting for his partner to come home. He would manage that bit, anyway.

Ashley arrived as he was still thinking this, and Leo hurried the door and pulled her into his arms. She hugged back, and Leo kissed her head. Normal, Leo, normal.

'It's so great to have you back, babes. I'm sorry, Ashley. But we'll get sorted now.' He hoped.

'Oh Leo, that's all I want. With Mum gone, we'll be fine. I'm sorry too.'

They stood in the kitchen for a long hug, then Leo opened white wine and Ashley told him about meeting Tom and his mother.

'Doris was great – not at all like those people you hear about sometimes, who don't want their child to contact his birth mother. And Tom did talk a bit too. Doris is going to bring him to Glasgow – when he's ready – and then she'll meet up with a friend, and Tom and I can do something together. He said he'd have a think, and then they'd get back to me. I wanted to kiss him goodbye, Leo, but I didn't. I didn't even touch him.'

Leo passed her a cold glass. 'Baby steps, my love. You have all the rest of your life to get to know him.' Leo swallowed sudden bile – if he didn't want to ruin the rest of her life, Eleanor would have to stay a secret for all time.

Over a plate of salad, he told her about Joya running away. Ashley was immediately concerned.

'Oh no, poor sweetie, how awful.'

'They've gone to the police station,' said Leo, reaching out to touch Ashley's arm. And whether Martine would ever be back was another question. She could be in a cell right now, and he could be in another very shortly. This might be the last 'normal' time he'd ever have with Ash. He should make the most of it.

'I've started to clear the annexe, did I tell you?'

To his relief Ashley was distracted, and they went on to discuss what they'd need for the holiday let. The furnishings topic lasted them all through coffee too, and a different kind of unease began to worm its way into Leo's head. It was as if Ashley was deliberately not mentioning her mother. Eventually he could stand it no longer.

'What do you think of Eleanor's trip to Spain? Do you know who she'll have gone to?'

Ashley shrugged. 'She has two old friends who went there. But you know what, Leo, I don't care. I'm done with her. If she wants to live in Spain I'm delighted, but I bet anything you like she'll be on our doorstep again soon. She never does well in heat. But when she does come back, we'll have a nice little flat ready for her right across town, and holiday people in the annexe.'

She raised her glass. 'To the new holiday let!'

Leo clinked, and sipped, concentrating on keeping his expression happy. He should have chosen France for Eleanor. Or Ireland, or somewhere else cool. But it was way too late for that. For better or for worse, Ashley's mother was in Spain.

'Joya, sweetheart? It's all okay, you're safe now. Are you hurt?'

The police lady held her hand tight as they walked out of the park. She didn't sound cross, and Joya squinted up, shaking her head. 'I want to go home.'

Another policeman was bossing people away, and the police lady, whose name was Sandie, took Joya into a police car.

'We'll go to the police station, and you can tell us all about it, and your mum and dad can come and get you there.'

Sandie got into the back of the car with Joya, and another police lady drove. They went past the new hospital and the little park, and stopped outside a low brown building. Joya had seen it before because the swimming pool her mum went to was across the road. Sandie took her hand again when they were walking inside, and to Joya's surprise the first person she saw was the social work lady who'd come to her house when her mum had got lost at the beach.

'Hello, Joya. Remember me? I'm Elaine.'

Joya managed a little smile. Elaine didn't sound cross either, and she came into a little room and sat down beside Joya at the table, and a big policeman brought juice and digestive biscuits. Joya took one. It was a long time since she'd had something to eat.

Sandie sat down at the table across from Joya and Elaine and switched on a machine.

'Can you tell us what happened, Joya? Did anyone frighten you?'

Joya took a deep breath. Grandma Vee always said it was best to tell the truth. 'I was sad because Grandma Vee's getting sicker and my mum and dad are fighting all the time and I don't know if Eleanor's gone to Spain or...' Joya stopped, hope welling in her heart. The police would know if Eleanor had gone to Spain, wouldn't they?

'Eleanor? Who's that?'

Sandie was looking very kind, and Elaine had her arm on the back of Joya's chair, almost like a hug. It felt good.

Joya sipped her juice and took another biscuit. 'She lives next door with Ashley and Leo, and she's Ashley's mum and she's a bit like a witch. Like Wanda.'

Sandie's mouth twitched upwards. 'Did she put a wrong spell on you?'

'No, I put one on her and then she went for a long sleep, but now she's gone to Spain. Except I don't know if she really went there or to—' Joya ducked her head and almost whispered the next bit, it sounded so funny. '—Zuzipzuland.'

'Almost definitely Spain. I wouldn't worry about that for a minute. Joya, can you tell me about when you ran away?'

Joya rubbed her face. Sandie and Elaine were waiting, so she told them about going to the park and sheltering in the playhouse when it rained, and when she had finished Sandie switched off the machine and smiled.

'Good work. I need to have a grown-up chat with your mum and dad and another policeman, so you and Elaine can stay in here. I'll get someone to bring you more biscuits.'

Joya nodded. All these policemen. Why couldn't she just go home? She sat picking her fingers until the biscuits arrived, but they were lemon wafers and she didn't like them very much.

Running away was a lot more bother than it was worth.

Martine sat on the hard police station chair beside Stu, her head swimming. The relief that Joya was found and apparently safe and well had given way to guilt, terrible guilt that she was to blame for what Joya had done. They'd been here twenty minutes; what was the child telling them in there all this time? If Joya confessed to giving Eleanor those pills… And Leo, what had he done with the body? What a stinking mess this was.

Stu was sunk in his own thoughts, he'd barely spoken since the police arrived to bring them here. Martine closed her eyes. She had no idea what her husband was thinking, and she couldn't even plan to do better in the future, until she knew if she was going to land in prison for concealing a – a murder? Or was it manslaughter, when a child was involved? Anyway, there was no way forward in sight, only a high brick wall, and all that was before you even started thinking about the Huntington's. And if they had to stay here much longer, she'd need to get someone to check on Vee.

'Mr and Mrs Proctor? You can come with me.'

Stu was on his feet and walking towards the two officers before Martine gathered enough wits to stand up. It didn't sound as if her arrest was imminent, but how would she know? She hurried after Stu. Not exactly Mr and Mrs Supportive, were they? Which was her fault as well as his, of course.

'Joya?' she managed, following the pair into a small room filled almost to capacity by a grey table and four chairs.

'She's fine, don't worry. The social worker's with her – Elaine Morton. She met Joya when you went missing from the beach.'

Martine thudded into a hard chair, and Stu jerked his away from her. Wait, she told herself. Don't say too much until they tell you what's going on. 'I'm sorry about that,' she said, making a huge effort to sound calm. 'It was a bad time for me, but I'm – we're getting past it.'

The younger officer, a woman in her thirties, leaned forwards. 'You should tell that to Joya. She's worried about her grandmother, which is understandable, but she's also worried about your relationship. Children feel terribly insecure when they see their parents arguing, especially if it happens often.'

'Was that why she ran away?' Stu's voice was wobbling.

Martine hesitated for a few seconds, then reached for his hand. He rubbed it. What did that mean?

'Yes. It might be an idea to set up family counselling. You're in a difficult situation, I know.'

Martine nodded, conscious that her breathing was shallow and fast. Unless this was a huge trap, Joya couldn't have said anything about Eleanor and the pills. The relief was numbing.

Stu was still holding her hand. 'All I want is to get my family home.'

Martine squeezed his hand, unsure if this was genuine, or

272

an act to persuade these police officers that everything was okay between them. She cleared her throat. 'Did Joya say – was there anything specific she was worried about, that we could talk about?'

'Not really. She mentioned fights, and her grandmother's illness. You can take her home now, and I'll ask Elaine Morton to get in touch about the family therapy.' Both officers stood up. 'Oh, and Joya seems worried about your neighbour who's gone to Spain. You can set her mind at rest there, too.'

She held the door open, and Martine walked through in front of Stu. They were going to get away with it.

'Who's in Spain?' asked Stu.

This was it. She could do this. 'Eleanor.'

'Mummy! Daddy!'

And Joya was in her arms at last. Martine held on tightly, feeling Stu's arms round them both, and oh, if only it was always like this.

'Come on, chick,' she said, carrying the child towards the door, where a car was waiting for them. 'Let's go home.'

Home to dying Vee, and Leo, and dead Eleanor, unless she'd been shifted by this time. Dear heavens.

Leo was drinking his hundredth coffee of the day when voices came from the garden next door. He hurried the window, and a tidal wave of relief crashed over him – Joya was home, and judging by the way the three of them were bent over the bloody rabbit hutch, everything was okay. Whatever the kid had told the police, she hadn't told them he had killed Eleanor. Or – had she? Suppose they were on their way for him now?

A chill spreading through him, he fumbled his mobile out to text Martine. *Ok?* He saw glance at her phone, then the answering text pinged in. *Ok*. Leo swallowed. A reprieve. For the moment. A few minutes later he saw Stu and Joya go round to the front of the house while Martine went inside. Leo ran to the living room window, and watched as father and daughter drove off. As soon as they turned the corner, he was outside and jogging next door.

Martine came out the front door before he reached it, and pulled it shut behind her. 'Mum's in the living room so keep your voice down. Joya's fine; Stu's taken her to get another rabbit. She told the police a load of stuff about being worried about Mum, and Stu and me, and she did say something about Eleanor going to Spain, but nothing that made them suspicious.'

Leo leaned on the wall. 'Thank God. What does Stu know?'

'That Eleanor's in Spain. I'll reassure Joya again, and you'll have to deal with Ashley, Leo.'

'I will, don't worry. I'm going to bury the – the container. The suitcase is in her storage unit; I'll dump it another time. We'll get through this, Martine.'

He moved to touch her, but she stepped away. 'I think you should go before Stu gets back. I'm shattered. And Mum's not well and she won't call the doctor, it's like she has a death wish. And she does, of course, but I'm not letting her die until Joya's recovered from all this. I'll see you whenever, Leo.'

She turned back inside, and Leo returned home more thoughtfully.

Okay. Eleanor was in Spain. End of. And now he had a relationship to save.

Chapter Twenty-Five

Tuesday, 29th July

Joya knelt by the rabbit hutch and swung the front open. Snowball and the new rabbit were great friends already. They jumped out and started on their breakfast of carrot and apple, with celery as a special treat. Joya stroked the new arrival. They were going to have a name party when her dad came home. Oh, it was lovely that things were better again, even though she still didn't understand what had happened with Eleanor. But no one was cross any more, and that was the main thing.

Thinking about Eleanor made Joya remember the driving licence she had found under Eleanor's sofa. She could take it over to Ashley, yes, that was a good idea.

Patting the licence in her jeans pocket, she ran into the kitchen. Her mum and Grandma Vee were in the loo so Joya shouted through the keyhole. 'I'm going to Ashley's!' and ran outside as fast as she could. There! If Ashley asked her in for juice she could stay.

'Joya, darling! Come in. I'm so glad you're safe. Come and have some juice. Leo's gone for fresh milk.'

Joya clambered onto a stool at the breakfast bar, glad to be alone with Ashley for a few minutes. She watched as Ashley poured juice into three glasses.

'Here you are. What happened yesterday, sweetie? Did something upset you?'

Joya hung her head. 'I tried to put a spell on your mum, so I was worried because I didn't know if she really had gone to Spain, or Zuzipzuland or where.'

Ashley propped her arms on the breakfast bar. She was smiling. 'You put a spell – like Wanda? Oh, Joya – spells only work in books, kiddo. If they were real, I'll have put a disappearing one on Mum myself, years ago.'

Joya giggled. What a good thing she'd come. 'Did you know Eleanor was going to Spain?'

Ashley sniffed. 'No, but I'm sure she won't stay there long. Leo's going to find her a nice flat right across town, so there'll be no need for spells when she comes back, don't worry. How's Grandma Vee?'

'She got a big fright when Eleanor was sick, but she's getting better now.'

'Was Mum sick? Poor Grandma Vee – you'll need to do lots of nice things with her, now that she doesn't have Mum next door.'

Joya sipped her juice. It was summer and everything was truly all right again. 'We're going to Largs for ice cream soon.'

The kitchen door opened and Leo came in with a paper bag and a carton of milk. 'Ah, Joya. I thought you might be here so I got a croissant for you too.'

Joya beamed. What nice neighbours they had.

Leo strode away from his newest building project, then flung his boots into the back of the van and pulled on his trainers. He hadn't done much work this morning, after their late breakfast, but hopefully things would settle down after today. He would go home for lunch, see what Ash was up to. Thankfully, his renovations were trundling along without him.

Ashley was in the garden, swinging gently on the patio sofa and looking very beautiful and very lonely. Leo's heart melted.

He dropped to the decking at her feet. 'Any lunch going?'

'I was about to stick a quiche in the oven.' Ashley jumped up. 'Guess what – Tom texted.'

She showed him the message. *Off to London for a week or two. Will call you when I'm home.* Ashley had replied. *Lucky you – London's fab. Have a lovely time. x* Tom hadn't answered.

Leo hugged her. 'A very positive baby step, I'd say.'

He followed her inside and stood with his back against the breakfast bar while she sliced tomatoes. Relief that she was back in his life as if nothing had happened was mingling with fear of what might happen if she knew what he had done to her mother. Tread carefully, Leo.

'Joya told me Mum wasn't well before she went to Spain.' Ashley glanced up at him. 'You didn't tell me.'

Christ – what had Joya said? Leo coughed, to give himself thinking time. There was a difference between, 'Eleanor was sick' and 'We thought Eleanor was dead and Leo was crying'. He aimed for middle ground. 'I think it was some kind of food poisoning. It gave her a fright but it was over quickly.'

Ashley pressed her fingertips together under her chin. 'I felt so sorry for Joya. It was Mum's fault she had such a fright. Do you know, the poor poppet tried to put a spell on Mum, and then she was scared she'd magicked her away?

God knows what the old cow did or said to make her do that.'

Leo gripped the breakfast bar, his head swimming. Holy shit. Joya thought she had... *Bloody* hell. Had Joya said something to Martine to make her think the kid had harmed Eleanor? The events of Sunday paraded through his mind. Heck, yes. That would be why Martine was so gutted when he'd found the empty pills back in the kitchen, and why she'd been so cooperative about hiding the body. Leo's cheeks burned. Martine didn't fancy him. She'd been trying to protect her child.

Ashley was staring. 'What is it? Do you know what she said to Joya?'

Leo forced his mind back to the present. 'Your mother? Haven't a clue. What did you tell Joya?'

'I said I'd have magicked Mum away years ago if I'd been able to. Leo, what is it? You look like you've been in the sauna.'

He tried to smile. If Martine was now aware that Joya had only wanted to magic Eleanor away, there would be no reason for her to keep silent about Eleanor's death. And she'd know the only reason he'd wanted to hide it all must be – because he had killed Eleanor.

Ashley's eyes were narrow. 'Leo, what's going on?'

The kitchen swam in front of his eyes. He had to keep Ashley in the dark ... then he should persuade Martine somehow to ... and there was Vee ... Leo clenched his fists.

'I'm – ah, wondering if Martine knows about Eleanor probably being mean to Joya. As far as I know, she thinks the poor kid ran off because of their situation at home.'

Ashley went back to her salad. 'Good thinking. I'll have a word this afternoon.'

Fresh sweat broke on Leo's forehead. 'It's all right. I said

I'd pop by after lunch with some tools for Stu; I'll mention it then.'

'Okay. That quiche must be ready – let's eat outside.'

Leo grasped the salad bowl and went out to the patio and flopped into a garden chair. Between now and his visit next door after lunch, he would have to think up something to tell Martine. Something that would explain everything and leave them all in the clear.

Martine set the sandwiches on the table and sat down opposite Vee and Joya. This was the famous first day of the rest of their lives. Joya was ecstatic about her new rabbit, and Vee's cough was better, thank God, but... Martine forced herself to eat her cheese and pickle, and smile at Joya's rabbit anecdote. It wasn't easy.

'Oh – I forgot to give Ashley Eleanor's driving license,' said Joya, in the middle of her rabbit story. She slapped the card down on the table, photo side up.

Vee choked, and Martine got up to rub her mother's back and help her sip some water, glad of the interruption.

'Where did you find it?' she said weakly.

'Under her sofa. Do you think she'll need it, in Spain?'

Martine grabbed the card while Joya was taking another sandwich. 'No. She'll have a Spanish one.'

Joya nodded, and Martine rushed on. Change the subject; this was best forgotten. Thank heavens Stu wasn't here. She caught Vee's eye.

'Nardini's on Thursday, Mum?'

Vee rose to the occasion. 'Great idea. The knickerbocker glories are on me.'

He had worked out the perfect solution. Leo literally felt lighter as he went next door and rang the bell. All he needed was for Martine to believe what he was about to tell her.

Joya opened the door. 'Have you seen my new rabbit?'

'I'll come and see him after work this afternoon, shall I? Ashley has some scraps for him at home – why don't you go and get them?'

'Ooh!'

Martine closed the door behind Joya. 'News? It's okay, Mum's asleep.'

Leo followed her through to the kitchen. This was where a couple of semesters at acting school would have helped. His plan wouldn't succeed unless she believed him. He leaned against the work surface and met her eyes. 'Martine, I found the pills. They didn't land inside Eleanor after all, they'd fallen down the back of the drawer at home.' He tossed the little plastic bag with the white powder he'd prepared onto the table, watching Martine's jaw drop.

She collapsed onto a chair and leaned over the bag. 'No! And the empty bag you found at yours?'

Leo pulled up the opposite chair. 'Was a bag. Ash has loads of them. But you realise what this means?'

Tears were coursing down her cheeks, and a tiny sensation of something relaxing deep within him began in Leo's middle.

'Joya didn't do it. Oh, Leo.'

He thrust the bag into his pocket and gave her his most reassuring smile. 'You must be so relieved. I'm guessing it was a – a heart attack, or the like – she did have high blood pressure.'

Martine wiped her face with a crumpled Little Princess

serviette. 'So, what now?'

He reached across the table and squeezed her hand. Go for it, Leo. 'That's the problem. By not reporting Eleanor's death and then hiding her body, we've become … criminals.'

She stared bleakly. 'What can we do? And why did Joya think—'

Leo interrupted before she thought too hard about this. 'Joya told Ash all about it. Eleanor must have narked her about something, so Joya put a spell on Eleanor.'

Martine gasped, and Leo gave her shoulder a little shake.

'Martine. Eleanor died a natural death. You and I then turned it into a mess. But only the two of us – and Vee – know she's dead. Everyone else thinks she's in Spain, so we should stick to that. Eleanor's in Spain, end of.'

Martine raised a clenched fist to her mouth. Her eyes were wild. 'What did you do with her? Eleanor.'

'Nothing yet, but don't worry. I'm onto it. No one will find her.'

He patted her shoulder and left before she could think of any awkward questions.

Ashley was at the breakfast bar, poring over the laptop. 'I thought I'd drive out to Braehead this afternoon, get some supplies in. Want to come?'

Leo kissed her head. It was wonderful having her back. 'No can do, I'm afraid. I have some building stuff to organise.' He slid an espresso cup under the coffee machine. Knowing what he was going to do with Eleanor was the best feeling he'd had all week.

Ashley closed the laptop. 'If I tell you something, Leo, will you promise never to tell a soul?'

'Sure.' One more secret this summer would make no difference at all.

'That evening when I left, I was so mad. I had a real go at Mum and she stomped out the room, and I – I put one of those E tablets into her pill box on the coffee table. I saw them in an egg cup here, and I lifted them, just in case… You know how she tosses her pills back. So, I guess that was what gave her food poisoning. Served her right, though.' She reached for a mug.

Oblivious to the heat of the coffee, Leo clutched his cup to his chest, his mind whirring in ghastly slow-motion through the scene in Eleanor's living room. Vee having wheezy hysterics in the armchair … the body on the sofa … the upturned coffee cup on the floor. Yes, the pill box had been on the coffee table until he'd put it in Eleanor's case. And the juice bottles in the fridge… Had he, or had he not, doctored them? And had Eleanor drunk any?

'It's all right, baby,' he said, surprised at how steady his voice was. 'If she swallowed it, it did her no lasting harm.'

Leo watched Ashley make a cappuccino, frowning in concentration as she shook the chocolate powder over the top, then he slid his cup into the machine for more espresso. Say nothing, be normal. Ash was here and they were all right.

He would forget that one of them had got away with murder.

Joya crouched in the run, giggling when Snowball and Ebony came sniffling up around her legs. Their noses were ticklish. They'd had a lovely name party – her dad had brought a welcome home carrot cake for Ebony, but it was more for them because rabbits didn't eat cake.

'Want some strawberries?'

Joya jumped up again. Ashley was standing at the fence,

the blue colander in her hand. Joya ran across.

Ashley handed it over. 'This'll be almost the last lot, but next year we're going to make a bigger fruit section at the side.'

Joya nibbled on a tiny little strawberry. It was warm from the sun.

Leo came around from the front with a big sack of something. 'Ash! Come and give me a hand, would you?'

Ashley ran over, and Joya stood watching while she and Leo lugged sacks and spades to the middle of the garden. Then Leo disappeared again, and Ashley came back to the fence.

'Can I come over and help?' Joya was itching to see what was going on.

'You're safer where you are, kiddo. Leo's bringing a digger, and we don't want any accidents, do we?'

Joya shook her head. Leo was driving a little digger around the corner of the house now – how clever he was. Her mum appeared behind Joya and cuddled her tight from behind.

'Nearly bedtime, chick.'

Ashley winked at Joya. 'You'll have a grandstand view from your room tomorrow, Joya. He'll stop after unloading, Martine – you won't have this din all night, don't worry.'

Leo parked the digger halfway up the garden.

Joya clapped. 'Ooh! Are you making a building site?' She felt her mum breathe in hard against her back.

Ashley beamed. 'Leo's going to dig out a big hole for a pond. It'll be brilliant; we can have Koi. You know – great big fish.'

Joya clasped her hands under her chin. This was just the best day ever.

Epilogue

Joya's ninth birthday

Martine opened the bedroom curtains; it was time to get Saturday started. Autumn leaves were flying around the gardens, and grey clouds were scudding overhead. And it was Joya's birthday.

Gratitude welled up in Martine's chest and she clasped her hands under her chin. It was a miracle that Joya had come out of the summer unscathed, but the child was her usual happy little self again.

She glanced down at the garden next door. It was impossible not to notice the pond, and every time she looked at it, a picture of what lay beneath swilled into Martine's mind. Deliberately, she pushed the thought away. This was Joya's day, a happy day. Though how Martine was to keep up the illusion of a perfect family party, she had no idea. It would be the last birthday they were all together; this time next year, Vee would have taken her one-way ticket to Switzerland. The recent breakthrough in Huntington's research had come too late for Vee, and who knows if they'd really be able to stop the disease. Martine clenched both fists. Her test results were due to come next week, and she intended to give them straight to her mother. If Stu saw them lying around he might open them, and their relationship was still too frail to survive the wrong result.Stu appeared from the bathroom, and Martine gathered her things. Time for a shower and time for a happy family face.

'...happy birthday to you!'

Joya gave a big puff when her mum and dad finished singing, and one two three four five six seven eight nine candles went out. 'Yay! I got them all!'

Her mum pulled the candles from the pile of pancakes, and put the biggest pancake on a plate for Joya, with more maple syrup than she was usually allowed. 'Here you are, chick.'

Joya got stuck in. This was a brilliant birthday because it was Saturday and her dad was home all day. They were having pancakes for breakfast, then they were going to Grandma Vee's for lunch. Grandma Vee lived in Hartford House now, but it was all right because Hartford House was just across the road from Joya's school. She went to Grandma Vee's every day after school, until her mum or dad came to get her.

Her dad finished his pancake and pushed his plate back. 'You sure you want to wait until we're at Grandma Vee's before you open your presents, Joya?'

Joya opened her eyes wide. 'Oh yes. Grandma Vee wants to watch, she said so.'

There was a plop in the hall, and the postman whistled as he went back down the path.

Joya jumped up. 'Cards! I'll open them now.'

Her mum lifted the plates. 'Good idea. Take them into the living room; this table's all sticky. We'll join you in a minute.'

Joya scooped up the pile of post and plonked herself down on the sofa. She had lots of cards; she always did. The first was from Stevie and his gran and grandad, and the second was from Stevie and his mum. Joya giggled. Maybe the next was from Stevie and his dad. She ripped it open.

Oh. This wasn't a birthday card. It was a funny-looking letter on white paper, and Joya didn't understand a word.

'Who are the cards from?' Her mum sat down on the armchair.

'Stevie, mostly. And I opened this by mistake.' Joya handed over the funny letter and opened the next card. *With love from Ashley, Leo and Tom, and all the fish. xxx* Tom was Ashley's big boy and he often came to visit now. How nice of them to send the card in the post. Joya looked up to tell her mum, and stared. Her mum was sitting straight as straight holding the letter and she looked as if she'd seen a ghost.

'Mummy?'

Her mum came over to the sofa and gave Joya the biggest hug ever. 'Oh sweetheart. Oh Joya.' She was crying now and Joya could feel huge shaky waves coming from the middle of her mum's body.

Her dad came in. 'Martine? What's going on?'

Joya's mum let go with one hand and passed the letter over. Joya peeked up at her dad. His face had gone red. He reached across and took her mum's hand.

'It's okay, Joya. Just a result we've been waiting for, but it's negative so everything's all right. Everything's wonderful, in fact.'

Joya's mum ran from the room, followed by her dad, and Joya gaped after them. What on earth could be negative and wonderful, all at once? She would never understand grown-ups.

Acknowledgements

As always, love and thanks to my sons, Matthias and Pascal, for help and support in all kinds of ways, also to my editors, Debi and Emma, to everyone at Fabrian Books, and to The Cover Collection for the fabulous cover art.

Thanks too to Caryl Crabb for advice about some of the medical issues in this book – any mistakes here are my own – and Fiona Ewers for information about UK schools.

And to all those writers, book bloggers, and others who are so supportive on social media – a huge and heartfelt 'thank you'! I couldn't manage without you.

Death Wish is set in my home city, Glasgow. Some locations and institutions mentioned are real, others are fictional.

For more information about my writing and books please visit my website www.lindahuber.net

If you enjoyed *Death Wish*, you may like to try Linda Huber's other books. Here's an extract from *Ward Zero*:

Prologue

Thursday, 20th July

He stared across the table in the crowded restaurant and his mouth went dry. Sarah. She was so lovely, smiling at him with shiny blonde hair just tipping her shoulders, and her blouse an exact match for the blue of her eyes. And now he would have to kill her too. It was too much to bear.

He reached for his glass, fighting to keep the 'I'm having the greatest time ever' expression fixed on his face. But her last remark had confirmed it – she knew way too much. And he, idiot that he was, had just made a monumental mistake. Sarah was busy with her fritters; she hadn't realised the significance of what he'd said. But she would, and the first thing she'd do was tell that bloody policeman. It was a risk he couldn't take. Time to switch his emotions off.

He took a deep breath, forcing himself to smile back. All he had to do was keep her busy thinking about other things, and after dessert he would suggest a quick coffee at home. His home. Once he had her safely locked up he could organise her death in peace and quiet. It shouldn't be too difficult – he'd already had a practice run.

When Sarah was gone too, he'd be safe.

If only he'd never gone to the hospital. He hadn't wanted things to end like this, not for one minute.

Chapter One

Two weeks earlier: Tuesday, 4th July

Sarah stepped into the arrivals hall at Manchester Airport. What a brilliant feeling – back on British soil for her first long break in two years. And she was ready for it. Teaching in Switzerland and travelling round Europe in the holidays had been exhausting, if exciting. And now – where was Mim?

A glance round the waiting crowd failed to locate her foster mother's strawberry-blonde head, and Sarah stood still. *She* hadn't spoken to Mim since last week, but they'd texted yesterday. At least... Sarah frowned. She had texted her new flight time and Mim had replied with a smiley, which, when you thought about it, wasn't typical. Mim had the gift of the gab even when she was texting.

'There you are! Sorry I'm late – I had to park at the back of beyond.'

Sarah spun round to see a short, very pregnant figure beaming up at her, dark curls damp on her brow. 'Rita! You're huge! Come here!'

A lump came into her throat as she hugged the other woman, feeling the hardness of Rita's bump against her own body. Lucky Rita.

Rita hugged back. 'That's pregnancy for you. Come on, let's get out of this rabble.'

Sarah grabbed her case and turned towards the exit.

'You're on. But where's Mim?'

She couldn't imagine what could have kept Mim away from the airport when the two of them were supposed to be setting off on their long-anticipated tour of Yorkshire that very afternoon.

Rita took her free elbow. 'Ah. Now don't shoot the messenger, Sarah. It's not my fault. My darling mother insisted you weren't told until you'd arrived. Mim's in hospital. She had an emergency knee operation on Saturday and she's doing well.'

Sarah stopped dead. 'No! What happened?'

Rita shot her a sideways glance, the ghost of a smile on her face. 'She was biking home from the DIY store with a large tub of paint under one arm and didn't quite manage the turn into Allington Road. She collided with the fish van and her right knee was damaged so much the docs had to replace it. And the fish van, her bike, and the road were all left with an interesting new yellow pattern.'

Sarah closed her eyes in affectionate exasperation. It was such a Mim thing to do. 'Oh no, Rita, poor Mim. So what's the plan now?'

'Back to mine for coffee, then I guess you'll want to get down to Brockburn to see her.'

Sarah nodded, acknowledging the unease niggling in her gut. Her own experience of Brockburn General hadn't been the best. It was horrible to think of warm, energetic Mim stuck in a hospital bed.

'Love to Mim! And call me tonight!'

'Will do. Thanks for the loan of your car.' Sarah waved as she drove off. Rain was streaming down the windscreen as she turned Rita's Opel towards the Manchester ring road, but by the time she reached Brockburn the sun had struggled through. For a moment her spirits lifted. It wasn't the prettiest town on earth, but even red brick looked better in sunshine. She took the short cut round the park then turned towards the east side of town, where Brockburn General had stood for a hundred years at least, and oh, Lord – was Mim okay?

The hospital was a sprawling collection of buildings flung up in different decades, most of them in depressing shades of grey. 'Colditz' was a good word to describe the place, and Sarah's mood plummeted, taking her back to the day of her grandmother's death. Black Tuesday. Blue-lighting up this road, sirens wailing, a paramedic pounding on Gran's chest and fourteen-year-old Sarah having hysterics on the seat beside him. Thinking about it still made the sweat break out.

Forcing down panic, Sarah flipped on the indicator. Nothing like that was happening today. She and Mim were going to turn Colditz into *The Great Escape*, weren't they?

The rehabilitation unit was a four-storey block at the back of the compound, beside maternity and opposite geriatrics, and Sarah parked as close to the main door as she could. A quick glance in the mirror confirmed her make-up was still in place and her hair no more chaotic than usual. She tucked her handbag under one arm and hurried across the car park. Two minutes more and she'd see with her own eyes how Mim was. She was being silly, worrying like this.

Glass doors slid open at her approach, and Sarah strode in before slowing down. The entrance area was busy and noisy, the cafeteria on the right providing an interesting olfactory challenge to the usual hospital smell, and the sounds of Wimbledon coming from a darkened TV room straight ahead. Sarah hurried towards the lifts. The wards here were named after rivers, but they had numbers too. Mim was in Clyde, aka Ward Seven, on the fourth floor. Sarah pressed the button. Going up...

The lift doors opened at the orthopaedic rehab floor and Sarah stepped out. A porter was waiting with an empty trolley, and she squeezed past with a muttered, 'Excuse me.'

He swung round and caught her elbow. 'Sarah? Sarah Martin? It is, isn't it?'

Sarah gaped at him. Tall, dark hair, thin face – handsome thin face, actually... Jack Morrison from Montgomery Road, way back when she'd lived with Gran, and golly, he'd changed since the days of teeth braces and school sweatshirts. 'Jack – goodness, it's been years! So you work here?'

He smiled, showing white, even teeth. 'I'm between proper jobs at the moment so I'm being a porter for the summer. What are *you* doing here?'

'Visiting my foster mum.' Sarah glanced at the clock on the wall behind him. She didn't have time for a long what-have-you-been-up-to conversation, even if he was the best-looking bloke she'd spoken to all year.

His face creased sympathetically. 'You had a hard time back then, didn't you?'

Sarah was touched. 'It was awful. But my foster family were – are – great. I'm fine. Are your parents still in Brockburn?'

'They've moved to a retirement complex down near the town centre. Unwillingly, I might add, but Dad's health... I've started doing up their old place. Not so easy – memories in every room.' His eyes were suddenly bleak.

Sarah bit her lip. Sensitive as well as good-looking, and he seemed to be having a hard time. Poor Jack. He was an only child, she remembered that, but oh, Mim was waiting...

His bleep saved the day. 'Sarah, I have to go, but why don't we have coffee sometime, catch up a bit?'

Relieved, she moved away. 'Great idea. Phone me at Mim's, huh? Miriam Dunbar, Allington Road.'

'I'll do that.' He touched one finger to his head and pushed his trolley into the lift. Sarah heard him whistle *The Song of the Clyde* as the lift started back down.

A young nurse directed her to room 145, and she opened the door with her heart in her mouth.

'Sarah, love! Come in and let me look at you!'

Mim was sitting beside a bed at the window, both legs resting on a footstool, and Sarah ran over to hug her. There was a long scrape on Mim's forehead and she was paler than usual, but her hair was shining and her lippie was on. She was wearing a tracksuit in her favourite turquoise, and the eyes fixed on Sarah were bright.

Sarah heaved a sigh. It was going to be all right. 'You bad woman, keeping all this from me. Now tell me how you are.'

Mim grimaced. 'Mediocre would be the best word, but it could have been a whole lot worse. As soon as I can bend my knee ninety degrees and straighten it enough to stand on safely, I can go home.' She dropped her voice. 'Which is more than can be said for some of the poor souls here. Rehab or not, it feels like an old folks' home, and I'm not ready for that.'

'Can you walk? Are you in pain?' Sarah settled down on the chair beside Mim's.

'I have elbow crutches, and I swallow every painkiller they bring me, but it is getting better. Now tell me about you. What's happening about the job?'

Sarah relaxed. Mim really did seem herself. 'The Zürich one is finished, but there's a vacancy for a primary teacher in the international school in Geneva this October, and I can have it if I want it. And oh, I don't know.'

'Why not?'

'Geneva's in the French part of Switzerland and my French isn't wonderful. And… you know. Andreas. I'll need to have a good hard think. I've to let them know by the end of this month.'

She glanced round the room as she spoke. It was pleasant enough for a hospital, with green-tinted blinds keeping the sun out, and a couple of flower prints on the opposite wall. The occupants of the other three beds were all elderly, and busy with visitors too.

A nurse appeared and parked a trolley beside Mim's bed. 'Mr Lawrence is coming to inspect your knee. Let's get that dressing off.' She nodded to Sarah. 'You can stay if you want to.'

Sarah shook her head. She'd never been good with blood. 'I'll wait outside. I don't want to go all weak and wobbly on you.'

Mim stood up on her good leg and hopped over to the bed. 'Go and have a coffee, Sarah love. I'll try to persuade Mr Lawrence to let me home this week, now you're here to keep an eye on me. Wish me luck!'

'The very best. Tell him I'll do all I can,' said Sarah, kissing Mim warmly.

Printed in Great Britain
by Amazon